HEART SMART

WORK FOR IT BOOK #2

EMMA LEE JAYNE

WWW.SMARTYPANTSROMANCE.COM

COPYRIGHT

CHAPTER 1

MAX

Everyone knows I'm an asshole. Everyone I've ever worked with, taught, or even met agrees. I'm a total dick.

I don't see what the big deal is. I don't demand people waste their time being nice to me. Why should I be expected to do the same for them?

The upside of being a dick is that no one expects me to act like anything else. Former students never want letters of recommendations. The head of the department has never once asked me to be on a committee. No one asks me for favors. No one ever just stops by to chat.

Except today. Today, when I let myself into lab, there's a woman reading the notes I wrote on the whiteboard before leaving last night.

"What are you doing in my lab?"

She's petite, with mousy brown hair pulled back into a bun low on her neck. She's dressed in a knee-length skirt, sneakers, and a sweater the color of something I might've poured out of a petri dish.

The lenses of her glasses are so big they make her look like an insect.

Despite her delicacy, she doesn't blanch at my tone.

Instead, she smiles. "You must be Dr. Ramsey."

She walks over and holds out a hand so tiny I'd probably shatter it if I touched her.

I've got my satchel in one hand and my cane in the other. I'm not about to shuffle all my shit around to shake hands with a stranger. And people say *I'm* inconsiderate.

She looks down, realizes I can't easily shake her hand and she jerks her hand back, blushing.

Yeah. There it is.

I stomp past her and can feel her gaze on my damn leg.

I'm aware of the weakness in my leg with every step. The way the muscles spasm seemingly for no reason, like they might suddenly give out.

I always feel it. Every step I've taken since the car accident that shattered my hip and left a mangled scar slashing across my cheek.

I don't mean to stomp everywhere I go, but the slight difference in my leg length plus the cane makes every step I take seem louder and clumsier. I don't growl when I walk past but I want to, because I hate being watched, especially by a woman. The fact that she's young and even passably attractive makes it that much worse.

I wish I hadn't brought my cane today. It draws attention to my limp. Nine days out of ten, I don't use it. But on the rare day I overdo it and I'm on my feet too long, I need it. The last thing I want when I'm already fatigued is for my leg to give out in public.

She just watches me as I pass her, like she's waiting for me to say something.

I don't.

So far, I haven't frightened her away.

Stubborn little thing.

"I'm Holly. Holly Dolinsky. From the Communications Department."

I shrug out of my coat and drape it over the back of my stool before sliding onto it. I toss my satchel on to the empty chair beside me so that she's not tempted to sit there herself. Because, Christ, that would be a fucking disaster.

The only thing worse than having a woman in my lab would be having one sitting right next to me.

I don't hate women. I hate being near women. I hate how good they smell. I hate their pitying looks. I hate their sympathy. I hate how fucking kind they are.

Kindness is the worst.

Women aren't kind to real men. They're kind to kittens and lost puppies. They're kind to ugly, crippled men they would never dream of fucking.

And no, it's not like I think every woman should want to fuck me. It's not that I think I deserve to have sex with anyone. I'm a dick, but I'm not *that* kind of dick.

I just hate knowing that no woman would ever sleep with me out of anything other than pity.

Worse, I hate that I fucking care at all.

I'm a scientist, God damn it. I work my ass off for the betterment of humankind. I shouldn't fucking care how good any woman smells—not a beautiful woman or even this passably attractive woman in an ugly sweater.

But I do care. And I don't want her any closer to me than she has to be.

I want her out of my lab before I notice if she smells like flowers or lemons or whatever the hell kind of perfume she uses. I look at her again. No. Not perfume. The kind of woman who wears a sweater that ugly wouldn't also wear perfume. Which means she probably smells like her shampoo.

Unless she smells like the puke-green of her sweater. That might help.

But somehow I doubt I'll be that lucky.

So I ramp up the rudeness. "This is the Louisa Franklin building. Communications Department is on the main campus in the Franklin Lewis building. Surprised they didn't tell you that at orientation. Another way to tell would be the fact that they don't have labs. This is for hard sciences."

She blinks in surprise, pushes her bug-eye glasses further up her nose and says, "I'm not looking for the Communications Department. I'm not a student—I'm a lecturer here."

As if I give a shit.

Still, I squint past the ugly clothes and severe hairstyle. Faint lines by the corners of her eyes. Frown lines between her eyebrows. She's older than her porcelain pale skin makes her look. Plus, the combination of a skirt and sneakers looks more like something a student would wear.

What did she say her name is? Dolinsky? Why does that sound familiar?

"What are you doing in my lab?"

"I was hoping I could have a few minutes of your time to—"

"Office hours are posted on my door." Jesus, even her pattern of speech is annoying. Can't she just get to the damn point? "Come back then."

"I did." She takes a step closer. "I waited at your office on the other side of the building for the last three posted office hours. Monday, Wednesday, and Friday of last week. You weren't there."

Even though the university mandates I post office hours, my students know better than to waste my time.

This woman obviously doesn't.

"Shoot me an email. I'll make an appointment for you."

"I did send you an email. Two weeks ago. And a follow-up email last week." I open my mouth to talk, but she holds up a hand. "Also, I made an appointment with you through the department admin. You didn't show up for that either."

I frown, unable to remember if Clarissa had handed me a note the previous week. "Make another appointment. I don't have time to talk to you today."

"No," the woman says. "I'm here now. And I'm not leaving. So you might as well talk to me."

I glance at the computer. It's still booting anyway. "Fine," I grumble. "You've got about two minutes before this is done booting up. What do you need?"

"It's not what I need. It's what you need."

She steps even closer. She's right next to my desk, her hip cocked to the side, one sneaker-clad shoe tapping in irritation.

And people say I'm not observant.

"I don't need anything." Which isn't precisely true, so I add, "A bigger budget." I quirk an eyebrow at my computer. "A faster booting computer, maybe." Her eyes narrow in irritation and I feel a spike of pleasure that I've annoyed her. "And apparently I need better security outside my lab. How did you get in here anyway?"

"When you missed our appointment, I asked Clarissa to let me in."

Hmm . . . Clarissa wouldn't have let just anyone in, which meant the woman knew Clarissa. She might be one of those people who just knew everyone. But it was a big campus.

Before I can ask her another question, she adds, "And your budget is big enough. Not as big as your ego, but big enough."

I glance back at my computer. A few more seconds to go.

As though she's annoyed that I'm ignoring her, the woman sets her handbag down on my desk, right beside my keyboard.

This part of my lab isn't sterile. There's a clean room at the back where we analyze soil samples from all over the world. Her purse near my computer isn't that big of a deal.

It isn't.

It shouldn't bother me.

But it does. Because this kind of carelessness could potentially lead to contamination of a sample.

I glare at her bag pointedly, but she doesn't move it.

At least not off my desk.

Instead, she nudges it aside and props her hip where the bag was a second ago.

And now it's not just her bag that's in my space. *She's* in my space.

I'm one deep breath away from knowing what her damn shampoo smells like.

Fuck.

"You don't need more money. What you do need are social skills."

"I'm a scientist. Not a debutante. I don't need social skills. And get your bag off my desk before it contaminates my lab any more than your presence here already has."

She doesn't move her bag. "Are you saying my bag is dirty?"

"Dirty is a relative and imprecise term. By the standards of a clean laboratory, every-thing is dirty. Everything is a potential contaminant." My computer dings, releasing me from the torture. "And your time is up."

I turn my chair toward my computer and wiggle the mouse to wake it up, dismissing her.

"Oh, you have got to be kidding me," she mutters.

Since she doesn't seem to be leaving on her own, I pick up her bag and hand it to her.

But she still doesn't leave. No.

She arches an eyebrow, somehow managing to get it higher than the rim of her ridiculously huge glasses. She takes her bag and drops it unceremoniously on the floor. She hoists herself onto my desk and sits with her ass about an inch away from my keyboard. That skirt that seemed demure a second ago hikes up to reveal about a mile of pale, creamy thigh. Which is now an inch away from my hand where it rests on my mouse.

She wiggles her ass as if settling in and crosses her legs. Which, through some miracle of physics, exposes even more of her bare thigh.

Jesus Christ. Just kill me now.

"If you refuse to talk to me," she says slowly, like she's talking to an idiot. Which, in all fairness, is what I feel like. "It could cost you five million dollars."

And that's when I finally connect the damn dots.

Yep. I'm an idiot.

Holly Dolinsky. Not just a communications lecturer.

She's the ex-wife of Dr. Thorndyke. The dean of Agriculture and Life Sciences. My boss.

No wonder she knows Clarissa.

God damn it.

I should have known Thorndyke wasn't going to let this go.

"You're here about the McPherson Fellowship."

"I am."

"Then you're wasting your time. I already turned it down."

I click a couple of windows open on the screen. I don't care what. Anything to look busy. Anything to keep my gaze off the swath of thigh an inch away from my knuckles.

I'm about one mouse click away from accidentally brushing her thigh with the back of my hand. Which would be torture. Or bliss. Or a sexual harassment suit. Or all three. Though she's the one sitting on my desk.

"Why on earth would you do that?" she asks.

And now I do look at her. Do what? Why would I touch her thigh? When it's right next to my hand? The bigger question is why wouldn't I?

Except that's not what she's referring to. I realize this a second later when she keeps talking.

"That makes no sense. The McPherson Fellowship is one of the most prestigious awards in the field."

Right. The McPherson Fellowship.

The McPherson committee reached out to me a month ago. Apparently, I was on the short list to receive the fellowship this year. A fellowship worth five million dollars.

In the past, recipients simply showed up at a reception, took a few pictures and went home with the money.

This year, there were strings attached.

Heiress Lily McPherson had taken over the selection committee and apparently she wanted to "take advantage of social media to strategically position the fellowship in popular culture."

The fellowship should be an honor. Instead, it's making my life hell.

I give a snort of derision. "It's not that prestigious."

"Some people says it's even better than a Nobel."

"Nothing is better than a Nobel," I grumble.

"It's more exclusive. They only give out one McPherson Genius Award a year."

I whip my chair around to face her, scooting back to put some space between us. "McPherson. Fellowship."

"Excuse me?"

"Call things what they're named. Not this trendy, popular nonsense." In the past several years, the media had latched on to the ridiculous term "Genius Award." The McPherson committee ran with it. What had once been a prestigious fellowship is now a platform for scientists who are more interested in showboating than doing real work. It's a damn shame. "It's not the Genius Award. It's a fellowship. Not an award. I didn't win a race in an elementary school field day."

"Well, you haven't won this yet either. And you won't unless you—"

"Unless I jump through a series of ridiculous hoops like I'm some sort of show dog."

She blows out a breath, her eyes fluttering closed like she's praying for patience. "It's not a dog and pony show. It's—"

"It's twelve filmed lectures in front of a studio audience."

Whatever moron thought I was a good candidate to be filmed in front of a studio audience like one of those flakes doing a TED talk needed to have their head examined.

"Yes," she says slowly. "For the purpose of educating a broader audience."

Her voice is soothing. Like I'm a fucking toddler she's trying to keep from throwing a fit in a grocery aisle.

That's it. I'm done.

Done being talked to like *I'm* the problem here. Like putting me in front of a studio audience is a reasonable thing to do instead of the worst fucking idea ever. Like I don't know my own limits.

I turn my chair to face her, leaning in. "You mean dumbed down for a broader audience!"

"Lectures geared to introduce the public to—"

"Dumbed. Down." I bite out the words with a fierce snap of my teeth.

"Just because they're going to be on TV, doesn't mean—"

"Most of the grad students who take my classes end up dropping out because the work I do is too complicated for them to understand. You think the average viewer in Bumblefuck middle America is going to understand it?"

"I think if your students can't understand your work, there's a chance the problem isn't with them. It's with your teaching."

Does she think I don't know that?

Does she think I'm a fucking moron?

Obviously the problem is with me.

Yes, analyzing the microbiology of soil is complicated, often tedious work. It's dense. But it's not impossible to understand. So obviously the problem is that I'm a shit teacher.

"Which is why I'm the last guy on this planet who should be giving lectures to a studio audience."

And I sure as fuck don't need her driving that point home.

I rise from my seat, bumping back the rolling chair with my legs. I stand right in front of her for a moment, breathing deeply, looming over her. Praying for patience. Waiting for her to panic.

Not because I want to scare the shit out of her.

That's never what I want.

But I'm a big guy.

At six-four, the combination of the build, the beard, the goddamn limp—it scares people.

Ninety-nine times out of a hundred, I don't do it on purpose. It's just me not reading social cues, because that's another thing I'm shit at. But every once in a while, when someone is really pissing me off, I use it to my advantage.

I have never—and I mean never—purposefully scared a woman with my size. But this chick is hitting every damn button I have and I need to get her out of my space.

But, again, she doesn't do what I expect.

She doesn't panic. She doesn't bolt. She doesn't fucking leave me alone.

Instead, she narrows her gaze, scoots her ass off my desk and stands. Which puts her way too close to me.

She doesn't take her gaze off mine. She doesn't so much as blink.

Her chin is tipped so far up she's probably going to need to see a chiropractor for neck strain. But she doesn't back down.

Instead, in a fierce and angry tone, she says, "I can help. This is what I do. I teach people how to speak in front of crowds for a living. If I can teach a generation of phone-addicted introverts to give presentations, I can teach you."

I want to argue with her. I'm about to. But then I make the mistake of a lifetime. I inhale deeply, preparing to light into her, and get hit with a whiff of her scent.

It's something warm and homey, but with the faintest hint of citrus layered on top. Like pancakes drizzled with lemon glaze.

The instant I smell her, my dick stirs.

I swear I don't mean to, but my gaze drops from her eyes to her lips. Which are surprisingly full when they aren't pinched into frowning disapproval.

Right now, they're not pinched at all. Her mouth is slightly open, like she's having as much trouble catching her breath as I am. Nope, not pinched at all, but full and moist and I'm struck by the almost irresistible urge to kiss those lips.

It shocks the hell out of me because I'm never struck by urges and I never kiss anyone. Ever.

Not in more than a decade. Not since the last woman I kissed called me a monster.

Despite all reason, logic, and common sense, I want to kiss Holly Dolinsky.

Badly.

Which is possibly the worst idea I've ever had.

No, not possibly. Definitely.

Though it would likely result in her running screaming from my lab.

But since it would also undoubtedly result in a workplace harassment lawsuit, I don't.

Instead, I back down.

For the first time in my entire adult life, *I'm* the one who backs down from a fight.

That's what this woman and her lemon-pancake-scented hair has brought me to.

I take a step back, and then another. My damn leg means I can't just turn and stomp off. Men of my size don't turn easily even when they aren't crippled. I have to back up nearly four feet before I can comfortably steer myself around her to stomp away.

Except, when I make it to the other side of the lab, I have nothing to do there. I have no reason to have walked away from her other than my obvious retreat.

But . . . if I retreat all the way into the clean room, that's the one place she can't follow. It doesn't matter that I have nothing to do once I get in there. She won't know that. She'll have to leave.

So I stalk the rest of the way over to the door on the opposite side of the lab and start the procedure for entering the clean room. Watch off. Shoes off.

She doesn't take the hint. Of course she doesn't take the hint.

When she speaks next, she's right behind me.

"Your work is no more complicated than Neil deGrasse Tyson's."

Her voice has lost that steely, defiant quality. Maybe my intimidation tactics actually worked. The thought should make me feel better, but doesn't.

"If he can explain theoretical physics, then—"

"Neil deGrasse Tyson is a showboating—"

"There is nothing wrong with needing help," she says quietly.

Like she's been cowed.

Which was what I wanted.

Except for one second there, I thought I'd actually met someone I couldn't intimidate. The idea had been terrifying, but also . . . what? Intriguing? Tempting? Appealing?

What the hell is wrong with me?

How did this tiny, lemon-scented, puke-colored, insect-eyed woman disarm me so quickly? How did she upend my entire day in mere minutes?

"I don't need help." I don't turn around to face her. I turn only so I can sit on the bench to change into my clean room shoes.

The frown on her face stabs at my conscience. I don't need help and I sure as hell don't need to feel guilty. She came here. She butted into my business.

"You need my help. You need this."

I stand up, shoes forgotten. "No, *you* need this. Well, you can run back to your husband and tell him you tried."

"My—my husband?" she stammers, blinking in obvious surprise.

"Yes. You think I don't know who you're married to? You think I don't know you're Mrs. Thorndyke?"

Her gaze snaps defiantly at the name. Her jaw tightens as her chin bumps up again.

"Dr. Thorndyke and I have not been married for four years," she says in clipped words. "My name is Holly Dolinsky. When you address me, you may call me either Holly or Ms. Dolinsky. Not. Mrs. Thorndyke."

"Whatever," I snap. Because once I get her out of my lab, I won't ever be addressing her again.

"Not whatever. It's—"

"Did he send you or not?"

"As Dean of Agriculture and Life Sciences, he thought—"

"Whatever." I stalk past her to the keypad beside the clean room door. "Go back to your ex and tell him you begged. You can tell him you blew me, if you think that will help."

Fuck. I can't believe I just said that aloud. She'll probably slap me with a sexual harassment lawsuit. And I'd have it coming. I'll deal with that later if I have to. But now ... Now I just need to get this woman out of my lab. "Tell him whatever the hell will get him to back off. Because there is nothing in the world that will convince me to prance around on a stage in front of a camera like some sort of second-rate cable talk show host. Nothing. Not five million dollars. Not some beautiful woman wiggling her ass on my desk."

She actually stumbles back a step in surprise.

Yeah. That should do it.

Before today I may never have scared a woman on purpose, but I do know that the idea of me finding them sexually attractive is enough to terrify most women.

I turn my back to her and swipe my badge to unlock the clean room.

I get two digits in when she wraps her tiny hand around my arm and tugs. Like she's actually trying to turn me around to face her. As if she could so much as budge me.

I take pity on her and turn toward her.

Her arms are crossed over her chest, her eyes blazing. "I didn't wiggle my ass on your desk."

Once again, she's mad, not scared. What the hell is up with this woman?

"Then what was that"—I point to the spot by my computer where she'd sat—"if not an ass-wiggling?"

"I was trying to get your attention."

I snort in disbelief.

"Not like that!" Her voice rises in indignation. "Because you freaked out about my purse being on the desk. I thought my ass would bother you even more."

Yeah. That does make more sense. Because no woman—ever—has wiggled her ass to get my attention.

"This is a lab," I say in a low, but steely tone. "Keep your ass, keep your bag, keep your opinions out of it."

She opens her mouth, but then snaps it shut.

Before she can say anything else, I type in the rest of the code. The door swings open and I stomp in.

I yank it closed behind me before she can follow and do any more damage.

I cross to the sink, roll up my sleeves, start the timer, and begin washing my hands up to my elbows.

When the timer goes off three minutes later, I turn to find her gone.

Thank God.

I sag against the counter, suddenly unsure what to do next.

Twenty minutes ago, my day was perfectly planned. And then she walked in.

I should have been at the computer analyzing the results that came in overnight. Instead, I'm standing here ready to walk into the clean room, except I don't have any work to do in there.

Worse still, when I glance down, I realize I'm standing here in my socks.

They're a pair of blue socks with eyes on them. I don't even recognize them. It isn't surprising given my sister, Tavey, buys me most of my socks and it amuses her to mess with me like that. The eyes stare up at me, like they're judging me.

Yeah. Judgy socks.

Guess I had that coming.

Even by my standards, I've been a colossal ass.

Worse, Holly Dolinsky distracted me to the point that I walked into the foyer of the clean room without putting on my lab shoes and sterile booties. I also neglected to put on a clean lab jacket. Which means the foyer will have to be sterilized before anyone can do any work in there.

Fuck.

Last semester, I fired a grad student for doing almost the exact same thing. I kicked the guy out the program. I made him cry.

I wish I could slam the door on the way out of the foyer, but I don't. Instead, I sit down on the bench, put my damn shoes back on, and roll down my sleeves.

Back at my computer, I type up an email to my lab assistant Gwen asking her to come in and sterilize the foyer.

She's the only one in the department I trust to do it right. Gwen is competent, attentive, and nearly as smart as I am. And she doesn't smell like lemon pancakes.

Probably because when I hired her, I forbade her wearing scented anything since I hate those kinds of distractions.

Holly Dolinsky is just one distraction piled on top of another.

The only good thing about her is that I will never have to see her again.

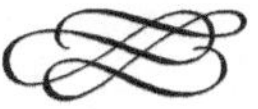

CHAPTER 2

HOLLY

D ick.

Asshole.

Douche canoe.

Monster.

Those were just some of the ways people had described Max Ramsey to me.

Had I believed them?

No.

He can't be that bad, I'd thought.

He's just misunderstood.

I'm used to dealing with difficult, brilliant men.

Ha!

When it's obvious that Dr. Ramsey isn't going to come out of the clean room in his lab to finish our conversation, I stand there, glaring at his back for several seconds before stomping back over to his desk for my bag. I shoot him the finger on my way out.

Not that he notices.

And then I just feel petty.

What is wrong with me?

Out in the hall, I pause, pressing a palm to my chest for a second. My heart is pounding, so I breathe in deeply through my nose, hold it, then exhale slowly through my mouth, mentally pulling up my dealing-with-difficult-people mantra.

Max Ramsey does not intimidate me.

He does not.

I am his equal in every way that matters.

He does not—

Before I can mentally repeat it again, I hear the ding of the elevator followed by voices from down the hall.

I don't want to be caught lurking outside his lab, so I quickly duck into the women's restroom, which is blessedly empty.

I set my bag down on the counter.

Then pick it up and glance around for a hook, because who knows what's on the counter here.

I can practically hear Ramsey sniping about contaminants.

I meet my gaze in the mirror, glare at myself, and set the purse back on the counter. No way I'm letting that jerk get in my head. No. Way.

Anger surges through me.

That man . . .

Had I ever met such an infuriating man in my life?

Everyone was right about him. He is a total . . .

At times like this, I wish I cussed more.

But Momma always said cussing just shows people you don't have a big enough vocabulary to say what you really mean. While the communications lecturer in me can appreciate the linguistic flexibility of certain curse words, the Southern girl in me knows my momma is right.

Besides, as Clive has told me repeatedly, when it comes to holding my own professionally, I have enough obstacles to overcome without cussing like a sailor.

I had weaned myself off curse words a long time ago. And now that I need them, they don't come naturally.

But that man . . . he is . . .

Extremely difficult.

Implying I'd wiggled my behind to get his attention?

Oh . . . if he only knew.

He thought I was trying to seduce him into working with me?

The idea is absurd. I purposefully wore one of my most demure outfits. I'd aimed for the least appealing look I could pull off.

My hair pulled back. My makeup minimal. My bra boob-flattening. My sweater set the color of a 1970s toaster.

I hadn't even worn heels, which I always wear on campus since that time I was mistaken for a visiting high schooler.

But not today. Today, I'd worn my Chucks.

If there's an outfit with less sex appeal than an avocado sweater set and Chucks, I don't know what it is.

And, I mean, I have sexy clothes. I have a body-skimming red dress that makes men drool. I have a pair of Daisy Dukes that literally brought Clive to his knees. It was back when I'd wanted him on his knees, but still. I wore a Hufflepuff schoolgirl outfit to a party last Halloween that had stopped a guy in his tracks. The dude proposed to me on the spot. He was drunk and probably joking, but still . . .

If I wanted to get Dr. Ramsey's attention, I damn well would have done better than this.

The jerk face.

How could that man have accused me of coming there to seduce him?

Of all of the . . .

So unprofessional . . .

I should . . .

But I wouldn't. Even if he had been unprofessional. Even if his suggestion had been outrageous. I wouldn't issue a complaint.

After all, I had put my ass right next to his keyboard. And despite his outrageous claim, no harm was done by it. He had no power over my career. He made no threats.

I may be outraged, but I hadn't felt threatened.

Instead, I'd felt all tingly and breathless.

I'd felt . . . aware.

No. I wasn't going there.

Nope. Nada. No way.

Yes, brilliant men are my weakness. My personal brand of catnip. My fatal flaw.

Doesn't matter. I've been burned by that type of guy before. I may not be smart enough to have earned my PhD, but I am darn well smart enough to have learned that lesson the first time.

And if Dr. Ramsey—the massively arrogant jack apple—is unexpectedly attractive in a burly, overly masculine kind of way, with his thick dark brown hair and steely gray eyes, that is neither here nor there. Because I will probably never see him again anyway.

Texas University has over 40,000 students. His office and lab aren't even on the main campus. I will never run into him accidentally.

Clive asked me to talk to the guy. I did. Now I'm done.

I dampen a paper towel and pat my cheeks with it. Despite my lack of makeup, my skin is all pink and glow-y in a way that not even the sallow green of the ugliest sweater set in existence can offset.

Darn it.

I blow out a breath. I think I need a new mantra.

Max Ramsey is not attractive. He's a bully and a jerk. He's not hot. He does not smell yummy, like warm male skin with the faintest hint of pine. Not in the least.

And I probably just imagined that pine scent anyway. Because he's definitely not the kind of man who wears cologne. Maybe he just has pine-scented soap.

And now I'm imagining him in the shower. Great. Just frickin' great.

I toss the damp cloth in the trash, dry off my fingers with a clean one, and get my phone out. I pull up Clive's number and shoot him a text.

Me: Talked to Ramsey. He wasn't expecting me.

Me: He isn't interested.

I delete that text before sending it and try again.

Me: He doesn't want my help.

Me: I tried. Sorry.

I'm not really sorry.

I'm relieved—deeply relieved—that I won't have to see Dr. Ramsey again.

Partly because of my reaction to him—okay, mostly because of my reaction to him—but also because this whole endeavor is a distraction I don't need in my life right now.

I glance at the clock on my phone. I have just enough time to grab a latte before making it to my afternoon class. Given the state of my nerves, I better make it decaf.

I'm about to slide my phone back into my purse, when Clive replies.

Clive: Go talk to him again. Convince him.

I glare at my phone. I ought to block Clive's texts. It would serve him right.

Before I can, another one rolls in.

Clive: The university needs this. You know you're the right person to do it.

Clive: Get it done.

Me: He doesn't want to do the speeches. There's nothing I can say to convince him.

Clive: Be persuasive. You're good at that.

Me: What does that mean?

Clive: You know what that means. I know how persuasive you can be.

Me: What does that mean???

Clive texts me an emoji of a winking smiley face.

God. Men over forty should not be allowed to send emoji texts.

Was he actually suggesting that I do what Ramsey had accused me of doing?

Dear God.

I break my no-cussing rule.

Me: Flock you.

I hit send before I notice the autocorrect.

Stupid, prudish phone. What the hell does "flock you" mean anyway? Why would my phone think that's what I meant?

Obviously I had taken this no-cussing thing too far if my phone didn't even know cuss words existed.

Clive sends me a laughing emoji, then adds,

Clive: Sorry, dear, we don't do that anymore.

Disgusted, I put my phone into airplane mode before Clive can send another text.

I would bet good money that Dr. Ramsey had made his suggestive comments just to get me out of his office.

Clive, on the other hand, knew exactly what he was doing. Clive is a hound dog. But there's no way I'll report him to human resources. For starters, I know Clive well enough to know he said that just to get a rise out of me. That's the kind of jerk he is, but I would bet good money he would never say that kind of thing to anyone but me.

Besides, I'm a mere lecturer. A peon to Clive's university royalty. I'm so far down on the university totem pole I'm practically buried in the dirt.

Clive is a battle I'm not willing to fight.

Dr. Ramsey is a fight I can't win.

Looks like I picked the right outfit after all. This sweater set is the exact shade of nausea.

CHAPTER 3

HOLLY

I am elbow deep in orange-scented bathroom cleaner and rubber gloves when my African gray parrot, Iago, starts cussing at me.

"Fuck off!" he shouts from his cage in the living room. Repeatedly.

This isn't a good sign.

Iago has anxiety issues, but he only cusses at strangers. Which means there's someone at the door. Since it's nearly ten at night, I can't imagine who.

Normally, I am not a cleaning-at-ten kind of girl, but I have a home visit from the foster-to-adopt social worker coming up. I have a lot of decluttering and organizing to do between now and then, but those activities take more brain power than I have at night. I can scrub a toilet when I'm tired, so that's when I do it.

I don't have time to mess with a visit from anyone right now, nevertheless, I strip off the gloves, rinse my hands in the sink and go investigate. Skip and Lou, my dogs, are huddled by the door, tails wagging eagerly, which explains how Iago knew there was someone there even though no one has rung the doorbell.

"Who's there?" I ask the dogs.

They look at me, then at the door, and then back to me. Lou wags her tail so forcefully she knocks Skip over. The pug normally has excellent balance despite having only three legs, but Lou, my labradoodle, is three times his size. Physics is not in

Skip's favor. He tumbles to one side and skitters around before getting his feet under him again.

Not unlike me this afternoon.

My steps slow as I weave my way through the boxes littering my living room towards the door. I'm in the middle of an epic purge and decluttering that would make Marie Kondo proud and I'm hoping will impress the social worker. Since my normal decorating style consists of mismatched thrift store finds, the additional boxes and piles of clothes just add to the overall ambiance of claustrophobic clutter. Between the boxes and the prancing dogs, the path to the door is an obstacle course.

There is only one person Lou loves like this: Clive.

Before this nonsense with the McPherson Fellowship, I could go months at a time without running into Clive, which was exactly how I liked it. Now I'd seen him twice in the past couple of weeks.

"Fuck off," Iago grumbles miserably from behind me.

"I couldn't have said it better," I mutter.

And then the doorbell rings.

I live in a tiny, mid-century ranch a few miles from campus. Like all houses of that era, it's got a big picture window looking right into the living room. Yeah, I've got curtains, but I'm sure Clive could see the shadows moving behind them. Besides, I'm a grown woman. I didn't go to therapy after the divorce so that I could hide from my ex, no matter how annoying he is.

I nudge Lou aside with my knee and crack the door open. Lou rams her head against my thigh, trying to escape.

"Hey, Clive," I say.

He glances up from the spot he's staring at on the wall beside the door. "Oh good! That really was the doorbell. It took me forever to find it."

I have sizable wisteria vines growing on either side of my door which hide the doorbell. This isn't an accident. I get lots of "people time" at the university. My tiny house is my sanctuary.

He smiles broadly. "Can I come in?"

Before I can tell him it's not a good time, Lou bumps me with the force of a rhino and makes a break for it.

She barrels into Clive, her paws going right up onto his shoulders. He stumbles back a step and gives her head a bemused rubbing. "Hey, Lou. How you doing, girl?"

He looks confused by her enthusiasm. Good lord, he is so oblivious. He's such a jack apple.

He gently lowers her back to the ground and she prances around his legs like a dog ten years younger than she really is as she tries to herd him into the house. I know when I'm defeated, so I step aside and let him in.

Clive is Lou's favorite human in the universe. The fact that he cheated on me during our marriage just pissed me off. The fact that he didn't even ask for her in the divorce damn near broke my heart.

How had I ever loved a man who couldn't love a dog like Lou?

I shut the door behind him as Lou continues to beg pitifully for his attention. In his corner, Iago has moved on from cussing to passive-aggressively kicking birdseed out of his cage.

"Want a glass of wine?" I offer, less out of hospitality and more because I think I'm going to need it before this is all over.

"Um . . . sure." There's hesitancy in his voice as he looks around my tiny living room. "What's going on?"

"Spring cleaning," I say as I pick my way around the stacks of cardboard boxes and head into the kitchen.

"You didn't do spring cleaning when we were married."

His tone—which has just a hint of pout in it, like spring cleaning is some kind of sexual favor I never performed on him—makes me want to hit him over the head. Preferably with something pointy and heavy.

"Seriously?" I ask instead of looking for a murder weapon.

Clive follows carefully, picking his way around the bags of trash and boxes for donation.

He stops in the doorway to the kitchen, apparently willing to go no further, and props his shoulder against the doorjamb. "Since when do you like to clean at all?"

I ignore his question—and the box of wine sitting on the counter—to dig in the pantry until I find a bottle of red decent enough that Clive probably won't wine-shame me. Thank God it's got an actual cork in it.

I take it and the wine opener and hand them to Clive before rummaging for wine-glasses. Clive is the kind of guy who likes to open nice bottles of wine in a display of manly strength. I'm the kind of woman who drinks boxed wine out of a tumbler and pretends it's because it's more environmentally friendly and not just because it's cheaper.

It's a wonder we'd lasted even five years.

Opening the bottle, he shakes his head as he follows me into the living room, once again taking in all the boxes and piles of junk. "What is going on with you?"

I set the glasses on the coffee table and then move a stack of papers from a chair to the floor and gesture for him to sit. My corner of the couch is free of detritus, but not of dogs, so I pick up Skip and put him in my lap as I sit.

"There's nothing up." Nothing that's his business, anyway.

He looks around the room pointedly as he hands me the glass he'd poured for me.

I shrug. "I'm a slob. I always have been. It's one of the reasons we got divorced," I remind him. "Why are you here again?"

That's an over simplification, of course. But Clive never could understand how my ADHD affected my ability to stay organized. How the very idea of organization made me feel incompetent and overwhelmed. It's taken me years to understand these things and make peace with them. I have zero interest in trying to explain these things to Clive, especially since his zero interest in trying to understand them is actually one of the reasons our marriage failed.

As soon as he's seated, Lou puts her head on his lap and sighs in blissful contentment. The jack apple doesn't even notice, but at least he rests his hand on her head absentmindedly.

He ignores my question and says, "That's not why we got divorced. And our house never looked like this. This looks like . . . what's that show about people who hoard?"

"Hoarders?"

"Yes. This looks like you're auditioning for that show. I'm worried about you."

"You came all the way over here at nearly ten to tell me that?"

"No, I was at the office late. And you hadn't been answering my texts all day."

"Because I blocked your texts," I say with a smirk.

His gaze darts to mine. "You . . ." He sighs, raises his glass like he's going to take a drink, but then stops, setting it aside like it might explode. "I'm sorry," he says with forced sincerity. "In our earlier text exchange, I did not mean to imply that our sexual relationship would or should continue or that I have any expectations that it will do so."

For a second, I just stare blankly, trying to process the odd formality of his words. Then I bust out laughing. "Oh my God, did you rehearse that?"

He blushes. "No."

"You did, didn't you?"

He presses his lips together. "The university takes all allegations of—"

"I know, I know." I wave my hand dismissively. "Yes. I got it. And thank you." I try to see it from his point of view and still have to smother a laugh. But bless his heart, he is really trying. "I did not take your text the wrong way. But I still appreciate you trying to clear things up."

He sinks back in his chair and scrubs a hand over his face. Lou raises her head and stares at him, clearly worried. "Thank God." Now he takes a sip of wine. More than a sip, actually. "You know my past. And it's hard to be careful enough."

I did know his past. He'd been the teaching assistant for one of my classes when we'd started dating. The woman he'd cheated on me with had also been a colleague. One or two more incidents like that and it would look like a pattern.

"For men in power, the world has gotten really complicated in the past few years," Clive says.

I know Clive. He's self-centered and egotistical, but he's not a predator. Still, he does have power over people's lives. As one of the few people he actually listens to, it's kind of my job to make sure he sees that. So I say gently, "For women, the world has always been this complicated."

He flinches and then sighs. He does the face-scrub thing again before meeting my gaze. "I know. I'm sorry."

He didn't offer a genuine-sounding apology during the divorce. But this . . . this sounds real. Like he means it. So I nod.

"So now that you know I am not over at HR drawing up a complaint, can I get back to cleaning?"

"Yes." He chuckles. "If this is really cleaning."

But instead of getting up, he settles back in his chair, his hand resting on Lou's head again. The bliss that washes over her is so potent I can feel it from across the room.

He shakes his head looking around. "What is up with you? Seriously?" He pins me with a look. "Is this about the letter from the county I got asking for a letter of recommendation?"

I try to hide a wince. The adoption specialist I'd been working with had wanted a letter from Clive. I'd hedged, hoping she'd give up on it. Apparently, she had not.

"Um . . . maybe."

"Foster kids?" he asked. "Are you sure you're ready for that, Holly?"

"You know I've always wanted kids."

He also knows why I can't have them myself. After the ectopic pregnancy that nearly killed me and had ultimately driven a wedge in our marriage that couldn't be breached, the doctors said my chances of ever conceiving again were slim.

"Well, sure, we both wanted kids. But then . . ."

He trails off, obviously unsure what to say.

Even after all these years, he doesn't have the emotional bandwidth to handle my grief.

"This really is what I want," I try to explain. I look around my tiny house, taking in the massive upheaval I'm putting myself through. My living room looks like a Goodwill collection facility.

Two years ago, I'd started saving to add a third bedroom on to my tiny two-bedroom house. Now that the addition is complete, I'm fully in stage two. The purge. I'm purging a decade's worth of stuff I'd bought hoping it would make me happy and whole. Getting rid of all that junk to make room for two more humans. The only things not on the chopping block are the pets. Everything else can go if it needs to. I feel good about this process. Really good.

"But foster kids . . ." Clive shakes his head. "That's going to be so much work. Especially now. You've got a lot on your plate."

I do. I always did. I have trouble saying no, setting boundaries, and turning away the needy. I over-commit. I under-plan. I charge into situations and obligations without thinking them through. At first, Clive had loved it. Ultimately, it drove him crazy and then drove him away. It had been hard for a man so rigid and set in his ways to live with a woman with ADHD. Just like it had been hard for me to live with a man with a stick permanently lodged up his rectum.

"My plate is just fine," I say. I set aside my glass, hoping he might take it as a sign that the conversation is done. "More to the point, my plate is no longer your business."

"But—"

"You're not my husband anymore, and you're not my boss. If you don't want to write the letter of recommendation for the county, then don't. Beyond that, it doesn't have anything to do with you."

"I just want you to be able to give this thing with Ramsey your full attention."

Ah. That makes more sense. Clive isn't really worried about me. He's worried about himself.

"I told you this afternoon. The thing with Ramsey isn't going to happen. He kicked me out."

"Maybe you misunderstood."

"He was very clear when I talked to him."

Inexplicably, I remember the dark expression in Ramsey's eyes when he'd looked at my legs. And the way he'd stomped around the room like some burly, angry mountain man.

"I'll talk to him again," Clive says, leaning forward to prop his elbows on his knees. Lou's doggy eyebrows knit in confusion when there's no more room for her head. "This is important. For me and the university. If I can get him to work with you, will you try again?"

I hesitate and Clive gives me sad puppy-dog eyes that rival Lou's.

"You have to know what this could do for Ramsey's career. For my career."

I raise my eyebrows and smirk. "How nice for you."

"What if I could free up some money for a consulting fee?"

"How much money?"

I wish I didn't have a price, but I do. I still have debt from the addition to the house.

He rattles off a number just big enough to make my heart thump a little. It's not extravagant, but it would definitely pay off most of the principal of my loan.

"I'll think about it," I tell Clive. I'm not playing hard to get here. Ramsey is intractable, arrogant, and obstinate. I'm not going to get too excited about the prospect of a debt-free future if it depends on Ramsey changing his mind.

"Please, Holly. This is important. To me and to the university."

Obviously, it would be a huge boon to the university. The McPherson Genius Award is a big frickin' deal. And since Clive is the one who hired Ramsey all those years ago, it'll make him look good, too.

"Just what I've always wanted," I quip. "The undying gratitude of my ex and his entire department."

Clive levels a serious look at me. "Don't be dense. The university's gratitude matters. Especially to you."

I study his expression as his words sink in and an uncomfortable knot forms in my belly. I even feel the tension creeping into my jaw as my teeth clench.

I see nothing but kindness in Clive's expression, but it still irritates me. *He* still irritates me. Not because he's being a jerk for pointing it out—though, he kind of is—but because he's right.

I don't have a PhD, which means I'll never be a professor.

Personally, I can live with that. I don't have the ambition or the patience to put in the kind of work it would take to get my doctorate. Even if I did, it wouldn't guarantee me a tenure-track professorship at the university, because the competition for those positions is understandably tight.

Since I am not and never will be a tenure-track professor, I get less pay and I have less job security. Theoretically, I have more "freedom," because I can leave this university and go to a different one any time my contract is up. Unfortunately, that's a freedom I don't want to take advantage of. I don't want to leave Hillsdale. It's been my home for nearly a decade. More importantly, I now have a relationship with the social workers here and the foster-to-adopt program in Texas is one of the best. The kids I want are here. My life is here.

I am so close to having everything I want.

But it will all go away if the university doesn't offer me a contract in the spring. That's just how it is when you're contract faculty. I have more job security than a lot of people, because I teach classes the tenured professors aren't interested in and because my classes are usually full. Despite that, everything I care about is dependent upon the whims of the university.

So, yeah. "The university's gratitude" is no small thing.

"You work for a different department," I say. "You're College of Agriculture and Life Sciences. I'm College of Liberal Arts. You have zero say over whether or not my contract is renewed."

I *hate* that I sound defensive.

"I know that," Clive says, scrubbing a hand down his face. "I'm not threatening your job. I wouldn't do that to you, even if I was in a position to affect your contract. However, if Ramsey gets this fellowship, *especially* if he gets it because of the work you do, I will make damn sure everyone who does affect your career knows that you're a miracle worker."

I don't know for sure if Clive's praise would make any difference in whether or not my contracts continue to get picked up, but Clive does move in the highest circles of the university. He has clout. This university is world-renowned for its Agriculture and Life Sciences programs. So, yeah, Clive pretty much trumps everyone in my department.

In a perfect world, my ex-husband would have no influence on my career one way or the other. Of course, in a perfect world, I'd already be a mother. I'd have a five-year-old little girl asleep in the other room, dreaming of starting kindergarten in the fall. I'd have two working ovaries instead of one and a blown-out mess of scar tissue from the pregnancy that had taken out my fallopian tube and damaged my left ovary.

But this isn't a perfect world. Far from it. So instead of the kids I always wanted, I have rescue animals. Instead of a daughter I gave birth to, I have two empty spare bedrooms I hope to one day fill with foster kids I will love just as much. Instead of career stability, I work my patootie off to be invaluable to the university. I strive to be so good they can't afford to let me go.

I blow out a long breath and will away the tension in my jaw.

"Okay, Clive, I will do whatever I can to help Ramsey." I hold up a cautionary hand before Clive can shower me with praise and thanks. "But it's him you have to convince. That man may be the most stubborn person I've ever met. I can't force him to accept my help and I can't fix what he won't acknowledge is broken. Please tell me you understand that."

The smile Clive sends me is smug and arrogant. Once upon a time, when I was young and stupid, I'd loved that smile.

"I do. But I know you better than almost anyone. You are clever and determined. Ramsey may be the most stubborn person *you've* ever met, but you're the most stubborn person *I've* ever met. My money is on you."

And then he winks at me.

I roll my eyes. Clearly, I've made his night.

A few minutes later, as he's leaving, Clive's enthusiasm slips just a little. "But also . . ."

"Also what?"

"Be careful with Ramsey."

"Careful? What do you mean?"

"I just don't want you to get hurt."

"How would I get hurt?"

Clive's mouth twists into a bittersweet smile, and he reaches out a hand, like he's about to touch my face or maybe my hair, but then catches himself. "Look at you, Holly. You take in every stray and misfit you come across. You find a way to love the most unlovable creatures around."

"No, I don't," I protest automatically.

He holds up his hand as evidence. It's covered with fur from Lou, the least hypoallergenic labradoodle ever bred. "You do." He brushes his hands together, clearly a little confused about how to handle the dog fur. "And Ramsey is brilliant and emotionally unavailable. He's exactly your type." He quirks an eyebrow and wryly gestures to himself. "Case in point. Exactly the kind of guy you'd fall hard for and who would never be able to love you the same way. The way you need to be loved."

I step back, putting some space between me and my ex. "Wow. Sounds like that therapist has been earning her three hundred bucks an hour."

I expect defensiveness from him, but instead he smiles. "Yeah. She has. Just think about what I said."

"Clive, the job you're asking me to do is not simple. You're asking me to help him write speeches that will win over minds of the McPherson committee. And then to teach him how to deliver those speeches with passion that will win over their hearts as well. Do you honestly expect me to do all that and not get at least a little emotionally involved?"

He frowns, clearly weighing my words, then shrugs. "Just keep it professional. It's just a job. I'm not asking you to become his best friend."

I bristle at the patronizing condescension in his voice. It is so like him to imply the problem is with me, not what he's asking me to do.

Once he leaves, Lou and I both spend a long time staring at the door. Lou is once again devastated. Me, I'm just confused.

I want to deny that there's anything to Clive's concerns. Ramsey isn't my type. He's burly. He's gruff. He's mean. He was clearly trying to intimidate me.

But . . . my inner voice whispers, *Not in a creepy way.*

He was more like a . . .

Like a porcupine.

All bristles and defenses.

I met a porcupine once at an animal rehab I'd volunteered at as a teenager. Despite all the quills on the outside, the poor animal still had a soft underbelly. That was where it had gotten hurt in a dog attack. Once the prickly creature had gotten used to humans, she'd been so tame she would roll over and let you pet her tummy.

Okay, yeah, I could see Clive's point. I was a sucker for a wounded animal.

But that certainly didn't mean I was going to fall for Ramsey. There was a huge difference between begging my mom to let me adopt a porcupine and falling for a grown man.

No matter what happened, I would be fine.

If anything, Ramsey's similarity to a wounded animal actually worked in my favor. If I could pretend he was just a vulnerable porcupine, I could ignore the awareness that shot through my body when he stood so close to me. Now all I have to do is make sure I don't get poked.

CHAPTER 4

HOLLY

As soon as I walk into Ramsey's lab, I'm glad I wore my four-inch heels. Dr. Ramsey is nowhere to be seen, but I do see a woman who I assume is either one of his grad students or a coworker. She looks like someone crossed Merida from Disney's Brave with an Amazonian warrior princess and then dressed her up like Scientist Barbie.

She's at least five-ten, with curly red hair that she's attempted to tame into braids. I say, "attempted to" because there are numerous escapees that she's pinned away from her face with a variety of barrettes and bobby pins. She's dressed in a classic white lab coat and has two pairs of glasses—one perched on her nose, and another shoved on top of her head. She is one makeover montage away from winning a Julia Roberts look-alike contest.

Thus my appreciation for my high heels. There aren't a lot of things that intimidate me, but women who are tall, smart, and gorgeous definitely check off all the boxes.

Still, I'm a grown woman, too mature to let intimidation get me down, and too smart to assume that her unblinking stare means she's not a perfectly friendly person.

So I march across the lab and hold out my hand to her. "Hi. I'm Holly."

She blinks rapidly, as though she's not sure how to react. As if no one has ever just walked in and introduced themselves before.

After a moment, she holds out her hand to shake mine. However, in the same moment she pushes her glasses off her nose up onto her head. Unfortunately, this knocks off the glasses that are already perched there. They tumble off the back of her head and fall to the ground. She whirls around, trying to catch the glasses, misses them and then bends down to pick them up. This sequence, causes her to knock a composition notebook and several pens off the counter and onto the floor. Through it all, she mutters a stream of words that start with a greeting and ends with several curse words.

"Hi, I'm— Shoot— Dammit— Fuck!"

I bend down to help her pick up the notebook and pens, but she snatches them out of my way before I can.

"No. I've got it." She stands up, clutching all of the things that touched the ground in her hands, staring at them like she doesn't know whether to throw them away or burn them.

"OCD much?" I ask with a smile, going for friendly teasing.

But in response she frowns. "This is a lab. And besides, OCD—"

I wave a hand to try to get ahead of the train wreck I started. "I'm sorry. That was a jerk thing to say. I know OCD isn't just being particular about cleanliness. And that it's a serious disorder. I was just—" I sigh and press my lips together. "I was nervous to meet you and trying to lighten the mood."

The woman blinks, flinching in what I can only assume is surprise. "You were nervous to meet me?"

I chuckle. "Um, yes. Tall, gorgeous, and brilliant? Hello, intimidation!" I shrug. "And I make stupid jokes when I'm nervous. It's an ADHD thing." Too late I remember Max's reaction to me putting my purse on his desk. "I guess cleanliness isn't something you joke about around here."

She gives me a hesitant smile. "Not so much. I'm Gwen. Dr. Ramsey's lab assistant." She looks down again at the things in her hands and then walks over to the counter by the door and sets them down with a sigh.

I guess she'll have to disinfect them or something. I don't offer to help. Obviously, this environment is not my comfort zone.

She turns back to me and makes another attempted smile. "You must be Holly Dolinsky."

"Yes. I'm here to see Max."

Her eyes go wide again and she clears her throat. "Dr. Ramsey," she says with a note of censure in her voice, "isn't available right now."

Okay. Note to self: Dr. Ramsey is the correct nomenclature when dealing with his minions.

"We have an appointment."

Her smile falters. "Yes, well, he actually asked if I could meet with you instead. Because he's not available."

Wait a second. He made the appointment.

"He's not available?" I ask.

I glance around the lab and immediately see the briefcase he was carrying the other day sitting in the chair next to his computer. Clearly, he's at least been here.

I take a step further into the room so that I can see through the double glass windows from here into the clean room on the other side of the lab.

Sure enough, through the windows I can see the back of a tall, broad-shouldered man with a mane of thick, sable hair.

Ramsey.

In my mind, I whisper his name like a curse.

I practically had to apply thumb screws to get him to agree to this appointment, but I let him pick the day and time. I had to rearrange my schedule to accommodate his. And now he's trying to foist me off on his underling?

My right eye starts to twitch.

I force a smile that makes my cheeks feel as hard as peanut brittle. "Isn't that him right there?"

Gwen follows my gaze, and then her eyes snap back to mine.

"Um, yes?" Her hand goes to her head, and she gives a tug on one of her braids. "But he's unavailable?"

She says both of those things like a question, clearly unsure as to whether or not I'm going to bite.

Needless to say, I don't. "So, he made the appointment, and he's here, but he's somehow unavailable?"

"He . . ." She gives her braid another tug. "Well, you see what happened is that an unexpected shipment of soil samples came in. Late last night. And they have to be analyzed right away. Obviously." She chuckles, tugs her braid, and then pushes an errant curl off her forehead. "Because, you know what it's like. With soil samples. Right?"

Good gravy! This poor girl could not be more nervous. I feel my peanut brittle cheeks softening into a genuine smile. My labradoodle Lou has more chill than this girl.

And yes, I fully recognize that in the past five minutes, I've started to think of this grown woman as a girl. I don't mean to infantilize her, but while she may have me in brains and height, she is clearly a flustered mess.

I can sympathize. I'm a flustered mess half the time.

I've just developed the skills to hide it. If I could teach those same skills to this girl, she would be a force to be reckoned with. It's almost a shame I don't have the time and energy to mentor two people in this lab.

"Max told you why I was here?"

"Yes. Dr. Ramsey said you were here to help with the McPherson grant."

"You know I lecture in the Communications Department, right?" I ask.

"Yes?"

"Can I give you a tip?" Okay, maybe I have a little time to nudge Gwen towards some people skills.

"Yes?" she asks.

"As a general rule, don't lie. Especially when you're talking to someone who's an expert in communications. You're not any good at it. And I'm very good at spotting liars."

Her face falls. "I'm sorry," she says.

This time, it's not a question. Thank God. I definitely couldn't have stomached an apology question.

"Okay," I say. "Let's try this again. You know about the McPherson Fellowship?"

She nods.

"I assume you know how prestigious it is?"

She nods.

"For Max." I deliberately use his first name. Not his title. He doesn't intimidate me. And she needs to know that. "And for the university."

For a second there, it looks like she's about to correct me on the "Max" thing. Again. But I don't give her the opportunity. "And for you."

Her mouth snaps shut.

"Don't you think it will look good on your resume? Having studied under the man who received the McPherson Fellowship?"

"Yes." She nods. And then a burst of words comes out of her mouth so fast and furiously I feel like she's been bottling them up. "He deserves this. He really does. He's so brilliant. And the work he's doing is groundbreaking. I just wish everyone could see and understand how important it is."

I try not to roll my eyes at her dewy-eyed worship of Max.

With minions like this, maybe I should be thankful he's not more arrogant.

"That's all I want, too," I say with exaggerated patience.

Gwen is nodding enthusiastically. "This kind of recognition would be huge for the entire field. And—"

"I'm going to stop you right there. You don't need to sell me on the idea that he deserves to win this grant. You need to sell him on it. *We* need to sell him on it. And as enthusiastic as you are, the McPherson committee is not interested in you. They're not interested in me. They want Max. So I need to talk to him. Because unless those soil samples contain proof of intelligent life outside of our galaxy, or the cure for cancer, or the answer to renewable energy, they are not more important than this meeting."

Before Gwen can respond, I set my bag down on the counter and head for the clean room. I almost make it to the door to the little foyer outside the clean room, when Gwen bodily throws herself in front of it.

"I can't let you go in there."

"I don't think you can stop me."

"It's locked."

I glance down and see a keypad by the door and badge reader.

Yeah. It's locked.

I'm not going to pretend I have mad skills as a pickpocket or anything. But I have four brothers. I've played a lot of keep-away in my life. And, locked or not, this place isn't exactly as secure as Fort Knox. Gwen has her badge around her neck and it's on one of those little retractable strings. I make a grab for the badge and have it in my hand and at the badge reader before she can stop me. The door clicks open.

"It's not locked anymore."

As I reach for the door handle, she squeals. "Oh my God! You're going to get in so much trouble for that! I can't believe you did that!"

I just shrug, not bothering to point out that my boss couldn't care less. And since Ramsey's boss is Clive, the man who begged me to do this job in the first place, I'm not too worried about the repercussions of using Gwen's badge without her permission.

She pleads, "Please, don't go in there. He will literally kill me."

I pause, sigh deeply, and turn back to her. "He will literally kill you?"

"Yes."

"Literally?"

She blinks. "Well, not literally."

"Good. Because if he would literally kill you for letting someone into his sacred space, I would have to call the police. And probably get you a therapist or something. Because you shouldn't be working for someone who would literally kill you for something as silly as this."

She lets out a strangled laugh. Which is exactly the reaction I was hoping for.

"Okay. He would figuratively kill me. I would have to clean the room again. Scrub it. And he would be really mad."

"The second rule for dealing with someone who specializes in communications is use the words you mean. You're a PhD candidate, Gwen," I tell her gently. "Say what you mean."

"Okay, what I mean to say is that it is a real pain if anyone goes in there and contaminates the room. Even the foyer has to be cleaned regularly. The clean room has to be kept pristine, or we risk contaminating the soil samples."

"He's in there."

"Yes. But he had to follow the procedure before going in."

I just look at her and arch an eyebrow, because if there are procedures that need to be followed, I can do that.

She may be tall. She may be smart. But she has definitely met her match.

CHAPTER 5

MAX

Few things in life annoy me more than a lack of focus. It annoys me when people around me can't focus. It straight-up infuriates me when I'm the one who can't focus.

It shows a lack of self-discipline I simply cannot abide.

Thankfully, it isn't a problem I often suffer from.

Unfortunately, it is definitely a problem I am suffering from today. I know exactly who to blame: Holly Dolinsky.

She is the thorn I simply can't get out of my paw.

In the four days since she first visited my lab, I've received a visit from Clive Thorndyke, three phone calls from him, an email from the president of the university, and no fewer than three phone calls from Ms. Dolinsky herself. Each requesting a meeting.

This is exactly the kind of shit I shouldn't have to put up with. I had already come to that conclusion, even before Clarissa met me outside my lab yesterday morning and refused to let me enter until I agreed to schedule a meeting with Holly. I might be able to ignore the president of the university—not for long, but for a while—but I cannot ignore Clarissa. She is the woman who buzzes in the delivery people when they bring me lunch. And coffee. If I piss her off, I may never get delivery again.

So yesterday I relented and scheduled an appointment with Ms. Dolinsky. Thankfully, I have no plans to actually attend the appointment.

After all, what is the point of having three lab assistants, if I can't assign them things like this? Since Gwen is always the first to volunteer for any job, I assigned the task to her. She will meet with Ms. Dolinsky and report back.

The matter should be simple. It should not be distracting me.

But all morning, as the clock ticked closer and closer to the meeting time, my ability to focus became more and more erratic. When I glanced up and saw that it was 10:02, I had to resist the urge to turn around and see if she was already in the lab.

The clean room is relatively silent, the way I like it, and with two layers of walls and glass between me and the rest of the lab, I haven't heard her come in. I've heard no conversation. With any luck, Gwen followed my suggestion that they have the actual meeting in the staff room down the hall.

It's only a few minutes past ten when I hear the series of beeps that indicates Gwen has used her badge and security code to open the foyer to the clean room.

I pause for a moment before returning to the task of isolating a single-cell protozoan from the soil sample. Since I'm still distracted, I'm aware that it seems to take longer than it should for Gwen to scrub up and change into her slippers and protective gear. Normally, that's not the kind of thing I would even notice. Several minutes pass after the initial beeps of the door opening before the clean room opens.

Without looking up, I say, "These slides here are ready to be analyzed."

But before I can return my attention to the work in front of me, I inhale and am hit with a whiff of lemon-scented shampoo.

Fuck.

Gwen knows better than this. She's worked with me for three years. She's never made this kind of mistake before. But if that scent of lemon means what I think it means, Gwen better have a backup plan that doesn't involve a PhD in microbiology.

I snap one last picture on the digital microscope, hit save, and turn around.

Sure—fucking—enough.

The person who entered my clean room is not Gwen.

Oh, she's wearing slippers over her feet, a clean lab coat, gloves, and a cap, just like Gwen would. But she's not Gwen. Not even a little bit. The person who enters is a bundle of lemon-scented energy here to wreak havoc on my life.

"What are you doing here?"

Above her face mask, her eyes narrow. "The next time you schedule an appointment with me, I expect to meet with you. Not your lab assistant."

"Gwen is a perfectly competent—"

"Gwen isn't you. Gwen isn't up for the McPherson grant. I need to talk to you. Not Gwen. And I need you to take this seriously."

"I do! Thorndyke wanted me to reach out to the committee to tell them I want to be on the short list. So I did it. I emailed them. I agreed to do whatever stupid shit they want me to. But not if it interferes with my work. My work has to come first."

"No one is saying your work isn't important. Clearly it is. But this is important too. Not just for you. For the university."

"I know it's important. I assume that's why Clive hired you. He said you're the best."

She seems to be gritting her teeth. "Clive assured me you were going to cooperate."

"I am cooperating. That's why I told Gwen to give you the information you need. I told her she can set aside all of her work until this is done. You have full access to her."

"That's not good enough. I don't need full access to Gwen. I need full access to you. You have to do this."

"I don't have to do anything."

"Think about how it will look if you don't."

I snatch my cane in my hand and take a step forward. She does too. Suddenly, the clean room, which isn't that big to begin with, feels even smaller than normal.

"I don't care how it looks to the university. I don't even care how it looks to the McPherson committee. Either they respect the work I do or they don't."

"Fine. But if you don't care how it looks to the McPherson committee, think about how it looks to the tenure committee."

"What the hell is that supposed to mean?"

The look she gives me implies I'm being dense. "You're up for tenure soon, right?"

"Yes." I've been at the university for five years. Next year, I'll be up for tenure.

Sure, I dabbled with the idea of getting a job in the private sector. But that isn't where my interests lie. I want to be at a university. This university in particular, since it has the advantage of being close enough to my sister that I can visit her occasionally. Moreover, I want the security that comes with a tenured position. I want to know the university isn't going to fire me just because my class numbers are low. Tenure means freedom from socializing and awkward faculty parties or worrying what my students think. Not that I actually care what they think, but I do care about things like funding, staffing—the kind of resources I need to get my work done. All things that come with tenure.

"What's your point?" I demand, because there's no way she's implying what I think she is.

"Come on, Max. You may not care about getting this fellowship." She jabs a finger in my face, her eyes narrowing. "Which, by the way, I don't actually believe, because no one goes to all the hard work of getting two PhDs if they don't care about getting recognition for their work."

"I—"

"My point is, even if you don't care about the fellowship, the tenure committee will care."

Suddenly it feels like I can't breathe. There's a tight pressure in my chest like someone has reached into my lungs, grabbed them in a fist, and started slowly twisting them. I clutch the handle of my cane more tightly, focusing on the feel of the wood against my palm, hoping it will ground me. It doesn't.

I had never once considered the possibility that I might not get tenure, not since my mom got tenure when I was eight, when I first learned what tenure was.

"The McPherson committee only gives out one of these fellowships a year." Shock makes my voice come out even more gravelly than normal. "The university can't deny me tenure just because I don't win it."

She takes a step closer, too. Bumps up her chin in that annoying way she has, like she's daring me to argue with her. "No, they can't deny you tenure just because you don't get the fellowship. Obviously. But the tenure committee will care about whether or not you try."

Fuck.

Is she right?

She can't be.

The tenure committee knows I do good work. My research is more important than any damn fellowship, even one as important and prestigious as the McPherson Fellowship. Even one worth five million dollars.

Because it's not like the university cares about prestige or money.

Fuck.

God. Damn it.

She's right.

They will care.

Almost as if she can read my thoughts, she keeps talking.

"The tenure committee needs to know that you're committed to doing the right thing for the university. They need to know that you are an investment worth making. You need to be an asset that they can't afford to lose."

"The work I do here in this lab, the groundbreaking work that's going to change the face of agriculture and possibly space exploration, should be more important than any stupid fellowship from the McPherson committee or anyone else."

"I agree. It *should* be more important. But a breakthrough that can *change* the world isn't worth jack if you can't *share it* with the world."

Her words hit too close to home. They land on every fear, every frustration I have. Despite myself, my emotions get away from me, and my words come out like a roar. "You think I don't know that?"

I've spent decades working on controlling my temper. And there are few things that frustrate me more than when I lose control of it.

But this tiny little bundle of a woman pisses me off like no one ever has. She pushes every damn button I have. And before I know it, I'm stomping closer to her.

My breath is coming in fast, sharp inhalations, so I rip my face mask off and toss it onto the counter.

Part of me expects her to turn and run. To be afraid.

Because she's tiny, and I'm huge. Every woman I've ever met—and most grown men —seem terrified when I lose my temper.

But she doesn't turn and run. She doesn't even back up. No. She takes a step closer and takes off her own face mask. By the time I speak, we're mere inches apart; she is looking up at me, and I am glaring down at her.

"You think I don't know this shit is important," I say. "I *do* know it's important. You think I don't wish I was good at it? I do. But I'm not good at it. That's why the university has hired three lab assistants to help me. Not because I need help with the research. Not because I need help analyzing samples. But because when it comes to talking to students, to other people, or when it comes to conveying my ideas, I fucking suck. I have other people who do it for me. That's why you should turn tail and run. Or just meet with Gwen."

Impossibly, Holly takes a small step even closer to me. She meets my gaze without flinching, unperturbed by the full blast of my fury.

"You may think that the university hires grad students for you so that you don't have to do this kind of thing. But they're not doing you any favors. And I don't care whether or not you're good at this. You don't have to be. *I'm* good at it. And I can make you good at it too. I can't do that if you only let me meet with Gwen. The McPherson committee doesn't want Gwen. They want *you*. They want you in inter-views. They want you on social media. They want your thoughts. Not hers."

Suddenly, staring down at her, I'm aware of three things. First, my heart is thundering because of how close she's standing. I didn't close the distance between us. She did. I'm looming over her and she's not even batting an eye, because this tiny fireball of a woman isn't afraid of anything.

The second thing I'm aware of is the inexplicable urge to kiss her. Quickly on the heels of that, I realize I'm staring at her lips as I imagine what it would be like to do so.

Shit. I'm staring at her lips.

Her unmasked lips.

"Why the hell did you take off your mask?" I roar at her.

"Because you took yours off first," she roars back.

"Fuck." I plow a hand through my hair. "Now I have to scrub down the entire clean room. Look what you made me do!"

"I made you do?" She jabs a finger in my chest. Over and over again to punctuation each word. "You. Took. Off. Yours. First. I didn't do anything you didn't do. How is this my fault?"

"You made me lose my temper," I snarl.

And, yeah, I know what an asshole I sound like. I know I'm being completely unreasonable.

Holly has the gall to laugh. "*I* made you lose your temper? I hate to break it to you, but this isn't on me. Your lack of control is on you."

For one terrifying second I'm tempted to tell her that I have plenty of control. If I didn't have control, I would have kissed her by now. I would know if she tastes like lemons as well as smelling like them.

I'd also probably be rolling around the floor in pain, because if I did that, she'd undoubtedly stab me with something. And even then she wouldn't run away. No, Holly would probably stab me, then bandage me up, then lecture me about how to grovel in front of the McPherson committee.

The simple truth is, what she just described is everything I've ever wanted. I know everything would be easier if I was better at sharing my ideas. I know it's important. I've tried. And I just fucking suck at it. I've had colleagues tell me they can't read my work without having a copy of the Oxford English Dictionary in one hand and access to Google with the other.

I want to explain that to her. To make her understand the frustration of having so many ideas churning through my brain and not being able to slow my mind down enough to get them out in a way that makes sense to other people. But I can't even convey that. Let alone the complexity of my work. There are few things that I want more than I want to be able to explain my ideas. That just isn't where my strengths lie. And that's something a woman like this can never understand.

I *know* that. I don't explain myself or justify my behavior to anyone. I gave up on that a long time ago.

I could even give her the ever growing list of books my aunt keeps sending me about how to manage these various disorders. God knows there isn't anyone who has tried harder to understand how to deal with me than my aunt has. If those diagnoses and those books haven't helped her, they sure as hell aren't going to help Holly.

And yet, despite that, I *want* her to understand. I *need* her to.

"My lack of control isn't the problem," I practically snarl. "My Asperger's is the problem. I fucking suck at reading nonverbal cues like facial expressions and body language. It's why I'm a shitty lecturer and an even worse teacher. To make matters worse, my Asperger's comes with a side order of sensory processing disorders, which means things are too scratchy or too loud or smell too strong. Plus, I'm a goddamn bull in a china shop everywhere I go because I'm too distracted to pay attention to my surroundings." I waggle my cane in between us. "And all of that was true before the car crash that left me with this goddamn limp."

The words are out before I think them through, before I realize what a fucking whiner I sound like. When I see that flash of pity in her eyes, that's when it hits me that I've crossed a line I never cross. The line between gruff asshole and pathetic loser.

The pity is only in her gaze for an instant, but it slices me all the way to the bone. I don't give her a chance to voice it out loud, and instead come out swinging.

 "Those are all the reasons I'm not the right guy for the McPherson Fellowship. I have a damn grocery list of shit wrong with me, none of which your degree in communications can fix." I make sure to add an extra splash of derision to the word communications, because I would always rather be a dick than be the object of pity. "What the fuck was Thorndyke thinking siccing you on me? You're so underqualified, it's a joke."

This is the point in my tirade where I expect her to turn tail and run. That's what any sane person would do. Especially since she's only doing this because her ex-husband has either bribed or bullied her into doing it. It's her fucking job.

"There's no way in hell you actually want to work with me, so I've just given you the perfect out. You're not qualified. You don't have to skill set to fix all the shit that's wrong with me. So take the easy out, and stop meddling in things you can't handle."

I'm still waiting for my words to cut her as deeply as that flash of pity in her gaze cut me.

Instead, her expression softens. Just a little, but I see it. Even me, as bad at reading emotions as I am, see it. Or maybe it's just her. Maybe I can read her emotions because she holds my attention in a way no one else ever has. Because I can't stop looking at her.

Then she does the last thing I expect.

She sighs, and says, "You're right."

"What?"

"You're right. I'm not a neurologist or a psychologist. I'm not an occupational therapist. I can't 'help' with any of the symptoms related to your autism spectrum disorder
or your sensory processing disorder." She makes finger quotes around the word
"help." "But you're wrong about almost everything else you said. First off, you're
not broken. You don't need to be fixed. Secondly, wake up. You're a professor at a
research university. You couldn't throw a microscope in this building without hitting
someone with an autism spectrum disorder."

"Why on earth would I throw a microscope?"

She blinks at me, then her lips curve. "It's an expression. Usually people say, 'You
couldn't swing a cat without hitting ...' whatever. But I figure there aren't many cats
in this building."

"Of course there aren't cats in this building."

"My point is, Asperger's doesn't make you special, and it certainly doesn't mean
you're broken. I can't and wouldn't change anything about who you are. I just need
to teach you how to give a speech. And that is something I'm good at. Something I'm
excellent at, as a matter of fact. I help people write speeches all the time. I teach
people how to give speeches for a living. I do it to lecture halls packed with students
who are less knowledgeable and less passionate about their topics than you are. I
know I can do this. All I am asking is that you give me a chance to prove that I'm
right."

She says the words calmly, but with a quiet determination that unnerves me.

After a long moment, standing there staring down at her, hoping she'll back down so
that I won't have to deal with her, with the distraction of her lemon-scented hair or
her warm brown eyes.

When she doesn't, I say, "Fine. If you're so fucking determined to work with me,
you've got it."

"Good."

"But not here. Not now."

"Why not?" Her gaze narrows just a little.

Why not?

Why not, indeed.

Not now, because I'm too unsettled. Because my pulse is racing, and my senses are filled with her. Because just standing this close to her makes me want things I shouldn't.

It makes me want to know what her breasts feel like in my palms and if her skin feels as incredible as it looks. What she tastes like. What it would feel like to be buried deep inside of her.

I shouldn't want those things because I can't have those things.

I made peace with who I am and what I can and cannot have a long time ago.

But I'm sure as hell not about to say any of that to her.

"Not now, because I have work to do that can't wait. And this is a clean room. You shouldn't even be in here."

"I wouldn't be in here if you'd kept my original appointment. The appointment *you* made."

I don't have anything to say to that, so I just shut my mouth and stand there glaring down at her.

Thankfully, she doesn't seem to need a response from me.

"The next time you make an appointment, be ready to meet with me. Stop wasting my time."

"Fine. The next time we schedule an appointment, it won't be in my lab. Don't you ever come into my clean room again."

"Oh, that won't be a problem. Because the next time we have an appointment, you can come to me."

She spins on her heel and marches to the door.

"If you think I'm walking all the way across campus to meet in your office, you're delusional."

She turns and props her hands on her hips. "I don't expect you to walk all the way across campus. I assume you have a handicap license. You can drive across campus and park near my building. I have exactly one assigned parking spot and it's two miles from here. Either you can come to me or we can meet somewhere off campus. Because I'm not walking this long distance again just to have you blow off our appointment."

Before I can respond, she's gone.

Thank God.

It hadn't occurred to me that she might have to walk from a parking space two miles away.

I feel like an ass, which is stupid. I never care whether or not I inconvenience other people. I make a point of that.

Because if I'm going to feel like an ass, it should be because I yelled at her. Intimidated her. Or because I stood her up for our appointment. Thankfully, I'm used to feeling like an ass. It's pretty much my thing.

CHAPTER 6

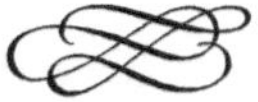

HOLLY

I'm forty-seven minutes into an hour-long lecture about Heidi Klum's evolving media presence when the door at the back of the lecture hall opens.

It isn't unusual for students to come in late, but most kids wouldn't bother coming in for the last thirteen minutes of a class. Somehow I know it's Max, even before I look up.

Of course, Max—who doesn't do anything discreetly—throws open both of the doors with enough force that they bang loudly. Half the students turn to look when I do.

Because I rely heavily on visual presentations, the lecture hall is dark except for the lit area on the dais where I am. So there's a long moment when we collectively stare at Max, backlit by the lights outside the lecture hall, his massive frame seeming to take up nearly the entire span of the double doors.

I stare for a full beat. It takes every ounce of willpower for me to not glare at him.

Because what in the proverbial handbasket is he doing here?

I muster more willpower and return my attention to the lecture.

This is content I'm familiar with. I've done some variation of this lecture every semester for the past four years. I know this.

And it still takes me several pounding heartbeats to get back on track.

Worse still, I falter. Several times.

At the end of a class, I should be driving home the point I'm trying to make—in this case the way Heidi Klum has smartly parlayed her initial fame as a model into a business empire. Instead, because he is watching, I stumble through the end.

Do I make my point?

Yeah. Probably.

But, darn it, why did he have to show up during my lecture about a supermodel?

Two days ago, I gave a rousing lecture about Bobby Kennedy's seminal speech on the night Martin Luther King was assassinated. It was an insightful look at race relations and the lingering impact on politics and our nation. I brought a student to tears.

Did Max Ramsey—one of the smartest men I will probably ever meet—walk in on that talk?

No. He shows up to hear me talk about a supermodel's Instagram feed. Just friggin' great.

But I finish the lecture. Because this content is important. And relevant. And I don't have to justify myself to Max Ramsey.

The timer goes off on my phone just as I'm finishing up, reminding me (and the class) that we only have a few minutes left.

I force a smile. "Obviously, I'd hoped we'd have time for questions. Since we didn't, you all know when my office hours are." As I turn off the projector, I remind them, "Don't forget, your speech on trending memes during the 2016 election is due by midnight tomorrow night. And I do mean midnight central time. However, I have office hours today and tomorrow if you need help."

Most of my students pack up and head out. A few linger to talk to me. There are always a few with questions. I'm answering as best I can, but a chunk of my awareness is focused on Max, who is thumping down the stairs as my students scurry out of his way.

The guy is like a bulldozer.

Or maybe just a bull.

By the time he reaches me, my bag is packed up, I've turned off the projector, and I'm almost ready to leave. There's a girl who wants to talk about the new Heidi Klum show on Amazon, but when Max scowls at her, she too flees.

He stops at the dais, right in front of me.

It's the first time I've seen him outside of his lab. Instead of the white lab coat, he's got on an ill-fitted suit jacket over a white oxford shirt. His tie is a gawd-awful paisley that someone should have thrown away a decade ago. His hair is even more disheveled than usual.

The first time we met, it had been . . . flatter. As if he'd at least made a recent effort to tame it. Now, I see that it's wavy and thick and that when he's not in his lab, he probably runs his hands through it.

Which shouldn't be sexy.

No . . . wait.

Allow me to rephrase that.

It isn't sexy.

Not at all.

Because this man is irritating and a total jerk and nothing about him is sexy.

Except maybe the way he smells. Clean and woodsy.

Darn it.

No. I will not think about how he smells.

Instead, I glare at him and try to sound professional.

"Is there a reason why you're here? Besides terrifying my students."

His gaze narrows as he looks around the room.

I swear a student breaks into a run.

"I'm not scaring your students," he says in his low, grumbly voice. "You said I should come to you. So I came."

That voice does things to me that it shouldn't. Warm, gooey things.

"When I said you should come to me next time, I meant that you should schedule an appointment and meet me in my office."

I cross my arms over my chest, wishing I could glare down at him.

The fact that I can't glare down at him when I'm standing on a dais that's at least six inches above the ground and I'm in four-inch heels is proof we live in an unjust and uncaring universe. I should be able to glare down at him from this height. Instead, I can almost meet his gaze eye to eye.

Almost.

Whatever architect designed this room should be fired.

"I came here," Max grumbles, "because I wanted to see if you're any good."

"Oh, I'm very good."

"Excuse me if I'm not impressed with your in-depth analysis of Heidi Klum's social media presence."

I grit my teeth.

I knew it.

I friggin' knew it.

I suck in a breath. And then exhale it quickly, because there's that yummy pine scent again.

No. I am not going to let this jerk get in my head.

"Do you even know who Heidi Klum is?"

"Based on your slides, she's a 'social media influencer.'"

"So, in other words, no. You don't know who she is." Ha! Yeah, look who's smart now. "But that's okay, because every one of my students does. More to the point, they knew who she was before today's lecture, because she's one of the most important women in fashion."

I see the beginning of an eye roll and cut it off by jabbing a finger in his direction.

"Also, you could learn a thing or two from Heidi Klum. Because if there's anything harder in the modern world than a beautiful woman over the age of forty remaining relevant, it's making dirt sound interesting."

I swear, he practically flinches at my jab about dirt.

A muscle in his jaw twitches as he looks me up and down.

His gaze is somehow both hot and cold.

I feel he's cataloging my every feature in a way that makes me intensely aware of everything about myself.

In particular, I'm aware of how different I look from the previous times we've met.

On both previous encounters, I'd gone to his lab. I'd known I'd be seeing him.

And, yes, that first time, I'd dressed down on purpose. Last time, I hadn't given my appearance much thought. I hadn't worn much makeup on either occasion.

As for today . . .

Well, today I was in full lecturing garb. Heels. Dress that skirted the line between professional and playful. My hair was in loose curls. My makeup worthy of the stage.

I look good. Like I always try to when I lecture.

To capture and hold the attention of nearly three hundred students, I need the confidence boost and they need to believe I'm worth listening to.

Max seems decidedly less impressed.

He steps closer, his gaze narrowing and his mouth curving into a sneer, and I know his next words are more about me than they are about Heidi Klum. "You expect me to believe that being beautiful is such a hardship."

"You're going to believe whatever you want to believe."

"Am I?" he asks. "Or are you going to try to manipulate me into believing what you want me to believe based on how you dress."

"What is that supposed to mean?" I ask the question even though I can guess what he's talking about.

Max Ramsey isn't exactly a master of subtlety.

"Both times you showed up at my office dressed like a mousy undergrad. Then I walk into your lecture and see you looking like ..." His mouth pinches as he drags his gaze up and down my body one more time.

I can't tell if he can't think of the words to describe my appearance or can't choke them out past his disgust.

At least, my mind and common sense can't. My body seems pretty darn sure it knows what he's thinking, because heat flushes my skin and every darn cell in my body snaps to attention in response. Even my nipples harden as if to say, "Look at us! Look at us!"

Thank goodness my arms are crossed over my chest.

"Like what?" I ask coldly.

"Like a . . ." He seems to be casting around for a vile enough description. Then he gestures broadly at the screen behind me, where moments ago my presentation slides were displayed. "Like a fashion model."

I nearly laugh. "I'm five-two. I look more like a Smurf than a fashion model."

"What the hell is a Smurf?"

"What does it matter? I don't look like a fashion model."

"You know what I mean," he grumbles.

"Why don't you explain it anyway?" I goad. Because I need him to say it. I need to hear it out loud.

"You're pretty. And you tried to pretend you're not."

His tone makes it perfectly clear that he means "pretty" as an insult.

Ouch.

Yeah. That one hurts.

I've had a lot of people dismiss me over the years based on my appearance alone. Having this jack apple dismiss me shouldn't hurt. But it does.

I knew it would. It's why I pushed him to say it.

Because he's a jerk. And I can't forget that.

I can't ever forget that.

Because if I do, I'll end up focusing on the fact that he's brilliant and smells faintly of pine and has hair that looks touchably soft.

"So what if I am pretty?" I ask, getting even closer. Getting right in his face. Because if he's going to be a jerk, then I will be too. "You think that means I can't also be smart? You think that means that I'm incapable of intelligent conversation? Of ambition?" My voice rises with each question, to the point that I'm almost yelling at him.

"Of having the skills and knowledge you need to get this grant? Is that what you think?"

"No. Of course not!" he practically roars, hands flying into the air in a broad gesture. He doesn't even seem to notice that he's holding his cane in one hand.

I take a step back automatically. Maybe to avoid his cane, but also because his roar makes me realize how loud I've gotten.

Sucking in a deep breath, I press a hand to my belly, trying to settle the sudden tension stirring there. Because I never yell. I just . . . don't.

That's how unsettled this man makes me. This brilliant, infuriating man who says he didn't dismiss me because of my appearance, but has obviously done just that.

I glare at him. "Don't."

"What?" he demands. "Don't shake my cane at you?" He gives it another shake. This one accompanied by a mocking smirk. "I'm not going to hurt you. But since you demanded I come to you, I needed my cane to get down all those damn stairs. And I can't very well throw up my hands in annoyance without shaking it."

My gaze flickers to the stairs behind him. It's a lot of stairs.

I haven't asked about the cane. About why he needs it. But I have seen him limp, so I assume his leg hurts when he walks. Maybe that's why he's so grumpy all the time.

Maybe.

But that doesn't mean I'm going to let him get away with treating me like I'm less competent just because I know how to use a curling iron.

So I take a step closer. Again. Back into cane-shaking range, just so he knows I'm not scared of him. "I didn't mean don't shake your cane. I meant don't dismiss me because of my looks."

"I . . ." He stammers for a second. Then looks me over again, before saying, "I didn't make your beauty an issue. You did when you purposely dressed up in that hideous sweater set designed to make you look like an avocado."

I snap my mouth closed, not sure how exactly to respond to that.

"What am I supposed to think? You were frumpy when you came to my office, but when I show up here, you look like this. Obviously, you didn't want me to know you're beautiful. I didn't dismiss you because of your appearance. You did."

"That's the stupidest thing I've ever heard. And I teach a lot of twenty-year-olds who say a lot of stupid things."

"You didn't want me to know you're pretty. Why not? Were you afraid I'd be attracted to you? That I wouldn't be able to resist you? Because trust me, that's not going to be a problem."

"Okay, I take it back. *That* is the stupidest thing I've ever heard."

"What else am I supposed to think when you deliberately hid the way you look?" he asks in a tone that's . . .

What?

There's something in his tone I can't quite pin down. Almost like he's hurt, like I hurt his feelings.

So I soften my tone when I answer. "That I wanted to be taken seriously. That I didn't want you to dismiss me based on a first impression."

"I wouldn't dismiss you based on what you look like."

"Oh sure," I say glibly. "But you did dismiss me based on my profession. My field of research. My lack of PhD. Do you really think you would have stopped at my outward appearance?"

"I didn't—"

"You're taken seriously simply because you're a man. Throw a couple of PhDs in the mix, and there's no one on earth who won't take you seriously."

"I didn't throw PhDs in the mix. I worked my ass off for them."

"Did you?" I ask archly, even though I know the answer. No one gets their doctorate without working for it. Not even people as brilliant as Max. But I'm desperate to get the conversation back on track. To talk about this professional relationship we're supposed to have instead of whether or not I want him to be attracted to me. "If you worked for your doctorate, then why aren't you willing to work for this?"

"Because I shouldn't have to prove myself to anyone. The work should speak for itself."

Yeah. There it is.

Every researcher I've ever met has that innate arrogance. It doesn't surprise me that when it comes to his research, Ramsey has it in spades.

What is surprising is his vulnerability when it comes to his people skills. His stubborn refusal to even try to learn. He's like a child so convinced he's going to drown he refuses to step into the pool.

"Your work can't speak for itself," I tell him, "if no one ever sees it because you're too lazy to learn how to share it with a modern audience."

"I'm not lazy," he barks.

"Then why can't you bother to learn how to communicate?"

"I shouldn't have to jump—"

I can tell he's about to launch back into the argument about how he's above all this, so I cut him off. "Wait. You don't think . . . you don't think I'm smarter than you, do you?"

"Of course not."

His indignation is almost amusing.

Almost.

Though it would be better if he wasn't quite so horrified by the implication.

"Yeah, that's what I thought." I turn around and march back over to the podium to pick up my bag. "If you're smarter than I am, and I learned how to do this stuff, then you can, too."

I cross the dais to the steps on the other side before heading toward the door.

"Wait. Where are you going?"

I turn back around to see him following me. I almost feel bad for the guy. "I have office hours."

"So we're not going to do"—he gestures broadly again—"whatever it is you think I need to do."

"Yes. We're going to do it. The next time we meet."

"But I'm here now."

"And I have students waiting for me. Which I could have told you, if you'd bothered to make an appointment. Like I asked you to."

He stops following me and his gaze settles into another scowl. "Fine," he barks. And then, as if he just can't stand not to have the last word, he says, "But the next time we meet, I don't want you dressed like an avocado."

I stop, turn back to him, and pin him with a look that would skewer a lesser man.

"Did you just tell me how I should dress? That I should look pretty for you?"

This time, it's his turn to laugh. "I don't give a fuck how you look. Just don't hide your looks because you think I care about it. If I am going to dismiss you, it's not because of how you look. It's because I don't need your expertise."

God, he is such a jack apple.

"That's three," I tell him.

"What? Three strikes and I'm out?"

"No. That's three extremely moronic things you've said. And that's just today. You need my help way more than you think you do."

CHAPTER 7

HOLLY

You would think that, given that it's Friday afternoon on a beautiful spring day, fewer students would want to visit my office hours. After all, a lot of the students in my Modern Comm class are seniors who are not comm majors and have put off taking a communications requirement until now. They should have better things to do.

Despite all that, it's after five before the last of the students leave my office. I've barely had time to open my laptop when my friend, Liz, knocks on the doorframe and sticks her head in the office.

Dr. Elizabeth Farrow isn't in the Communications Department, but a lot of the English profs have offices on the fifth floor. Liz is my best friend at the university. One of my few friends, if I'm honest.

It's no secret that I got my job as a lecturer because the university was trying to entice Clive away from his previous position at a prestigious private university back east.

That made it hard—okay, impossible—for me to make friends in the Communications Department. Never mind that I'm good. Never mind that my sections are always full. Never mind that I teach filler classes most full professors have no interest in. Never mind that Clive and I are divorced now. There are still people who think I'm just an unqualified bimbo. Thankfully, the head of the department isn't one of those people. Still, it means my friends all teach in other departments.

"You busy tonight?" Liz asks, distractedly.

She's got her shoulder propped on my doorjamb, but she's leaning out in the hall to watch the last student walk away.

"What do you have in mind?" I ask. I still need to update my slides for Monday's lecture, but technically I can do that at home this weekend.

"I'm thinking a comparative study of modern interpretations of classic literature."

"So, another Jane Austen marathon."

She looks back at me, shooting me puppy-dog eyes. "Please? Pretty please?"

I nearly groan. "I love Mr. Darcy as much as the next woman, but haven't we seen every version of *Pride and Prejudice* like, six times?"

"Ah!" She holds up a finger, eureka-style. "But we've only seen the newest *Emma* once." Clearly she assumes she's already won the argument, because she comes into my office and plops down on the chair opposite my desk. "By the way, why didn't you tell me Colton Solimar is one of your students?"

"Um . . . Colton Solimar is one of my students," I tell her. It takes me a minute to pair the name from my class roster to the face of the kid who just left. And, yes, by kid, I mean grown man who is at least twenty-two. But he still feels like a kid to me. "Should I know who Colton Solimar is and why you'd want to know that he's in my class?"

"Colton Solimar? Pitcher for the university's baseball team? Probably going pro when he graduates in May?"

I shrug. "You know I don't do sports."

Liz rolls her eyes again. Sometimes, I wonder how she doesn't have eye strain.

"I know you don't do sports. But you're a living, breathing, heterosexual woman. Don't you . . . you know, *do* hot guys?"

She puts a hard emphasis on "do." As if there was any chance I could mistake her meaning.

"Ew. That young man is one of my students."

"Only for a few more months." She leans forward and waggles her eyebrows at me. "And if I had to guess, that young man is hot for his teacher."

"Double ew. And I'm pretty sure he isn't."

She leans back, shaking her head. "You are so clueless sometimes. He graduates in May. Why else would he be in your office talking to you until after five? On a Friday."

"Because he's worried about his grades."

"Do you have any idea how many tutors the athletes have access to? If he was worried about his grade, he wouldn't have to walk all the way over here to talk to you about it."

"Oh." See, now I feel stupid.

Yeah. Sure. I know men find me attractive. But the idea of a student finding me attractive? Eh.

"He's a child," I point out.

"He's in his twenties," she counters.

"I would absolutely get fired. Besides, he's . . ." I picture Colton in my mind.

Yes, he's handsome in a very GQ kind of way. All chiseled jaw and muscles.

Before I can finish my thought, Liz finishes her thought out loud. "He's hot is what he is." Then she gives a dramatic sigh. "But, yes, I suppose climbing that like a monkey would violate the university's fraternization policy. More's the pity."

"How can you be both the woman who talks about climbing a man like a monkey and the woman who demands regular Jane Austen marathons?" I throw up my hands. "That makes no sense."

"Oh, make no mistake. I would absolutely climb Mr. Darcy like a monkey. One hundred percent."

I stand and pick up my bag and my purse. "Let's get out of here. If we're going to have a Jane Austen marathon, can we at least do it at my place?"

She stands too, grabbing her own bag off the floor. "Sure. But that means you're buying the wine."

"As long as you don't mind boxed wine, we're good." I turn to lock my office door on the way out, then add, "You know what I think? I think you're a big faker." I point my finger at her. "I don't think you would climb any of these men like a monkey if you had the chance."

She shrugs as we walk towards the elevator. "Maybe. Maybe not. It's not like I have hot baseball players hanging out in my office. And since you do, I think it's your moral obligation to indulge yourself and then report back so I can live vicariously."

"First off, as I already pointed out, I would lose my job. Secondly—and I can't say this often enough—he's too young. And thirdly, he's just not my type."

Liz rolls her eyes. Again. "Like you have a type. You haven't dated anyone since the divorce."

That is—strictly speaking—not entirely true. I had a short bout with a dating app right after I signed the papers. That was back before Liz and I had become closer. Even then, I hadn't wanted romance or love again. But Clive had been the only man I'd ever been with. I'd needed to know what I was missing. Now I knew. And it wasn't much—at least, nothing I couldn't live without.

I had never told Liz about my stint with the dating app, because . . . well, for all of Liz's talk about climbing men like a monkey, she'd had real love. The kind of big, deep, real love I'd dreamed about growing up. My brief string of hookups seemed tawdry by comparison. Liz wouldn't judge me for them; that's not her style. But maybe I hadn't told her because I judged myself. A little, at least. Not because there was anything wrong with a woman exploring her sexuality, but because even while I was doing it, I knew it wasn't what I wanted. I think I did it as an "eff you" to Clive. And that just made me feel petty. I wanted more from my post-Clive life than that.

Instead of explaining any of that, I say glibly, "I don't have to date to have a type."

We reach the elevator and I push the button. The foyer is empty, since apparently everyone else has already cleared out.

"Okay, then," Liz says as the elevator doors slide open. "Describe this mythical type of yours."

"Smart," I say automatically. Then quickly add, "Well-spoken. Kind."

"We're still talking about for sex, right? I mean, you're not describing your perfect man to start a book club with?"

"Yes. I'm still talking about a man I would want to have sex with." Now it's my turn to roll my eyes. Thank God we're in the elevator alone, because I'm not sure that would stop Liz. "And I don't think intelligence is a bad trait to look for in a partner."

"But well-spoken and kind? Come on!"

"Hey, Austen fan! Mr. Darcy is well-spoken."

Liz busts out laughing. "No, he's not! He's rude and abrupt. He's all growly and hot."

"But, kind—"

The elevator door slides open, but Liz stops me from leaving the elevator by planting a hand on my chest. "No. Mr. Darcy is not kind. Don't fall for that Women's Home Journal bullshit. You don't want a man who is kind. You don't need a man who is kind. Clive was kind."

I push past her and leave the elevator. "No. Clive was a jerk."

She falls into step beside me as we leave the building through the door at the back that leads to faculty parking. "No. Clive was a jerk to you because he was a cheating bastard. But in normal life, Clive is kind and well-spoken. He is also very intelligent. Which only proves my point."

For a moment, I'm tempted to correct her. Clive isn't kind. Not really. However, he is extremely self-aware, which means he's great at *seeming* like he's kind around anyone who might someday help his career. To everyone else, to anyone he thinks is beneath him, he is usually condescending and patronizing. His cheating may have ended our marriage, but learning how he treated people had ended my love long before that.

I don't say any of that out loud to Liz though. Even though they worked in different colleges and their paths almost never crossed, it wasn't in anyone's best interest for me to still be complaining about Clive's failings all these years later. So instead, I deflect.

"So you're saying that I have horrible taste in men. Is that the point you're trying to make? Because I'm not loving this point."

I've almost reached my car when she puts a hand on my arm.

I turn, still feeling a little stung.

She gives me a smile that's a little sad and a little wistful. "Look, you know I mean well, right?"

"Of course." She means well. She's my best friend. Has my back. Best buds. Heart of gold. All that jazz.

"You had the guy you just described. He didn't make you happy."

"Yeah." I pull my arm away to fidget in my purse, ostensibly to dig out my keys, but also to avoid her gaze.

"All I'm saying is, I had a guy who was none of those things. And he made me very happy."

I look up at her then, just in time to catch the glimmer of tears in her eyes.

She never talks about the husband she lost too young. Six years of friendship and he's only come up once before now. I know more about him from her faculty bio and from Google than from conversations.

"Liz—"

She cuts me off. "All I'm saying is that whatever your type is, it should be more about how he makes you feel. It shouldn't be about some set of qualities you can tick off a list."

I nod, wordlessly. Because what can I say?

She cracks a grin, suddenly back to her normal self. "And I still think you should give some thought into how that hot baseball player might make you feel." She holds her hands up, palms out in a sign of surrender. "Not now. Not while he's your student. But May is right around the corner. And I'm pretty sure he'd at least stay for a long weekend if you asked."

I pop the lock on my car. "Okay, I'll consider it," I say, climbing into the driver seat.

"That's all I ask," she says, heading for her own car a few spots over. "That and six uninterrupted hours of Mr. Knightly."

"Wait. Six hours? I only agreed to one *Emma*!" I call out. But she's already in her car and waving like she can't hear me.

The sneak.

As I start the car and head for home, I know I will not consider sleeping with the too-young, too-student Colton Solimar. Not in a million years.

I'm not lying when I say he's not my type.

But I'm also not being entirely truthful when I say my type is well-spoken and kind.

The truth is as soon as I listed off smart as the defining quality of "my type," one man came to mind. And it certainly isn't Colton.

It's Dr. Max Ramsey.

I added well-spoken and kind to the list precisely because they are qualities Max does not possess.

Which is just silly. Because it's not like Liz can read my mind. It's not like she would know how my body responds to Max's presence. The way he makes my pulse hammer and my breath quicken. The way I'd wanted to lean into him today, when I'd been standing on the dais in front of him.

The man is ridiculously big.

Even though I was standing there in heels, he was still taller than me. How is that even possible?

Is the man part giant?

More to the point, why do I care how big he is? I should not be thinking about him that way. I should not be thinking about him at all.

Even if I'm supposed to be helping him get the McPherson Fellowship, I shouldn't be thinking about him.

I have enough on my plate without adding in this nonsense.

On impulse I use my car's interface to pull up Liz's number and I call her.

"Yeah?" she answers on the second ring.

I don't even greet her. Instead, I start with, "Even if I wanted to, this isn't the time to get involved. Not with anyone."

"It's never the time," she answers without missing a beat, as if our conversation never ended. "That's the thing about being a single woman in your thirties. It's never the right time. There are so many reasons not to get involved."

"So you agree with me? This isn't the right time. I've got enough on my plate."

"I didn't say that. What I meant was, okay, so it doesn't seem like the right time. It's never going to be the right time. You think a year from now is going to be better? It's not. Especially not if you get the kids. But I'm not talking about starting a long-term relationship. That's why he's perfect. Have a fling. You'll never see him again."

"You don't know that. I could run into him a hundred times a year."

"Why would you run into Colton Solimar a hundred times a year? I know you're not a baseball groupie."

Oh for . . .

For a hot minute there, I'd forgotten Liz and I were talking about two different people.

"I wouldn't," I say quickly. "Of course I wouldn't. I was just being hypothetical. You know. In case Colton Solimar doesn't get recruited by the pros or whatever and ends up getting his master's here. In whatever field jocks get degrees in. Hypothetically."

I pull to a stop at the light outside my neighborhood and, since I'm stopped anyway, bang my head on the steering wheel a couple of times.

"Are you okay?" Liz asks.

I sit up. "Of course I'm okay. Why wouldn't I be okay?"

"Well, you're doing that weird rambling thing you do when you're upset. Plus, I'm in the car next to you and can see you banging your head on the steering wheel."

I exhaled sharply with a breath that ends on a burst of laughter.

"Yes. I'm okay," I say. Pulling on all my reserves of chill and all my years of experience speaking in public to sound less like a crazy person. "I just have a lot on my plate right now."

"Yeah, that's like the fifth time you've said that."

The light changes and I drive on to the main thoroughfare of my neighborhood. In my rearview mirror I see Liz's Prius change lanes behind me so that when I turn onto my street, she's there, too.

My neighborhood is a few miles from campus. It's a collection of midcentury ranch-style houses built when the university first started expanding. It's not trendy or cool like the turn-of-the-century bungalows closer to campus. Here, the lots are too small for builders to tear down and rebuild. It's mostly faculty and staff—all the grunt workers. Liz lives a few blocks over. What was once a garage has been converted to the third bedroom, so I pull into the driveway as Liz parks on the street.

I climb out of my car quickly. If I make it inside before Liz can grill me more, the animals will distract us both.

But Liz can move surprisingly fast for a woman who spends her days reading.

"What is up with you?" she demands.

"Nothing," I insist.

"This"—she waves a hand at my general appearance, or maybe my demeanor. It's hard to tell—"isn't like you."

I slide the key into the lock and open the door to the expected barrage of barking. I hold the door wide and gesture to my house and then back at myself as I walk in.

"This is exactly like me. I'm a mess and a half. I'm unorganized. I'm a flibbertigibbet. You know that."

Liz shuts and locks the door behind her, then follows me to the crates where Skip and Lou are pawing excitedly at the ground. I let them out and Liz and I endure the usual marathon of exuberance.

She doesn't say anything more as I let the dogs out back to do their business and tend to the other animals, first checking Iago's water and food while he mutters the occasional curse, then on to Tinky, my rabbit, to give him fresh hay.

Liz is quiet through it all. Suspiciously quiet. Liz, who has never had an opinion she didn't share, doesn't say anything.

I leave her to stew in silence while I let the dogs back in and pour us both wine.

Finally, as we settle into the living room, I break.

"Okay, hit me."

She blinks innocently as Lou settles at her feet. "I don't know what you mean."

"You're never this quiet. You've never had a thought in your life that you haven't said out loud."

She presses a hand to her chest in mock indignation. "Well, that's a little mean-spirited."

"Come on, you know what I mean. You're better at digging out secrets than a CIA interrogator. If you're keeping your opinions to yourself on this, there is something seriously wrong."

She shrugs, taking a sip of wine. "Well, it's obvious, isn't it?"

"What's obvious?" I nearly take a sip of my own wine, but I'm a little afraid I might guzzle it out of pure frustration, so instead, I set it on the side table.

The second it's out of my hand, Skip hops into my lap. Or rather, he tries to. His three tiny feet scramble for traction on the edge of the sofa and I have to hoist him up.

When she still says nothing, I ask again, "What's obvious?"

She leans forward and helps herself to my TV remote. In the moments it takes the TV to turn on and my landing page to load, she says casually, "It's obvious you've met someone."

I suck in a breath, then press my lips together, hoping she didn't hear me.

She glances at me only briefly before flipping through the navigation screen to the app she wants. "You've met someone. Someone you're interested in. But you're not ready to talk about it." She gives a little shrug. "That's okay. You'll talk about him when you're ready."

She reaches the screen she wants and clicks away until the movie starts.

Like this is the least interesting thing that has ever happened in the history of uninteresting things.

Which is perfect. Because this *is* the least interesting thing.

And it's not even a thing.

Not. Even.

And I haven't met someone.

So there.

I glare at her for several moments as music sweeps through the room.

She ignores me.

I stroke Skip's ears. He drools.

I reach over, calmly pick up my wine and take a sip. I set my glass down. I stroke Skip's ears some more. My eye twitches.

I lunge for the remote, knocking Skip off my lap, and pause the movie.

"I haven't met someone."

Liz just looks at me. Skip gives me the saddest eyes ever.

I exhale, pull Skip back on my lap, and glare at Liz. "I haven't. Not someone I'm interested in. Not someone I could be with. Not like that."

"Okay . . ." Liz eyes me cautiously, like I'm a bomb she's trying to defuse. "But you have met—"

"He's impossible. He's arrogant. He's rude. He's this huge, burly, beast of a man who could squash me like a bug. And I'm supposed to work with him for the next few months. Months during which, can I just remind you, I will also be applying to be a foster mother to two kids I really want to adopt someday. So, when I say I have a lot on my plate, I mean that this is the worst possible time for me to meet a man I'm physically attracted to who's not even physically attractive, so I'm not attracted to him. End of story."

I press the "play" button on the remote with a little too much force. It doesn't respond, so I pound it three more times before tossing it on the coffee table in frustration.

And then, because I hate that Liz accidentally snipped the blue wire and I exploded like an emotion bomb all over the room and I hate that there are tears prickling at the back of my eyes, I pick Skip up and cuddle him close to my face, breathing in his clean doggy scent and getting a face full of pug fur. I don't even mind because at least then I have an excuse for my eyes to be watering.

For a long moment, Liz says nothing.

Then she gets up, takes both our wineglasses into the other room. I guess for refills, because when she returns she has the box of wine tucked under her arm, like she decided that would just be easier.

She pours me more wine and says softly, "Yeah, that is a lot," as she presses the wineglass into my hand.

I take a sip, kind of wishing she'd gotten me a straw so I could sip wine while still hiding behind my dog.

"Who is this guy who's got you all tied into knots anyway?"

I set the glass aside and lean my head back, looking up at the ceiling. "Dr. Maximillian Ramsey. He's—"

"Oh, yeah, I know who he is." She blows out a whistle. "Yeah, you are so full of shit. Because he is not well-spoken or kind."

I tip my head up to look at her. "You know him?"

"I know of him. I've got a friend in the registrar's office, Anika. And every semester they have an office pool on who is going to have the most students drop their class. He won so many years in a row they voted to exclude him from the running." She pins me with a look. "This is the guy that's got you all tied up in knots?"

"I'm not tied up in knots," I protest weakly. Man, I am such a wuss. But then it hits me and I sit up, pointing a finger at her. "You know what? I'm really not tied up in knots."

"That's what you just said."

"No, what I mean is I'm not really tied up in knots. This is just an illusion. It's like a fantasy, right? I mean, I barely know the guy. We've only spoken three times! So what if there was chemistry. Or whatever. That's not real. That doesn't matter."

"Ooo-kaay . . ." Liz says, sounding doubtful.

"I mean, I had chemistry with Clive when we first met. And it's not like that lasted. That's what I mean about this just being an illusion. Once I get to know the guy, I'll see what he's really like and then physical attraction won't matter anyway. It's not like I can avoid him. I'll just have to grit my teeth and muscle past the attraction until I get to know him well enough to realize he's a jerk."

"I thought we'd already agreed he's a jerk?"

"Oh, he's definitely a jerk. But I mean, once I realize he's not a sexy jerk but a jerk jerk."

Liz tips her head to the side. "Tell me again why you can't avoid him."

I explain as quickly as I can about the McPherson Fellowship.

Liz lets out another one of her low whistles. "Wow."

"I know, Clive is such a jerk for making me do this."

"Um, no. I meant, 'Wow, the McPherson Fellowship.' That's a really big deal."

"Yeah, I know."

"I mean, I knew Ramsey was considered one of the smartest guys on campus, but that's hard core. He must be brilliant. What's his field of research?"

"Something about dirt."

"Well, if he's up for the McPherson Genius Award, it must be like, the most important stuff about dirt ever. Because this is a really big deal."

I shoot Liz a scathing look. "This isn't helping."

"Sorry. I'll try again. I'm sure he's a total douche canoe."

"That's better."

She sits back, nodding toward the TV. "Okay, *Emma*?"

"Yes. *Emma*."

She pauses, her thumb poised above the play button. "Just to be clear, my role as best friend here is to bad-talk Ramsey whenever possible and remind you that he's a jerk. Right?"

"Yes."

She looks around my living room, which, admittedly is still a wreck from all the cleaning I've been doing. "And possibly come over tomorrow to help you haul some of this shit to Goodwill?"

"Yes. That would be awesome."

"Cool. Cool, cool, cool." She starts the movie, but then pauses again before the opening shot even narrows in. "And I'm not supposed to encourage you to sleep with him?"

"No!"

"Not even just to get it out of your system? Like, you know, a stress relief?"

"No. Absolutely not."

"Okay, just wanted to be clear here."

"Now play the movie."

Liz plays the movie, but despite the sweeping love story and gorgeous costumes and the wine and sweet dog on my lap, I keep thinking about Max Ramsey.

What is it about this guy that makes it impossible to get him out of my head?

He's annoying and rude. He's a huge, mean bear of a man. And because of his unruly hair and that obnoxious beard, I don't even know what he looks like! I've only seen a four-inch swath of his face. So instead of enjoying the movie, I'm sitting here wondering if the right haircut would make those steely-gray eyes of his less intense.

Which is super annoying.

Because I have so many things I should be thinking about.

I have a plan. A detailed, long-running plan.

That's one of the things about having ADHD. You need a lot of plans. And if there's one thing I've learned about myself, it's that when you have a plan, you have to stick to it. You can't let your resolve waver. You can't give yourself an out.

You've got to stick to the plan.

You don't stick to the plan, you end up married to a jerk like Clive, moving halfway across the country to live in Texas with the hope it will save your marriage, even though it won't.

And, yes, I'm happy with where I am in my life. I love my job. I'm happy living in Texas, and once I'm approved by the social workers, I'll be one step closer to that family I've always wanted.

But the truth is, the last time I veered away from my plan, it took a lot of years for me to get my feet back under me. I don't want to go through that again.

No. I won't go through that again.

Not for a man like Max Ramsey.

The only question now is how do I transform Max Ramsey into a man the McPherson committee can't resist while making sure that I can resist him?

CHAPTER 8

MAX

I exercise every single day, because if I don't stretch and use my leg muscles, everything hurts more. The car accident that killed both my parents also shattered my sacrum and my acetabulum. There are some breaks even the best surgeons in the world can't repair, but keeping my muscles strong helps. I have a series of Tae Kwon Do forms I do every evening and a rowing machine I use every morning after warming up with yoga. This morning, I do my exercises back to back and I push myself. Probably harder than I should.

The workout I do today is brutal. I'll regret it tomorrow when my muscles ache. That's okay—I need the distraction. I want the distraction.

The distraction from her. Holly fucking Dolinsky.

I shouldn't be putting "Holly Dolinsky" and "fucking" in the same sentence, even in my head.

Unfortunately, they are already together in my thoughts. Worse still, when they are linked in my mind, "fucking" is not in the form of the descriptive adjective I usually use, but rather the verb I almost never use. The verb I have never used in the same sentence with a colleague's name before. Especially not a sentence like, "Last night in the shower, I jerked off as I imagined fucking Holly Dolinsky."

Not that I actually did that last night.

No. I did that the night after we first met. And again on Monday night after she came into my lab.

But not last night. Because now that I know just how fucking gorgeous Holly Dolinsky is, it didn't seem . . . right somehow.

It was one thing to stand in the shower stroking my cock while I imagine fucking a woman who is plain, but smells amazing. Or a woman who smells amazing and has the sheer guts to stomp into my clean room and go toe-to-toe with me.

It's another thing entirely to do so now that I know how beautiful she is. Now that I know she didn't actually want me to know she's beautiful.

So now that I know, it's not happening again. Which is why this morning's workout was so completely grueling.

I'm nearly done on my rowing machine when my cell phone rings. I don't recognize the number, but answer it anyway. The name attached to the number is Charlene and the avatar on my phone shows a picture of a busty blonde.

Sometimes Tavey calls me from unfamiliar numbers because she thinks it keeps me on my toes. I have no idea how she hacks my phone like that. I keep that filed under Questions About My Sister I Don't Want the Answer To.

"What do you think?" she asks as soon as I answer.

"About what?" I ask.

"About the gift. Did you get the gift?"

"No. What gift?"

"Go look on your front porch."

I pull the phone away from my face and glare at it, tempted to hang up on her.

I'm sweaty and tired. My leg is aching. I want a shower and some ice.

I exercise because I have to, not because I like it, but because the combination keeps my leg muscles from seizing up. But, yeah, sometimes it makes my leg hurt like a bitch. And sometimes it makes me even more of an asshole.

"Just tell me what it is and I'll pretend to like it," I grumble.

She laughs. Tavey is always laughing. Most days, her perennial good mood is forty-five percent annoying and fifty-five percent lovable.

Today isn't most days.

"Go get the package," she coaxes.

I grab the towel and water bottle from the chair by the door, wiping off my face and chest as I walk. "There better actually be a package on my front porch," I grumble.

"It's there," she assures me.

"Let me guess, you hacked my doorbell camera again?"

There's a loud smooch from over the phone line. "I hack because I love. Besides, you're going to love it. I promise."

It takes me several minutes to make it to the front door from the guest room at the back of the house that I use as a home gym. Tavey doesn't comment on how long it takes.

She knows me well enough to know that it takes as long as it takes. Besides, for all I know, she has cameras planted throughout the house and is tracking my progress. Or maybe she has me tagged like wildlife. Who the fuck knows with Tavey.

I may be the reclusive hermit in the family, but she's the weird one.

I find the package—not from Amazon like I thought it would be, but mailed from her home in Houston—and bring it inside. The box is big enough that it's awkward to carry in one hand while I hold the phone in the other, but thankfully, it's lighter than it looks.

When I step into range of the Ring security camera, Tavey gives a squeal of mock horror. "Put a shirt on before you go outside! You'll give your neighbors a heart attack."

"I was working out when you called."

"Still!"

I give my Ring the finger.

On the end of the line, Tavey laughs again. "Very mature."

"Stalker."

"Hey, if I didn't stalk you, I would never know what was going on in your life. Because you never call me."

"Why would I need to call you? You call me."

"Yeah, yeah, yeah. Just open the present."

In the living room, I switch the phone to speaker, set it and the package on the coffee table, and open the box.

"It's full of socks," I say wryly.

"Sox in box! From Dr. Seuss. Get it?"

"Yeah." Like I said, Tavey's the weird one.

There are socks with penguins. Socks with polka dots. Socks with sandwiches and graduation caps.

"There have to be like fifty pairs of socks in here," I grumble, but I'm working hard to keep the smile out of my voice.

"You better count," she says slyly.

"Let me guess, the socks are part of one of your elaborate puzzles."

This is what Tavey does.

Professionally, she's a cryptographer who does a little light hacking on the side for fun. Her hobby is harassing me with puzzles and weird games she devises.

I keep digging in the box. Eventually, the socks give way to boxer shorts—which are all just as ridiculous as the socks. At the bottom of the box are puzzle pieces. Loose. All red.

"Jesus H. Christ. Can't you just text like a normal person?"

But even as I ask, I'm moving the socks and boxers to the sofa so I can dump the puzzle pieces onto the coffee table.

"Send a text?" she asks. "Like a boring person, you mean."

I sit down on the sofa and start sorting out the edge pieces. Yeah, I'm still sweaty and gross. And I fucking hate the way sweat feels as it dries on my skin.

Tavey is the one person I would put off a shower for. If I tell her I'll call her back in ten minutes, she might not pick up. In ten minutes she could be off focused on something else or off settling some international crisis. With her, you never know.

So, I sort pieces and talk to my sister.

"So why'd you send a package today?"

"Do I need a reason to send a gift to my big brother?"

"You always have in the past."

"Maybe I just think you need a hobby."

I pause sorting the puzzle pieces to frown at my phone. "I don't have time for a hobby."

"Right, because you're all work, work, work. Did you learn nothing from The Shining?"

"What—"

But before I can ask her what the life lesson from The Shining is supposed to be, she cuts me off. "Holy shit, who's that?"

"Who's who?" I ask. I don't even look up from the puzzle. Tavey is always doing ten things at once and for all I know she's watching surveillance from somewhere on the other side of the globe while she talks to me.

"Who's that at your door?"

Apparently, she's still got my hacked Ring feed up on her end. "I don't know. Let me pull up—"

"No! There's no time to pull up the app. Go get a shirt on!"

Her voice is so high I can't tell if it's excitement or horror that has her barking out orders.

I stand, but then she adds, "No! Wait. Skip the shirt. You're ripped. And there's no time."

Tavey is six years younger than me, but bossy as fuck.

"Jesus, calm down, Tavey," I mutter as I head to the door.

I have no idea who or what could be on the other side of the door. I haven't ordered any groceries or takeout. I'm not expecting any deliveries. Frankly, this feels like part of Tavey's elaborate puzzle.

I've got the phone in my hand and the towel tossed around my neck when I throw open the door—expecting . . . I don't even know what. A flock of geese. The cast of Cats. With Tavey, you never know.

When I open the door, it's not a flock of geese or the cast of Cats.

It's Holly.

Fuck.

If I'd thought she looked pretty that day in her class, today she looks fucking stunning.

Or maybe stunningly fuckable.

She's in a dress that's short enough to expose her legs, which are tan and muscular and gorgeous. It's got those thin straps that leave her shoulders and arms bare and immediately make me wonder if she's got a bra on. If she does, how the hell is it keeping anything up without straps?

Her hair is up in a ponytail on top of her head that somehow makes her neck look even longer.

In class she looked like a sexy librarian—elegant, but aloof—and it nearly killed me.

Now? With all this exposed skin? Looking relaxed and touchable? And on my doorstep?

I am absolutely screwed.

I'm a dead man.

All my plans of contributing to the good of humankind, of revolutionizing crop sciences, and solving world hunger?

Yeah. None of that shit is going to happen, because my heart is going to pound out of my chest like that alien in . . . well, Alien.

And I'm just standing there in the doorway.

Like a fucking moron.

While the most beautiful woman I've ever seen stands there, staring at me.

No. Not at my face. At my chest.

My bare chest.

Because my fucking sister told me not to put on a shirt.

CHAPTER 9

HOLLY

Despite being a Southerner and watching Gone with the Wind with my memaw every Thanksgiving of my childhood while the "boys" watched football in the living room, I have never swooned.

I'm not a swooner.

I am too practical. Too reasonable. And despite being a self-proclaimed flibbertigibbet, too level-headed.

But when Max Ramsey opens the door to his house dressed only in some kind of workout pants, bare-chested with a towel draped around his neck, I just about swoon.

Just about.

Through some miracle, I manage to keep sucking air into my lungs, albeit at a greatly increased rate. Due to all my panting.

Because, Jesus H. Lettuce Crisper, Dr. Maximillian Ramsey has the body of a Nordic god. Specifically, a Nordic god of the cinematic variety. And for the first time since we've met, he's not even scowling.

Who knew he was hiding all that under his ill-fitting jackets and repulsive ties?

If it had ever occurred to me to wonder about his body—and it hadn't, despite (or maybe because of) this weird energy between us—I would have assumed his oversized clothes covered the doughy body typical of a man who spent his time in a lab.

Not that there was anything wrong with that.

Who was I to judge?

It wasn't like I had a set of rock-hard abs.

But Ramsey was ripped.

And sculpted.

And—unless the sight of his sheer masculine beauty had brought tears to my eyes that were messing with my vision—he was covered in a light sheen of sweat.

Holy Brewer of Coffee.

There is a long moment where we both just stand there. Him, staring at me with the same slightly dumbfounded, slightly horrified look he always wears around me. Me, gawking back in abject lust, trying to decide if I need to wipe the drool off my chin before or after the ground opens up beneath my feet to swallow me whole.

Which I am definitely praying it will do any minute now.

Any.

Minute.

Now . . .

Nope.

There is no sudden geological shift to save me.

Max breaks first.

"I've got to go," he says into the phone in his hand, which I hadn't even seen until he hung it up.

I catch a glimpse of a name and a woman's face in the caller's avatar as he ends the call without ever taking his eyes off me.

All the lack of oxygen must be getting to me, because I still don't say anything.

Because I'm still staring at all those muscles.

But my brain slowly chugs to life.

Okay, Holly, say something.

You're the communications specialist. You know how this works.

He says words. Then you say words. Repeat as needed.

So I say words.

"You opened the door."

Not good words. But I do say some.

Out loud and everything.

I should have been more specific when I was giving myself directions.

"What I meant to say," I babble, "is that you opened the door before I could ring your doorbell." Probably because I'd been standing on his doorstep for several minutes working up the courage to ring the bell. Trying to decide if confronting Ramsey at home was a good idea or a bad idea. "But then you opened the door and so I never rang the bell." I clear my throat. Praying again for a freak geological incident. And then blurt, "Were you going somewhere?"

As I say all the words—all the stupid, brainless words—his expression slowly hardens into his normal scowl.

"I was working out," he says.

"Okay." But that's not really an answer to the question of whether or not he was on his way out. "Because I can come back if this isn't a good time."

"No. It's fine." But he still just stands there. Looking at me. His gaze moving over my face and my neck and my arms.

And for one crazy moment, I think, *What if he feels this too?*

What if this weird, crazy pull I feel isn't one-sided? What if he can't not look at me? Just like I can't not look at him?

What if he's just standing there because his brain is as foggy as mine is?

But then his scowl deepens into genuine dislike and he steps aside, opening his door wider with a noise something between a sigh of resignation and a grunt of disapproval.

"No. It's . . . fine."

He says "fine" like what he means is, "It's absolutely the worst thing in the world, but you're here, so we might as well get it over with."

I cross the threshold into the most pristinely clean, austere house I've ever seen.

From the outside, it is a typical, upscale suburban ranch, common among neighborhoods all over Texas.

Inside, it's minimalist and modern. Hardwood floors, mostly bare walls, a sleek leather sofa and a single chair. No TV. Big surprise there. The only signs anyone lives here at all are the single pair of running shoes by the door, a puzzle on the coffee table, and a pile of socks on the sofa.

I take my cue from his bare feet and the shoes by the door and slip out of my own low heels.

"You don't have to do that," he grumbles, frowning down at my feet.

"I don't mind." A lot of people don't wear shoes in the house, so I'm used to being accommodating.

He makes a grumbly, dissatisfied noise. Like maybe my bare feet disgust him.

Yeah. That's the Max Ramsey I know.

Clearly, I was momentarily blinded by the gleaming muscles.

"You can wear your shoes. It doesn't bother me."

Except now that I think my bare feet do bother him, there's no way I'm backing down.

I give him a tight smile. "I'm okay."

He glares down at me.

I even bob up onto my toes to show just how comfortable I am. And unfortunately, the bobbing-up-on-my-toes thing backfires.

Because we're facing each other.

And standing close.

And for one horrible second it seems like I'm going to kiss him.

I mean, I'm not.

I absolutely do not intend to kiss him. Ever.

But the action is vaguely reminiscent of going up for a kiss and we both seem to realize it at the same moment. I stumble back. He lurches out of the way.

Then he winces, like he landed wrong on his bad leg.

Which says it all, doesn't it?

The guy is so horrified by the hint of kissing me that he'd risk injury to escape.

I want to lick his abs, while the mere sight of me seems to repulse him. Just great.

On the bright side, licking his abs would be a horrible idea when we have to work together for the foreseeable future. So maybe I should be glad one of us is being logical.

"What do you want?" he asks, his tone low and gruff, like he spent his Saturday morning gargling battery acid.

I give a blithe shrug. "Same as everyone. World peace. The end of hunger. A cure for cancer."

Clearly not amused by my answer, he says, "I meant, why did you come here?"

"Ah. I came here because I emailed you yesterday asking if we could get together this weekend to set up your social media. You didn't answer. So I decided to follow up in person."

"I didn't answer because this weekend isn't good. I'm busy."

I look around the room pointedly. "You're busy with . . .?" I trail off to give him a chance to answer. When he doesn't, I supply, "Laundry and a puzzle?"

He opens his mouth to answer, but then snaps it closed when his phone rings.

He looks at the phone, frowning.

Naturally. Because when isn't he frowning?

I glimpse a different name and a different avatar.

He dismisses the call and props his hands on his hips. Which draws my eye to those perfect muscles at his hips.

At the risk of swooning again, I sit in the sole chair.

As the phone starts ringing again.

"You can take the call if you need to." I feign interest in the puzzle. "Don't mind me."

He's clearly just started the puzzle, because none of the pieces are together and he's only just started sorting out the side pieces.

He dismisses this call too and sits on the sofa, catty-corner to me.

Legs spread wide, elbows on his knees, he adopts a posture of being deeply put upon.

"Is this really necessary?"

"This puzzle?" I ask, because . . . okay, I know it will annoy him.

And, I can't help it. Annoying him is more fun than being ignored by him.

If I have to do this, if I have to give up my free time to do this "favor" for the good of his career and for the good of the university, then by God I'm going to do it my way. Not his.

"No. You being here. Is it really necessary?"

Ha! So I was right! He doesn't like that I'm here in his house.

Probably worried about germs. The jack apple.

"Yes." I flash him a serene smile. "Me being here is really necessary. Setting up your social media is a priority. And it's something I can't do for you, because you need all the login information. Once it's set up, a certain amount of it can be done by Gwen or whatever university lackey you want to push it off on. But this part has to be done by you."

"It has to be done right now?"

"Yes. It just so happens that this is the only free time I have in the coming week. So it has to be done now."

The home inspection is scheduled for Monday, which means I have to do the rest of the prep work for that this afternoon and tomorrow. Then I have a series of interviews early next week.

None of which he needs to know about. Not that he would care about them if he did know. Because he clearly thinks his schedule is more important than anyone else's.

The jerk.

I hold out my hand. "Let me have your phone."

He eyes me suspiciously. "Why?"

"So I can load the apps for you."

"What apps?"

"The social media apps. Pay attention."

If he wasn't one of the smartest people I'd ever met, I'd be tempted to tell him it's a good thing he's pretty.

He puts the phone in my hand and I immediately hand it back. "You have to unlock it first."

"You didn't say that."

It's obviously one of those facial recognition things, because he just holds it up to his face and it unlocks. No surprise he can afford all the latest tech. I bought my last phone from a very shady eBay site out of China. It took me three weeks to figure out how to get websites to load in English.

I click over to the app store and start downloading a couple of apps, handing it back to him every so often for the phone to scan his face.

I talk while the phone does the work. "Because the McPherson committee is looking to expand their influence, your social media reach will be important. Since—"

"How do you know that?"

"Know what?"

He gestures vaguely to the phone, his expression suspicious. "That social media stuff."

He looks so confused by all of this, I don't have the heart to mess with him this time.

"Well, for starters, it's just common sense. Lily McPherson has always been an influencer. Now that she's taken over the committee, she'll want to put her own stamp on it."

Sitting this close, I can smell his amazing scent. And it's occurred to me that I should probably get this done as quickly as possible. He still hasn't put on a damn shirt and the quicker we finish, the less likely I'll be to climb into his lap and lick his neck like it has a Ben & Jerry's logo slapped on it.

"Plus, since you've been dodging my calls and emails, I reached out to the committee on your behalf and had them forward me the information packet."

His jaw twitches. "And they just sent it to you?"

I roll my eyes. "Calm down. This isn't a huge invasion of your privacy. Besides, I just told them I was your press secretary. I also got them to tell me who else has been short-listed for the fellowship."

His gaze sharpens.

Ah-ha. I knew that would get his interest.

Which is why I don't say more, but focus on the apps loading onto his phone.

Barely a minute passes before he asks, "Who else is on the list? Just out of curiosity."

Yeah, right. He's dying to know who they are and whether or not he thinks they're as smart as he is. I list off the first couple of names. He nods like they're people he's heard of.

I had to google them, but it's not like I follow the work of the world's more prominent researchers. I can tell by his reaction that the list gratifies his ego. These are all people he wouldn't mind losing to.

"I thought you said there are five of us," Max says. I nod. "You mentioned three names, in addition to me. So who's the last one?"

Which brings us to the dark horse.

"Martin Sandeke."

Max frowns. "Dr. Sandeke? Haven't heard of him."

Martin Sandeke doesn't have his doctorate, but I don't correct Max. Not yet, anyway. I'm saving that gem of information. "He went to your alma mater."

Max nods, looking placated, as if that alone is testament to the man's brilliance.

"But he didn't graduate," I add casually. Like it's no big deal.

Even though it is. Not to me, of course. Not to most people. Because Martin Sandeke, once the heir to the Sandeke Telecom Systems fortune, had dropped out of college before graduating to start a charitable foundation and develop satellite technology that could change the world. That was what most people cared about.

"What?" he demands, sounding shell-shocked. "What do you mean he didn't graduate? Even with his undergraduate degree?"

Of course Max would focus on the dropping-out part.

I shrug innocently, pretending that I didn't save Martin Sandeke for the end precisely because I knew this would irritate Max. That this wasn't, in fact, the reason I'd brought up the other people on the short list. If there's one thing I know about brilliant men who worked their asses off to be the top in their field, it's that they can't stand to lose. Especially to someone they don't see as their equal.

"Why is he even a contender if he doesn't have a doctorate? Isn't that against the rules?"

I raise an eyebrow, trying to hide my smile, because—God help me—indignant Max is . . . well, he's cute. I say gently, "There aren't rules for this. The committee gets to pick whoever they think is most worthy of the fellowship. And Sandeke is doing groundbreaking work with communications satellites that—"

"He's not even a scientist?" His voice rises, this latest affront clearly too much. "He's an engineer?"

A lesser woman would have laughed out loud. It's really a sign of my moral fortitude that I don't. Instead, I explain about the Sandeke Foundation and the work Martin has done since turning his back on his father's fortune.

"So he's an engineer? And he doesn't even need the money?" Max's frown fades.

And then something happens I didn't expect. Something I could never have prepared myself for.

Max's mouth curves into a smile.

Of course, on Max, this looks like a subtle shifting of the mass of hair covering the lower half of his face. Still, there's a glint in his eyes. The combination hits me like a wrecking ball.

How on earth is his smile even more devastating than all those muscles he was hiding under his ill-fitted shirts? Is it the confidence? Or that masculine arrogance?

Either way, it's deadly.

Thankfully, before I can drop to my knees and pledge my eternal devotion, Max says, "The committee will never give it to Sandeke."

"Because he's an engineer?" Max gives a smug nod. And now it's my turn to smile. "Before Lily McPherson joined the committee, probably not. But now, I think he's the frontrunner."

Max blanches. "He can't be."

"He's brilliant, tech savvy, and"—I waggled Max's phone—"he knows how to play the social media game. He is exactly the kind of candidate who would parlay this fellowship into great things." I let Max stew on that for a minute. And then I add, "But you're right. He's not as brilliant as you. The only thing he has that you don't is a social media presence."

Max looks from me to the phone in my hand and back again. Obviously, he's still reluctant.

"Don't forget, this is what I do. I can fix this for you. But first you have to create the social media accounts."

I hand the phone back to him, because the apps have mostly loaded now. But he's still frowning. "But won't you know all my passwords, then?"

"You are digging pretty deep for excuses there, big guy. I promise I will not use them to hack your accounts. It's not like I'm your stalker."

Right as I say that last bit, his phone rings again in my hand. This time, I see the name and avatar. The avatar is an outline of a buxom woman, tire-flap style. The name is "Your Stalker."

He snatches the phone from me, his cheeks flushing bright red.

"I need to take this."

"Go right—"

But he's stormed away before I can get the word "ahead" out.

It's a big house but it's mostly empty, so his voice carries even though he leaves the room. Or maybe he just doesn't mind that I hear his side of the conversation.

"I'm not doing this now," he growls as soon as he answers the phone.

Which means whoever it is, is someone he knows well enough to answer without greeting her.

There's a pause and then he says, "No. I'm not doing that. Ever." Then, "I will call as soon as this is done."

He says the word "this" like he's undergoing an unanesthetized root canal.

When he speaks again, his tone is softer. Almost fond. "Yes, I promise."

Well. That's interesting.

And by interesting, I mean depressing.

Because this guy I am attracted to—the first guy I've been attracted to in years—has had three calls from three different women in the span of . . . if I had to guess, it's been less than twenty minutes. And at least one of these women is someone he speaks to in that voice. That not-a-jerk voice he's never once used with me.

All of which is really friggin' annoying.

Because I've only known him a few days. And I shouldn't care who he uses his not-a-jerk voice with. And I shouldn't care that he acts like a misanthropic jerk to me. But it's just an act. Because apparently there's a whole legion of women he chats with on the phone often enough that they freely call him on the weekend and have snarky avatars in his phone.

They're probably all tall, beautiful, PhD candidates. Or they already have a doctorate. Or two.

But you know what really gets me? What annoys me the most?

It's that I shouldn't care about any of this. Because I do not have the time or space in my life to be attracted to anyone. Misanthropic, judgmental jerk or not. I don't care how good he smells. Or whether or not he has an eight-pack. He could have a twenty-four for all I care. (Though, I'm pretty sure he'd have to be some kind of anthropoid to have a twenty-four pack.)

The point is, I shouldn't care how many women are calling him.

But I do.

CHAPTER 10

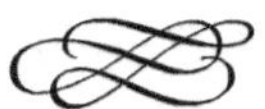

MAX

"Okay," Tavey says twenty minutes later. "When I said you should call me later, I meant after she left."

"I did wait. She's gone."

As soon as I got off the phone with Tavey, Holly breezed through the rest of the steps to setting up my social media in less than ten minutes. I'd even had time to take a shower before calling Tavey back.

Which, for reasons I don't understand, only irritates Tavey.

When I tell her that, she grumbles. Then hisses, "What did you do?"

"What do you mean what did I do? She left. I took a shower." During which I absolutely did not jerk off while thinking about Holly. "Then I called you back. Like you made me promise to do."

Holly did all the social media stuff so quickly, I couldn't help wonder why she needed to come all the way to my house to do it.

And now that she'd been here?

Fuck.

My house smelled like lemons, she'd sat in my chair, and I'd seen her bare feet on my floor.

Why did that matter?

I didn't know.

Yeah, the house-smelling-like-lemons thing is a pain. But why does it matter that she sat in my chair or had her bare feet on my floor?

Why had the sight of her tiny shoes next to mine seemed . . . weirdly intimate?

I didn't know that, either.

And I don't want to talk about any of it.

But this is Tavey and she never fucking lets anything go.

"That beautiful woman was there. At your house. And you were shirtless. And somehow she left after twenty minutes? Why did you let her leave?"

"Because forcing people to stay in your house is kidnapping."

Tavey groans. "That is not what I meant and you know it."

"No. I don't know it. Because I don't know what you're talking about."

"That woman was into you."

Tavey's words make my heart stutter. And then beat faster.

"No, she wasn't." I correct myself. "Isn't."

"Um? Hello? Yes, she is. Why else would she be at your house on a Saturday?"

"She was here for work."

Tavey gives an indignant snort that would make Aunt Jules gasp in horror. "She was not there for work."

"Yes. She was."

"Unless you've taken on a side job of producing porn at home, that woman was not there to work with you. She was a hundred percent into you. Two hundred percent."

"Tavey," I say, a note of warning in my voice. I know she used the phrase "two hundred percent" just to piss me off because I hate it when people ignore the impossibility of a percentage greater than one hundred. And I'm already about as pissed off as I can take.

She should fucking know better than to fuck with me about something like this.

Tavey doesn't know the details—I may be a jerk, but not the kind of jerk who talks about women he's slept with—but she does know that I've had exactly one relationship in my life. Beth was a fellow grad student. A few years older than me—because they all were. She'd been more ambitious than smart. All these year later and I still hadn't figured out if she'd been with me out of pity or because I'd always been so pathetically grateful that I'd done her work for her. It sure as hell hadn't been because she'd actually wanted me or even liked me. She'd made that abundantly clear when she'd dropped out of the program. We'd been together for nearly six months, but even fucking me hadn't been enough to keep her grades up.

Given my history with women, the idea that someone like Holly might be "into" me is a little hard to believe.

"What?" Tavey asks now. "You think I'm wrong?"

"I know you're wrong. Holly Dolinsky is not into me. The idea is preposterous."

"Why is it preposterous?"

I nearly laugh at the confusion in her voice.

"Have you seen her?" I ask, knowing full well that Tavey has seen her. Even if it was a grainy hacked video of Holly via my Ring camera.

"Yes, I saw her," she replies. "I sat here and watched the two of you on your doorstep. You guys just stood there looking at one another for a really long time. And her eyes practically popped out of their sockets at the sight of your muscles."

"No. They didn't."

"You know there are women who are smarter than that bitch Beth," Tavey says, her tone softer.

"Yeah. I know all women aren't Beth. I'm around smart women all the time. If I was the kind of man women were attracted to, I think I would have noticed before now."

"Oh, you think you would have noticed? Because you're so good at picking up on that kind of thing? And because you're awesome at putting yourself out there?"

"Trust me. Holly Dolinsky is not into me."

"And why was she at your house on a Saturday anyway?"

I quickly explain about the McPherson Fellowship and Holly's insistence that I need a social media presence.

Naturally, the explanation takes longer than it should. Tavey asks a lot of questions. Yells at me for not telling her sooner. Pauses so she can text Aunt Jules the news. Yells at me again, this time on Aunt Jules's behalf, even though I'm pretty sure Aunt Jules never heard of the McPherson Fellowship until today.

In the end, the conversation circles back to Holly.

"I'm telling you, bro, she likes you."

The "bro" sounds so unnatural from Tavey, I nearly laugh again.

Only Tavey can make me laugh.

Especially when I don't want to. And when I think about Holly, laughing is the last thing I want to do.

I'm not sure what I want to do, but I know laughing isn't it.

"I assure you, she is not. It's just business."

"She dressed up to come see you on a Saturday morning. With her hair up and her makeup on. In that cute little dress. She put effort into that. And that was before she saw how jacked you've gotten."

I don't argue with Tavey, but just let it go. Tavey hadn't seen what Holly looked like when she was lecturing. Today was nothing compared to that.

Which just proves what I already know: Holly isn't the least bit interested in me.

I'm the first person to admit I know nothing about women, but I do know I'm absolutely not the kind of man any woman would want to be around, romantically or platonically.

Besides, Tavey is as stubborn as I am and can't admit when she's wrong.

The only reason Holly is even working with me is because her ex-husband is making her.

CHAPTER 11

HOLLY

I know when I'm getting in my own way. When I'm in my own head too much. When my fear of failure is pushing me down the long dark road of procrastination.

Yeah. I know.

The best way to deal with all that stuff is to sit my butt down, make a list, plan out some kind of reward, and then work my way down the list.

This is what works for me, at least.

It's what got me through grad school. It's what got me through my thesis. It's even what got me through my divorce.

And if I can make a list that starts with "find a lawyer," ends with "buy my own house," and has "divorce Clive" smack-dab in the middle, then I can certainly make a list that starts with "email Max" and ends with "send Max a congratulations card and then forget him forever."

Nothing was harder than leaving Clive.

Okay, that's a lie. Losing a baby I desperately wanted to an ectopic pregnancy was way harder.

Recovering from that was way harder. Realizing that putting my life back together meant ending a relationship that was making me miserable was the only path to recovery. Choosing to not run home to my family afterwards. Yeah, all of that was harder.

Way harder.

If I can do all those things, then I can make darn sure Max wins that fellowship.

But . . . you know . . . ADHD and fear of rejection means I put off starting my FIX MAX to-do list for several days.

In my defense, I have a lot on my plate. Things I've been working on for years.

Saturday, after the naked-chest/social media debacle, Liz came over and helped me finish the massive cleaning and organization project to get my house ready for the home visit from the social worker.

Most of the week itself was taken up with the normal routine of classes and office hours, but with the added nerve-wracking adventure of the home visit.

And then, suddenly, by Wednesday, my master to-do list was empty and I was left with nothing to think about except the fact that the deadline for the McPherson Fellowship is still looming. Max still isn't ready. And no amount of procrastination on my part is going to help.

So I make the list.

It's long. It's detailed.

For the record, it does not include things like "bleach the image of his abs from my brain," "stop smelling woodsy candles at the grocery store in hopes of making your bedroom smell like him," or "stop fantasizing about what his beard would feel like against your skin."

Because I'm professional like that.

Instead the list has items like, "create content calendar for his social media," and "figure out what Max actually does."

There is a whole subsection devoted to "Make him look less scary."

Items on that list are things like, "Buy him clothes that fit," and "get him a decent haircut," and, perhaps most importantly, "shave his beard."

And, no, the beard-shaving thing isn't on the list just so that I will stop wondering what he looks like without it. As I've said, I'm a professional.

So instead of fantasizing about a man I know has zero interest in me romantically or sexually, I work my way down the list, starting with the easy jobs. Because that's always the way to go.

I send Max a text asking if he has a preferred barber. When I don't hear back, I text and email him a list of local shops with good reviews. When I don't hear back, I call Clarissa, get his schedule for the week, text Gwen to confirm his schedule and make him an appointment myself.

Which I then send to him in multiple formats.

And he still misses that appointment.

And the next two I schedule.

By the following Wednesday, I still haven't heard back from the state social worker about the home visit, I've fielded three calls from different hairdressers regarding the two appointments he's missed and received a very distressed text from the hairdresser I sent to cut his hair at his actual lab. I didn't know it was possible to know a person is crying over text. But I knew.

On the upside, my weird fascination with Max is definitely waning.

No amount of woodsy-scented abs make up for this kind of bad behavior.

On Thursday I don't have classes. Which leaves me an entire day to torture Max.

Or, rather, to get his hair cut and get him measured for a well-fitted suit.

I hire a tailor to come with me.

If there is one good thing about being the height of a Smurf, it's that I know a good tailor. Several actually, since I have to have all my pants and most of my skirts hemmed.

Rodrigo is either a sweet old man with fourteen grandchildren or a hardened criminal who learned his skills in prison and was the inspiration for the Morgan Freeman character in Shawshank. He tells a lot of stories and I haven't figured out which ones are true.

Either way, he's the best tailor in town and I know Max can't bully him.

Plus, I recruit help. I convince Clarissa to convince Stu in maintenance to temporarily change the digital passcode on the lab.

I may be professional, but that doesn't mean I can't fight dirty.

CHAPTER 12

MAX

I'm not some superstitious Neanderthal. I don't get my palm read. I also don't cast bones to predict the future or read my horoscope.

However, recent research has revealed that the intestinal tract contains as many neural cells as the brain. Which means there is truth to the adage about having a gut feeling.

When I get out of the elevators on the sixth floor on Thursday morning to find all three of my grad students waiting outside the lab, my gut tells me it's going to be a rough day.

"Why the hell aren't you already in the lab?" I ask.

Priya flinches at my tone like a goddamn drama queen. Gwen puts a hand on Priya's shoulder and whispers something to her. Jaxon, the only guy in the group, steps in front of the other two protectively.

I try not to roll my eyes.

They've all been working under me for at least a year. They are the ones who've stuck it out, despite what a pain in the ass I am to work with. They should expect it.

I don't normally have to put up with this simpering bullshit from them.

"What's wrong?" I ask.

Jaxon, despite his initial show of bravery, glances at Gwen.

In the end, she's the one who answers. "We can't get in the lab."

"What? Did you all lose your badges?"

They immediately protest, fumbling to pull out badges as visual proof. I wave them aside. "Never mind, let me try mine."

They scatter to grant me access to the door and its keypad.

It doesn't open with my badge either.

Not that I actually expected it to.

"Did you—" I start to ask.

"I already called Clarissa," Priya answers. "She called maintenance. They're already working on it. Apparently there was some sort of surge during the night. And now our badges have to be reprogrammed."

"Can't maintenance just unlock them remotely?"

"No?" Gwen answers, her voice rising like it's a question, which is something she only does when she's nervous. "Apparently they have to come do it in person."

"So all the rooms in the building are locked?"

"Just the ones on the north wall," Jaxon answers.

Which means I can't get into my lab. However, my office is on the south side of the building. So I can go there. Or I can go home and catch up on my reading.

"When is maintenance going to get to manually reset the badges?" I ask, already unhooking my badge from its retractable holder so one of the grad students can do the job for me.

"They should be here within the hour," Jaxon says.

I pause and look at each of the grad students. They look nervous. None of them look any happier about this than I am.

We all have work to do.

In that lab.

But this weird delay to my workday has all the trappings of some sort of prank. The offices are locked on only one side of the building on only one floor? Please.

No doubt I'm going to head to my office—because why would I go all the way home when the matter will be resolved in an hour?—only to find it full of helium balloons. Or rubber snakes or something.

This is exactly the kind of thing Tavey would do. The kind of thing she has done. In college, I once returned to my dorm room to find it stacked full of National Geographics, May 1984 through January 1997.

I am tempted to go back home just to thwart her plans, but head to my office on the other side of the building anyway. Just in case her prank involves something with an expiration date, like tapioca pudding—which she knows I hate.

When I reach my office, there is no tapioca pudding.

There is, however, a wiry man of indeterminate age pacing in front of a stool. And Holly perched on the edge of my desk, dressed in her sexy librarian costume again. Another slim skirt and fitted button-up blouse. The skirt and her position on my desk make her legs look impossibly long. Much longer than they can realistically be given her short stature.

"You're not pudding," I grumble.

Pudding would have been better.

Pudding would have been easily disposed of and forgotten.

Holly merely arches an eyebrow and smirks. "I never said I was." She gestures to the man, who smiles broadly. "This is Rodrigo. He's your tailor."

"I don't have a tailor."

"You do now."

"I don't need a tailor."

She glances quickly at my chest before hopping off the desk as her cheeks pinken. "Your clothes are all too big."

"My clothes are fine."

"They don't fit you."

"They're comfortable."

"Which was fine when the only thing you had to do was work in a lab." She takes a step closer and once again we're standing too close and arguing. "If you're going to be giving a ten-part lecture series for the McPherson Fellowship, you can't do it looking like a homeless person."

"I don't look like a homeless person," I snarl.

Her eye twitches and I see her inhale slowly. Like this conversation is as frustrating to her as it is to me.

She turns to Rodrigo. "Does he look like a homeless person?"

Rodrigo smiles at her and winks. "He does."

I instantly dislike Rodrigo.

"This isn't a democracy."

I'm still glaring at the man when Holly walks around my desk and sits in my office chair. She picks up my phone, hits a few keys and then says, "Clarissa, can you come in here. Oh, and bring whoever else is in the office with you."

Fucking Clarissa. I should have known she was involved.

"That's my desk," I tell Holly. "Get up."

"You don't use it. Why shouldn't I?"

I round the desk to stand in front of the chair.

She swivels to face me, leaning back.

"Because this isn't your office."

She just smiles and then toes off her shoes and curls her legs onto the seat beside her. Like a damn cat. And because she's so tiny, she fits. Her elbow is propped on one of the arms. Her bare feet pressed against the other. Her skirt has inched up to reveal those creamy thighs that I swear to God haunt my dreams.

I am tempted to pick her up bodily and toss her out the door.

But I don't. Because I'm not a Neanderthal. Though I am starting to wish I'd listened to my damn gut and fled for home when I had the chance.

I take another step closer to her, but she just tilts up her head to keep her gaze on mine.

This woman never even flinches.

Ever.

At that moment, Clarissa bursts in the room like she ran the whole way. Like she was afraid I'd be in here murdering Holly.

She skids to a halt when she sees me looming over Holly and several other people skid to a halt behind her. It's practically a pileup on the highway.

"Holly, are you alright?" Clarissa looks from Holly to me to Rodrigo and back to Holly. Then she widens her eyes significantly and jerks them in my direction.

"Yes. I'm fine." She turns her chair—my chair!—to face the door and flashes one of those serene smiles of hers, the kind that makes strangers melt into puddles of goo. She tips her head to look around Clarissa at the other people who came too. "Hey, Stan. Jill. Dave! I haven't seen you in so long. How is Gail?"

She greets each of the people like they're old friends. Maybe they are, since her ex used to work in this building. Still, I've worked here for four years and barely recognize them.

This is not something I'd normally feel self-conscious about because I'm here to work, damn it, not socialize. And I don't have the time or energy to keep track of a bunch of strangers.

"We're doing a little informal survey here." She unfolds her legs and stands.

Since I don't move—why should I when this is my fucking office?—this puts her within arm's reach again.

"You guys all know Dr. Ramsey, right?"

They all nod and make noises of acknowledgement.

Okay, they clearly all do know me. So now I feel like an ass.

I glower down at Holly. This is her fault.

"I have a question. Do Max's badly fitting clothes, ridiculous beard, and general appearance make him look like a homeless person or not?"

As if to illustrate her point, she reaches up and plucks at the shoulder of my jacket.

Clarissa, Jill, and Rodrigo all nod and agree. One of the men—Stan, I think, who is starting to look familiar—gives a loud, "Yes. Hell, yes."

Only Dave gives a shrug and says, "It's not too bad."

Stan just shakes his head. "Not exactly a ringing endorsement from a man wearing a short-sleeved shirt and clip-on tie."

Rodrigo chuckles.

Holly shrugs her shoulders. "See? Five out of six people think you look homeless."

"I do not look homeless," I growl.

She just shakes her head, making a shooing gesture to the other people indicating she's done with them and they start to leave. "At worst, you look homeless. At best—absolute best—maybe a young Hagrid."

"Who the hell is Hagrid?" I ask.

Already on his way out, Dave turns back to say, "I think he's over in Poultry Sciences."

Holly rolls her eyes again. "Dave, you have three kids! You should know who Hagrid is!"

When she looks back at me, I can see the remnants of that sassy eye roll in her gaze. It feels wrong that she looks so fucking good when she's annoyed.

I'm ninety-nine percent sure it's not emotionally healthy to be so attracted to someone who doesn't like me.

Not that I'd ever have a chance with someone like her, even if she did like my personality. She could think I was made of puppies and rainbows and she still wouldn't want to fuck me.

I am, in fact, two hundred percent sure of that.

Holly props her hands on her hips and says, "You can glare at me like that all you want. It doesn't change anything."

"Glare at you like what?"

"Like you want to murder me."

"Is that how I'm glaring at you?" I ask the question honestly.

Thank God she can't read in my eyes what I actually want to do to her. Because this whole thing is humiliating enough.

"Yes. Like you want to murder me. Or maybe lock me in some kind of stockade in the town square reserved for uppity women. My point is, it doesn't matter. Glare all you want. You still need a new suit. Maybe a whole closet full of new clothes. I can shop for you, but first I need to know your size. Therefore, Rodrigo is here to take your measurements."

"Fine," I bark.

This time she flinches.

This is what breaks her? Me agreeing?

"Jesus," I growl. "I'm not actually going to hit you. Or murder you."

Or fuck her. Obviously.

She blinks and then lets out a strangled laugh. "I didn't think you were. I was just surprised that you agreed so easily."

"This was easy?" I ask.

"Good point." Like she's afraid I'm going to bolt, she takes me by the elbow and gently leads me over to Rodrigo. "Look, all he's going to do is take some quick measurements."

"You convinced me. I don't know jack about fashion, but even I know clip-on ties don't cut it. So if the only person in the room who thinks I don't look homeless is wearing a clip-on tie, then that's pretty fucking pathetic. You don't need to keep lecturing me."

She grins.

At me.

And it's such a shock I almost can't breathe.

Which is just stupid. Because obviously, I can breathe.

I still have an autonomic nervous system. I can fucking breathe.

It's just that she's never given me that grin before. That amused, we-share-a-secret grin.

Then she blinks rapidly. Like even she's surprised that she's smiling at me.

Her hand drops away from my elbow and she turns to Rodrigo, suddenly serious.

Obviously she doesn't want me to get the wrong idea from that shared smile.

She rattles off a series of instructions that I barely listen to, throwing around terms I haven't heard before. Big surprise.

She and Rodrigo talk. I climb up onto the stool he'd brought. Jesus, I hope that didn't look as awkward as it felt.

He measures. He asks me to take off my jacket. When I do, he hands it over to Holly and she carefully drapes it over her arm, one hand stroking the fabric absently as she and Rodrigo continue discussing . . . I don't know, fabric options or something.

I can't focus on anything other than the sight of her hand stroking my jacket. The way her fingers move over the jacket is mesmerizing to the point of distraction.

Great. Now I'm getting hard. While some old guy is about to measure me for pants. Just. Fucking. Great.

And this must be what a protozoan in one of my soil samples feels like—being examined under a microscope by people who are only vaguely aware I'm even alive.

My mind wanders to the soil samples from Argentina that I'm expecting next week as Rodrigo measures me for pants.

I don't love being touched by a stranger. Does anyone?

It makes my skin crawl. But at least his touch is impersonal. And through my clothes, it's bearable. On the plus side, I'm not getting hard anymore.

He orders me down from the stool and starts measuring me for a jacket.

He measures my shoulders, my chest, my arms.

I'm only vaguely aware of him calling her over. They talk in whispered tones. He measures my shoulders again.

I blow out a breath of frustration. How much longer is this going to take? How many damn times does he have to measure my shoulders?

Because, yeah. I get it. I have the shoulders of a huge, ungainly bull. But am I really so freakishly big it requires this much discussion?

I'm ready to demand this be over, when the unthinkable happens.

Holly touches me.

She runs her hand along my shoulder, tracing the path of Rodrigo's measuring tape, from the center of the back of my neck to the crest of my shoulder.

Her touch is light and slow and I feel it everywhere.

It's not sexual. She doesn't mean it that way.

I know that.

Jesus, I fucking know that.

But my cock doesn't.

All my cock knows is that the most beautiful, alluring woman I've ever met is running her fingers along my shoulder. And then down my arm. Then down the center of my back all the way from my neck to the small of my back.

That touch—the feeling of her fingers on my back, just above the waistline of my pants—nearly kills me.

Because that touch fills my mind with images of her trailing her fingers around to the front of my pants. Undoing my belt. Cupping my cock in her delicate . . .

I'm done.

I jerk away from her touch and stumble to the side.

"Enough." I whirl to face her. "We're done here."

"What?" She takes a step back, surprise and confusion warring on her face. She looks to Rodrigo.

He gives a shrug. "I have enough to get started." He waggles a finger at me. "Don't get any bigger, okay?"

And then he laughs as he packs up his stuff. I fume as Holly gives him a hug.

"Thanks." She gives him a kiss on the cheek. "I really owe you on this one."

He pats her shoulder. "You don't owe me anything. You are a joy to work with." Then he pins me with a look. "As for you, you are going to pay through the nose. Because I can already tell you're going to be a pain in my ass."

Yeah. Like I need a tailor to tell me that.

I'm a pain in everyone's ass. Isn't that the problem?

As soon as we're alone, I ask, "Are we done here yet?"

"No, we're not." She turns back to face me as she shuts the door behind Rodrigo.

My jacket is still draped over her arm. Once again the fingers of her right hand stroke the fabric like it's a cat or some other kind of pet.

If I didn't know better, I'd say she was nervous.

But I hate the thought of her feeling nervous to be alone with me.

I have no idea why that should matter. I make a lot of people nervous. That's their problem. Not mine.

So why does her emotional state feel like it's my problem?

"Do I make you nervous?" I blurt.

"No."

"Because you're still holding my jacket."

"Oh." She thrusts it back to me. "Sorry."

I take the jacket from her and slide my arms back into the sleeves, all too aware of the way she's watching me. Aware of it, but confused by it as well.

It's not critical or assessing. It's almost . . . regretful. Like she wishes I wouldn't put the jacket back on.

Are my clothes really that bad?

"Who's Hagrid?" I ask.

Her gaze snaps to mine. "What?"

"That person you said I look like. The one Dave should know because he has children. Is this Hagrid person some kind parenting authority?"

She laughs.

For someone so tiny, her laugh is unexpectedly husky. Unexpectedly sexy.

Not that I'm surprised. Everything about Holly is sexy. I should be used to that by now.

"No, Hagrid is not a parenting authority. He's a character from the Harry Potter books." She tips her head to the side. "Let me guess—you haven't read Harry Potter, have you?"

"Should I have?"

"They would have been popular when you were a teenager."

Which explains why I've never heard of them. My childhood wasn't exactly normal, even before the death of my parents when I was twelve. For them, having children was more of a grand experiment than a life experience.

Hypothesis: When two highly intelligent, highly educated people reproduce, the IQ of resulting offspring will exceed that of either parent.

Conclusion: Definitively yes.

By the time they got around to repeating the experiment to confirm their conclusions (i.e. having my sister, Tavey), they had already lost interest in me.

I don't blame them.

They had interests and careers of their own. And I was, undoubtedly, a difficult child to keep occupied, let alone to love.

"I was in college when I was a teenager," I blurt out.

She looks at me, her expression a little sad. "Yes, I know. I've seen your CV. I know how young you were in college."

"Don't do that," I order.

"What?"

"Don't look at me like that."

She blinks and takes half a step back. "Like what?"

"Like you feel sorry for me."

"I don't—"

"I get it. I didn't have a normal childhood. My parents didn't read to me. I didn't learn any of the normal social skills. I'm a freak. I get it."

"I never—"

I slide my arms into the jacket and tug it on, jerking the lapels together. "Not everyone wants parents who read them bedtime stories or coddle them. Not everyone needs that. Some kids—smart kids—they need other things. They need mental stimulation. Intellectual challenges. The freedom to study without feeling like they're a freak. I got all the things I needed. I was fine. I am fine."

Suddenly, I'm aware of two things.

First, my voice has gotten loud. Even for me.

So loud I'm nearly shouting. Which I never do.

Okay, that's bullshit. I shout all the time. When I'm mad. When someone fucks up. When I fuck up.

But I don't shout when I'm upset.

I don't get upset.

Not about this kind of shit.

The second thing I'm aware of is that Holly is still looking at me like she feels sorry for me.

Like me telling her that I'm fine has absolutely convinced her that I'm a pathetic loser.

Which is just fucking great.

I'm willing to put up with a lot of shit.

I'm used to people thinking I'm a freak. Whatever.

Even here. Even at one of the best research universities in the country, I don't fit in. Partly because I'm smarter than everyone else. Partly because I'm big and I take up too much damn space. But mostly—to quote one of my former grad students—because I'm "a misanthropic dick who gets off on being mean."

I don't.

I don't get off on being mean. But I also don't have the patience to deal with people who cry every time I lose my temper. Or who make mistakes all the damn time.

So yeah, I'm used to being reviled.

But I'm not used to being pitied.

I don't like it.

Not at all. Not from Holly.

Especially not from Holly.

I would rather she look at me with anything other than pity.

Even hatred.

CHAPTER 13

HOLLY

I know the moment I've gone too far.

I see it in his eyes.

I know that no matter what he says, he's not fine. Whatever crap his parents put him through, he's not at all fine with it.

I know people well enough to know that.

I also know people well enough that I should know better.

When someone who is smart and proud and hurt says they're fine, that is absolutely the time to nod, agree, and walk away.

Because smart, proud, and hurt is a tough combination to crack.

But do I nod, agree, and walk away?

No.

That would have been the prudent thing to do.

Instead, I do the really stupid thing.

I reach out my hand and take a step closer to him.

What's the plan here?

Am I going to hug him and stroke his hair and promise it will be okay? Have him curl up in my lap and read him Harry Potter, which his damn parents clearly should have done when he was a kid?

I don't know.

I don't have a plan beyond the mindless urge to touch him. To comfort him somehow.

To connect and soothe.

And that's my mistake right there.

Because I should know by now that Max Ramsey isn't the kind of guy you soothe. He isn't the kind of guy you connect with.

Shitty parents or not, brilliant or not, wounded or not, the guy is an asshole.

The second I reach out to him, he steps back, his gaze narrowed in anger.

"I don't need your pity," he says darkly. "I don't need anything from you but your fashion sense."

Okay. That stings a little. Because, yeah, at a university like this one, there are plenty of people who assume I'm just a pretty face. Particularly because I used to be Mrs. Thorndyke and I only have my master's. I've got a lot going against me.

But if Ramsey thinks that little jab is enough to send me running in tears, he's got another thing coming.

I cross my arms over my chest. "You're going to have to do better than that."

His gaze narrows just a little. "Am I?"

"What? You think you're the first arrogant professor on this campus to dismiss me solely because I'm a woman? And because I know how to pick out clothes? Think again."

"Don't kid yourself. It's not just you I dismiss for caring about clothes. And it's not just women, either. I understand there are plenty of people in the world who aren't smart enough to study the world's big problems. But those of us who are shouldn't be judged by the asinine standards of people like you."

People like me?

He probably thought it was the perfect insult.

The jack apple.

Even knowing what he's doing here—that he's purposefully being a jerk because I hurt his feelings about the parent thing—it still pisses me off.

Not only does he know what he's doing—being intentionally cruel—he's also just being honest. That garbage about how people as brilliant as him shouldn't be held to the same standards . . . I bet he actually believes that.

"Well, guess what?" I take a step closer to him. "Lily McPherson is apparently a person with asinine standards just like me. So like it or not, you need me to help you impress her and the rest of the committee."

"Yeah, I get that." He matches my advance, taking a step closer, too. "But so far, you haven't done much, have you?"

"That's because you keep fighting me, every step of the way."

"I'm fighting you every step of the way because your suggestions are stupid. Okay, so I look like a homeless man? So what? The committee should look at my ideas, rather than my wardrobe. That's what should matter."

"Maybe. In a perfect world. But this isn't a perfect world."

"Or maybe you don't know how to impress the McPherson committee any more than I do. Maybe your suggestions are crap because the only thing you know how to do is look good."

I just roll my eyes as I jab a finger in his direction. "Look, you are out of options. Maybe I can help you. Maybe I can't. But I'm tired of fighting you. If you want to play hard ball, fine. It's on. But don't say I didn't warn you."

"What the hell does that mean?"

"It means that the only thing worse than your clothes is your beard. So that"—I waggle my finger in the general direction of his face—"is coming off. Whether you like it or not."

There's only a flicker of panic on his face before he tamps it down. "You can't make me shave my beard."

"Watch me."

"I like my beard."

"Too bad. It's off-putting."

"Beards are popular."

I try not to roll my eyes. "Like you would know what's popular."

"I have eyes," he snaps. "I see students with beards all over campus. Ergo, they are popular."

"Some beards, maybe. Not that one. It looks more like a bramble designed to keep knights out of Sleeping Beauty's castle than an actual beard."

"My beard can't matter that much. I'll wear whatever damn suit Rodrigo makes for me, but I'm not shaving my beard."

I give him a cold, assessing once-over.

He has no idea who he's messing with.

If he'd asked nicely, maybe I would have let him keep it. I would have settled for getting it trimmed. But now?

Now that he's acting like such a jerk?

Now that beard is a line in the sand. It is the Rubicon he'd chosen to cross.

That beard js the cross I will die on.

I don't even care if he gets the McPherson Fellowship at this point. That beard is coming off.

"Just remember," I say to him.

"Remember what?"

"This could have been easier."

And with that, I turn around and storm off.

I make it as far as the elevator before I remember that I kicked off my shoes before I curled up in his chair and I never put them back on.

I almost abandon them there to die like fallen soldiers.

They're only my favorites, after all. A small price to pay.

Except they are my favorites. And I paid nearly two hundred dollars for them. On sale. And I'll never find another pair that cheap again.

So I turn back around and stomp back to his office.

Thank God the door is still open and I don't have to go through the indignity of knocking.

His office is huge. Of course.

It's befitting of a tenure-track professor of his status.

I'd noticed it earlier, but now that I'm extra grumpy, it's even more irritating.

I march back in and stop in front of his desk.

He's sitting there now, in the chair I was in not that long ago. He takes up the entire chair, dwarfing it like the behemoth he is.

I give him my best gunslinger-showdown glare. "I need my shoes."

"What shoes?" he asks, clearly as annoyed to see me again as I am to be here.

Instead of answering, I walk around to the other side of his desk.

As I round his desk, he swivels his chair to face me, his hands resting on either arm of the chair, his legs spread wide so he takes up as much space as possible.

My shoes are right there beside him, practically behind his knee. But now, he's in the way.

Like, really in my way.

And he's just glaring at me. Like I'm the problem here. Like I'm the one being a jerk.

Sure, I could just ask him to hand me my shoes.

I should just ask him.

Obviously, that's the reasonable thing to do.

But I'm tired of being reasonable and I'm tired of him jerking my chain and being a pain in my patootie.

So I do the unreasonable thing.

The profoundly unreasonable thing. I walk over to him, brace one hand on his chair arm right beside his own hand and I lean down. Slowly. Until we're eye to eye. Until I'm practically crawling into his lap. And then I bend and pick up my shoes.

This close to him, I catch his super faint piney scent. I can almost feel the heat coming off his body.

I straighten slowly, my gaze searching his. His pupils are so huge his gray eyes look almost black. But he's not meeting my eyes. Instead, his gaze is fixed firmly on my mouth. I have to fight the urge to lick my lips. I bite down on my lower lip, because it keeps me from doing something really stupid. Like kissing him.

Because, dear God, I want to kiss him. But I don't move, because what I actually want is for him to kiss me. For him to want me.

I stay there, for what feels like forever, hoping he makes a move, but somehow knowing he won't.

And then I straighten and dangle the shoes from my hooked fingers.

"I needed my shoes," I repeat.

He just blinks. I can't tell if he's even more annoyed.

Or worse, if he's as turned on as I am.

CHAPTER 14

MAX

I don't expect Holly to back down.

I'm surprised when I don't hear from her about my beard right away.

I could have sworn—based on the sheer determination in her eyes—that she was going to fight me tooth and nail over the beard.

Instead, days pass.

I even hear from Rodrigo before I hear from her.

Rodrigo comes to the lab for a fitting.

And I still don't hear from Holly.

No calls. No texts. No emails.

I don't call or message her. That would be silly.

But I have started to wonder if maybe she's given up. Maybe I've simply made this all too difficult for her and it's just not worth the trouble anymore. After all, it's my fellowship that's at stake. My career. Not hers.

Moreover, I've been making it hard on her.

I've been a pain in the ass.

Which should surprise no one, but does give me a pang of guilt.

So much so that by the time I reach the lab on Thursday afternoon, I'm actually considering ways I can make it up to her. Obviously, shaving my beard is out of the question. If she knew what the scars on my face looked like, she wouldn't even consider it.

But maybe I could get her some sort of gift basket.

Maybe muffins?

But fruit would be better. Healthier, at least.

I'm getting to the university much later than I normally do because of a teeth-cleaning appointment that morning. The lab is quiet when I let myself in. Gwen and Jaxon should both be here already.

I set the bag down and start the computer before looking around the room.

Yes, Gwen and Jaxon are both here. Priya as well. However, none of them are at their workstations. Instead, they're all in the clean room, huddled around the digital microscope.

Their areas of research are distinct. They wouldn't need to all look at the same samples unless something highly unusual has happened.

Intrigued by the possibility that one of them made some kind of breakthrough, I change shoes and jackets quickly, then do my standard pre-clean room scrub. When I enter the clean room, they are still all huddled around the digital microscope.

And they all jump when the door opens.

Gwen and Jaxon both whirl to face me. Priya looks over her shoulder with wide, terrified eyes, before returning her attention to the computer screen.

These are not the actions of grad students who have made a breakthrough.

This is the behavior of grad students who have fucked up.

God knows I've had enough shitty grad students to know the difference. I just didn't expect it from these three, because they usually have their shit together.

"What the hell happened in here?" I bark.

Priya flinches, but doesn't turn around again.

Jaxon blinks, looking like he might actually cry.

Jesus H. Christ.

Only Gwen has the courage to meet my gaze, but even her chin trembles a little before she starts talking in her usual rambling vomit of words.

"The soil samples from the Costa Rican rainforest finally came in. You know, the ones you requested from that conservation group. The one you've been waiting for? Apparently they finally made it through customs and they arrived last night."

"Did they get left out over night?" I ask. "Because I've fucking talked to Clarissa about that."

Gwen moves her glasses from her nose to her head and then back again. "No. Clarissa knew to watch for them. I was still on campus. So I came over to accept them from the delivery company. I unpacked the boxes and stored the samples in the refrigerator just like I was supposed to."

That all sounds very . . . competent. And efficient.

"So why are you all acting like you've unleashed a plague?"

When no one answers, I cross to the microscope. They scatter out of my way.

I sit down on the high rolling stool to examine the sample on the current slide. And then flip through to the next screen. And the next. I increase the resolution and then decrease it. Trying to make sense of what I'm seeing.

I know what I should be seeing. Samples carefully collected from a dozen different sites from the rainforest, some of them healthy, some areas that had been deforested and are now over-farmed, some from places where the soil is considered essentially dead. Each sample should be unique. The healthy samples should contain hundreds of thousands of microscopic life forms.

That is not what I see.

I abandon the digital microscope, turn the chair around and scan the counter for the larger bagged samples Gwen would have used to make the slides. The bags contain more of the same.

I hold one up as I turn the chair to face my grad students.

"Is this …" I look at the bag, shaking my head, because I cannot believe what I'm about to say. "Is this Miracle Grow?"

"Well, you see," Gwen begins. "We've been trying to isolate the unique properties of these samples and the best we can—"

"Is it Miracle Grow?" I ask again, more slowly.

Gwen and Jaxon exchange a panicked look, but it's Priya who nods. "Yes, sir. I think so."

I look back at the bag in my hand, considering it.

I don't know how she did it. I don't know where my real samples are. But I know who is responsible.

Holly.

I look at the bag in my hand and then hold it up to examine the label more carefully. The labels should all include the date, location, and time the sample was collected, as well as the name of the person who collected it, as well as other relevant information like the soil depth of nearby plants.

Except this label has one additional line, on which is written the word, "Your."

I pull out each of the bags and catalogue all the extra words. Then I rearrange the bags until the words form the message, "Want your samples? Pete's Flat Top Shop, 7:00 p.m., Friday."

I stare at the bags and the message they display for several long moments.

And then I laugh.

CHAPTER 15

HOLLY

I expect the proverbial shit to hit the fan early on Thursday.

After all, one does not merely steal the soil samples of the university's most prestigious researcher and replace them with Miracle Grow.

Worst-case scenario, I expect Clive to call, furious, to yell at me. Maybe he'll even make the hike over to the Blocker building to yell at me in person.

Okay, I guess the actual worst-case scenario is that the police will come arrest me. But I have trouble imagining that happening. After all, I didn't commit mail fraud. I waited until after the samples had been accepted by a qualified member of the department. And then I stole them. Or, as I like to think of it, "removed them to an alternate storage location" for the greater good.

Though, I suspect Max might disagree with my use of the phrase "greater good."

But I don't think he'll tell on me. It's not his style.

Besides, he doesn't seem to like Clive any more than I do. So he won't want to get him involved. And he won't want to report it to anyone other than Clive because he won't want anyone knowing I got the better of him.

So I wait all day to feel the aftershocks of my prank.

When they don't come, I leave campus at three, just like I always do on Thursdays.

Texas University is one of the biggest universities in the country.

And while it's a state school, it's very prestigious. Particularly in science and engineering, but every department has a superstar or two. Most days, you can't throw a cell phone without hitting an overinflated ego. And that's just the professors. That's doesn't include the students who need hand-holding and a sympathetic ear.

Yes, I love my job. I love working with the students, even when they're difficult. I like most of my colleagues. I don't even mind my tiny office—which, sometimes I think they installed a false wall in, because I swear my office is smaller than every other office in the building.

Or maybe it just feels that way. The pressure of living in academia when I am not an academic can feel very Death Star trash compactor-y.

Which is why my favorite part of every week is Thursday afternoon when I leave campus in early afternoon and drive literally and figuratively across the train tracks to Bryan High School.

Texas University is located in the small town of Hillsdale. Due east is Bryan, Hillsdale's blue-collar, rough-and-tumble older brother—home of a meat packing plant, a community college, and housing cheap enough for the poorer students and the university's maintenance staff.

All of the professors live in Hillsdale. Breeding plus mere proximity to greatness meant Hillsdale High School had one of the highest college acceptance rates in the country. Bryan High School . . . not so much.

Most faculty and staff never think about it. Me, on the other hand?

I'm obsessed with evening the odds.

Clive described the weekly after-school class I taught for economically disadvantaged girls as part of my "quixotic obsession with nurturing." Our marriage counselor had agreed. Of course, then he'd slept with a colleague, we'd gotten a divorce and, six months later, he'd slept with our marriage counselor, too. So I may have a quixotic obsession with nurturing, but I was inclined to think it was a healthier way of coping than his sleeping around.

Of course, what he saw as quixotic, I saw as survivor's guilt. Well, maybe not guilt. Maybe obligation.

I'd gone to a high school like that. I'd been poor like that. I had had a lot of odds stacked against me, but these girls had even more.

I have the life I have now because I'd been lucky. I'd gotten a small scholarship to a small college because I'd been in the right place at the right time.

The college prep class I taught was my way of giving back.

"College prep" was a generous way to describe it. There were ten girls in the class. While all of them were smart enough to go to college, they were all miles away from having the social skills to prepare them to get into a college and actually attend it.

We covered everything from how to fill out college applications, to how to write an essay, to how to register to take the SATs, and how to fill out the financial aid paperwork that they would all certainly need.

Some of them would actually go to college—probably only the local community college, but still. Some of them wouldn't. But I figured they all needed someone who believed they *could* go to college. That kind of faith is important.

This year, five of the girls are sophomores and new to the program. Three of the girls are juniors and two are seniors. The juniors and seniors had all been in the program since sophomore year. Even though they were hearing some of the information for the second or even the third time, I refused to kick anyone out of the program. If they were willing to show up, I was willing to help them.

I run the program the way I wished I could run my classes at the university. Small groups, open conversation. Give-and-take.

I may enjoy teaching at the university, but I love this after-school class.

The kids in my college classes all wanted to learn, but these girls were desperate for it.

I love that about them. I love the time I spend with them. Today, we're reviewing SAT skills, something the sophomores in the class desperately need, since their testing date is right around the corner. By the time we all do a check-in and class starts, I'm starting to relax.

The girls are sitting in a semicircle close to the front of the room staring up at the SAT question I had projected on the whiteboard.

"Okay, who can tell me a strategy for answering this question?"

Rosa is the first to raise her hand, which doesn't surprise me in the least because she's wicked smart. Two of the other girls groan. One mumbles, "At least give us a chance to think about it."

We all chuckle and Rosa dips her head, blushing.

I look at Julia, the girl who spoke. "Okay, you go. How would you solve it?"

But before she can answer, the classroom door flies open with so much force I hear it slam into the doorstop on the wall behind it.

My back is to the door, so I don't see who's there. But I *know* who it is.

No, I don't have some preternatural awareness of him.

I can just see it in the faces of the girls. The way Julia snaps her mouth closed. The way Tria, who dislikes all men—which is no surprise given her relationship with her dad—narrows her gaze in instant disgust. The way Rosa goes pale.

Yep. These are exactly the reactions any room full of teenage girls would have to Max Ramsey throwing open the door and stomping into the room.

I turn just in time to see the door bounce back towards him. He stops it with a palm and then glares at the door, clearly affronted the door would dare swing back at him.

I briefly wonder how he got in the building since all the doors lock automatically, but if he terrorized some poor teacher, student, or janitor into holding the door open for him, I don't want to know. I don't want to be the person who gets someone reprimanded for that.

It's raining outside—because it's spring and the rain storms in this part of Texas are legendary. He's dressed in some kind of long duster. It's obvious he has no umbrella, because his hair is wet and disheveled. He's dripping rain and trailing muddy shoeprints. His face is twisted into the scowl of a man who is tired of being messed with.

This is Max Ramsey at his most terrifying. So, yeah, I get why the girls look so taken aback.

What I don't get is why my heart is suddenly pounding. And no, it's not pounding in fear.

Nope, my thundering heart is definitely of the excited variety.

And, yes, it's partly because it took me days of preparation to plan this prank. And I can't wait to see how he's going to respond. But it's also because Max, standing there in the doorway, looking like he might break the doorframe if he breaths too deeply, in that duster and dripping rain, is all very Mr. Darcy stalking across a field at dawn.

Darn it.

Then he levels his gaze at me. "I need to talk to you."

Why is his voice so growly? His gaze so intense?

Double. Frickin'. Darn it.

How am I supposed to not melt into a puddle of goo?

Thank goodness I have a reason to put him off.

Because I am a strong independent woman. Who is doing her darnedest to be a strong independent role model for these girls.

And immediately jumping to do his bidding would not set a good example. Nor, for the record, would be melting into a puddle of goo.

I muster all the molecular cohesion I can and say, "I'm in a class." I glance at the clock on my open laptop. "I'll be done in thirty minutes, if you want to wait."

"No. I need to talk to you now."

Okay, this is good. Max being a jerk helps with the molecular cohesion issue.

"I can't talk now. I'm teaching a class."

He scans the room like he's only now noticing the presence of other people.

As if the second he saw me, everyone else in the world ceased to exist. Which isn't sexy at all. Nope. Not at all.

His brow furrows, making his scowl that much fiercer. "This isn't one of your classes. You teach twelve hours of class. Two sections of introduction to modern media and one section of professional communication. Neither of them meets on Thursday at four."

Before I can muster an appropriate response—not that I even know what that would sound like—Tria asks, "Stalker much?"

I shoot her a *"Be respectful"* look. She smirks back, giving me a *"Is this guy serious?"* shrug.

Tria's attitude is way more likely to get her in trouble than her lack of testing prep.

I turn back to Max. "This is a class I volunteer to teach." I gesture to the girls. "These are my students."

"What are you teaching them?"

"Ironically, I teach them things very similar to the skills I'm teaching you. Skills they need to survive at the university."

He narrows his gaze, his scowl deepening. I try not to find his petulance cute.

"But I still need to talk to you."

Cute or not, I don't interrupt this class for anyone. Even people I've purposefully baited.

Not that I've done this kind of thing with anyone else. Ever.

"Well, I'll be done in thirty minutes," I say to Max, like I don't know exactly why he's here. "I can talk to you then."

He makes that growly noise in his throat again. I cross my arms over my chest and step closer to glare him down. For a long moment, neither of us budge.

"You can talk to him now," Faith, ever the peacemaker, says in a bright tone. "Rosa can take over while you talk to this guy."

The other girls nod. Tria, however, eyes Max with open suspicion. "If this is a guy you want to talk to, that is."

Tria looks like she can't imagine anyone wanting to talk to Max.

I should totally do the mature thing and not exacerbate this staring contest with Max. In the interest of modelling mature behavior for the girls.

"Rosa, if you think you're up to it, I certainly trust you to teach the girls about these questions."

Rosa opens and closes her mouth, clearly uncomfortable being put on the spot this way. But it'll be good for her, so I pat her on the shoulder as I cross to the door.

Now, to deal with my other student with authority issues.

Max follows me out into the hall. As the door shuts behind him, I cross my arms over my chest and tap my toe, exaggerating the signs of my annoyance. After all, he did say he misses social cues.

"You're mad at me," he says after several second of studying me.

"Really? What gave it away?"

"Your body language. You're—"

"That was a rhetorical question."

"Oh." He narrows his gaze, glaring down at me. "What right do you have to be mad at me, when you're the one who stole my soil samples? You've wasted my department's time and money. You've done incalculable damage to—"

"Calm down, your soil samples are fine."

"Then return them."

"I will. After you get your hair cut on Friday." I reach for the door, but he wraps his hand around my wrist, stopping me.

"I don't need a haircut. And I don't think the university would tolerate this kind of irresponsible behavior from you. So—"

I pull my wrist from his hand. Because I don't like being manhandled. Not because his touch felt disconcertingly good. I arch an eyebrow at him. "Oh, are you going to tell on me?"

"I'm not going to tell on you. We're not eight-year-olds tattling on the playground."

"You're lucky we're not. Because if the university doesn't appreciate my irresponsible behavior, how do you think they would feel about yours?"

"I haven't done anything irresponsible," he growls, jutting out his jaw stubbornly.

"You haven't? You're refusing to put in even the bare minimum of work to earn a very prestigious fellowship that half the professors at the university would kill to be considered for. You don't think that's irresponsible? You don't think that's worse than the fact that I relocated a few Ziploc bags of dirt?"

"That dirt—" He cuts himself off, exhales, and then continues. "Those soil samples are crucial to my research. And if they—"

"They're fine," I tell him again.

"If they aren't stored at precisely the right temperature—"

"Trust me. I know how to use a thermometer. And it's not like the Frigidaire in your lab is some high-end specialty equipment."

"So are the samples at your house? In your refrigerator?"

"Ew. No. I don't want nasty bags of dirt in my fridge. But they are in a safe place. And I promise they will be returned to you as soon as that jaw of yours is bare."

"That isn't going to happen."

"Then you aren't going to get your samples back. It's that simple."

He glares at me. I glare back. His chin juts out a smidge more as he studies me.

If I had a gun on me, my hand would be twitching at the holster.

After several heartbeats, he says, "Fine. Let's go."

He turns and starts down the hall, drippy coat, muddy shoeprints and all.

"What?" I ask. "Go where?"

"To the shop. That flat top place. I'll get my hair cut."

"Ignoring for a second that you agreed to a haircut and not a shave, your appointment isn't now. It's tomorrow evening. And besides, I can't leave."

"Why not?"

"Because I have a class. Which you interrupted. Which is pretty rude."

He gestured toward the door behind me. "How was I supposed to know that was a class?"

"What else would I be doing at a high school? How did you even know I was here?" I counter. "How did you know where to find me?"

"I went to your office. When you weren't there, I knocked on the doors of the other offices around until I found someone who knew where you were."

"Oh my God!" I blurt out.

Max, walking the halls of the comm building, knocking on doors until he found someone who knew where I was?

I'm friendly with a lot of people, but there are only a handful who know about my class at the high school. "You must have talked to at least twenty-five people."

"Thirty-three," he says gruffly.

I honestly can't tell if he's put out or expects me to praise his persistence.

"Why didn't you just text me?"

"I did. You didn't text back."

"Right. Because I'm in class. It didn't occur to you that I might be busy and that you should just wait?"

His scowl deepens, the nerve by his left eye twitching in obvious annoyance.

Good lordy. If this is what he'd looked like stomping around the comm building looking for me, he's lucky the villagers didn't come after him with pitchforks.

"You are the one who keeps telling me how important all this stuff is. That I need to follow your directions. That this is the most important thing for me to do right now."

"Yeah. It's the most important thing in *your* life right now. But not in mine."

For a second, he flinches. And looks almost hurt.

I even feel a stab of regret. "Look, you have to understand, these girls are important to me. I'm important to them. They don't have a lot of stability in their lives, so I have to be there when I say I'm going to be there. For an hour and a half, once a week, on Thursday afternoons I'm here for them. I need them to believe they can trust me. Just like I need you to believe you can trust me."

That squinty look in his eyes relaxes just a little, like the reality of this situation is slowly sinking in.

"I can't ever tell them that you're more important to me than they are. They have enough people in their lives telling them that educated white men are more important. If I bug out of their class thirty minutes early to take you to get your hair cut, they'll think I believe that too."

He studies me for a moment, looking at me like he's trying to figure something out. Like a puzzle he has to solve. It's disconcerting.

I'm used to men looking at me. Leering at me.

This is different than that. He doesn't look at me like he wants to possess me, but rather like he wants to unravel some mystery.

After a moment, he asks, "Can I come into the class? Can I meet them?"

He wants to meet them?

I have no idea what to make of that.

My first instinct is to protect them, to shelter them, in case he acts like an ass.

My second instinct is to protect him.

Because there is not a tougher crowd in the universe than a group of underprivileged Gen Z girls.

Geez, maybe that's just what he needs.

If he can hold his own in this room, then how hard can the McPherson selection committee really be?

"I suppose." I reach for the door and then pause. "You can't talk to them. I mean, you can greet them. But you can't dominate the conversation. Just listen."

Maybe if he doesn't talk too much, there won't be too much damage.

"Can I say one thing? Just one?" He must've seen my hesitation, because he says, "I'll be brief."

"Okay."

God, I hope I'm doing the right thing. That he's not going to be a total dick to them. I work hard to make these girls believe this is their space. That they are safe here. If he messes this up . . .

Well, it would solve one problem. It would kill this weird attraction I feel. Because crossing this line is the one thing a guy could never come back from, at least as far as I'm concerned.

I open the door and lead Max in.

Rosa is standing by the whiteboard, pointing to a paragraph of text. When she sees us, she trails off.

"You can keep going," I say.

But Rosa just shakes her head and slinks back to her seat, keeping her eyes glued to the desk in front of her like the swirls of faux woodgrain might transform into a magical incantation if she stares at them long enough.

The other girls are looking at Max like he's the enemy.

Not that I blame them. He is fresh from terrorizing the comm building.

I give them my most reassuring smile. "This is a colleague of mine, Dr. Maximilian Ramsey. He's a professor at the university. He would like to meet you. Max, these are my students. This is Rosa Hernandez. And—"

I expect to rattle off each girl's name. To get this over with quickly.

But as I introduce Rosa, he steps forward and thrusts out his hand.

Rosa looks terrified for all of a second, then she gets it together.

We've practiced professional introductions. That was the very first class. The second she figures out what's happening, she visibly relaxes. Yes, she's shy, but mostly she just hates not knowing what to expect.

She stands, shakes his hand and looks him in the eye as she offers a quiet, "Nice to meet you, sir."

I don't know who looks more awkward, him or her, but I'm certain I'm the one who looks the most surprised. They shake hands as he gives her a respectful nod and says, "Likewise."

Somehow, this man—this gruff, impatient man who regularly makes students, and sometimes even other professors, cry—greets Rosa like she is his equal.

And I swear she's three inches taller by the time she sits.

I have to swallow a lump in my throat before doing the rest of the introductions.

It's not _not_ awkward. Not for any of them. But it could be a lot worse. A lot, lot worse.

Once I'm finished with the introductions, I'm not sure what to say next.

Sure, the introductions went well, but I'm sure the girls won't be comfortable continuing our SAT prep with him watching.

But before I can figure out how to shoo him out the door, he says, in a rush of words like he's been mentally practicing them, "Ms. Dolinsky is an excellent teacher. You're very lucky to have her. And I am sorry that I interrupted your class."

Then he looks at me, a question in his eyes. As if he wasn't sure he'd said the right thing. But he had. Oh, he had _so_ said the perfect thing.

Even Tria gives him the faintest nod. Almost of approval.

"I'll wait outside until you're done here," he says to me. And then he's gone.

It takes all of us a moment to get back on track after he leaves. Not surprisingly, the girls recover before I do.

I do an okay job faking it—I've been teaching some variation of this information for six years now. Besides, whenever possible, I let the older girls coach the younger. It's a reminder of how much they know and how far they've come.

So I don't think any of them notice how disconcerted I am for the rest of class.

I'd been so annoyed with him when he'd first shown up, with his thoughtless invasion of my space and privacy.

It hadn't even occurred to him that I might have other plans. Plans that were more important to me than him.

Because that's the kind of arrogance men like him have.

Wasn't it?

But that apology . . .

Oh, man.

And the fact that he treated the girls with respect, like they are worthy of his time and attention . . .

These girls, who were at the bottom of every possible food chain, are not used to men apologizing to them, respecting their time. Let alone a powerful, respected white man.

His apology makes them feel valuable. Important.

Gah.

It wrecks me.

It would never in a million years have occurred to Clive to do that.

Clive had never understood why I wanted to teach this class. He had called me impossibly naïve for believing I could help them. He'd even told me I was cruel to let them hope for a better life that would never be theirs.

We had fought over it. Back before we had bigger things to fight over. Even before he'd slept with someone else, I'd been so hurt by him. By the slow realization that he wasn't the man I thought he was.

We'd first met when I was eighteen and he was twenty-five. He'd been getting his master's. I was barely out of high school and not that different from the girls I taught now. Poor, but hard-working. No real future ahead of me.

If Clive hadn't pushed, I might not have even finished college. My second year, between the stress of school and work, I floundered. My grades dropped. I was close to bungling it all. I was one failing grade away from dropping out and heading home to the small town in Georgia where my mom worked at the soda factory and my older brothers worked at the paper mill. If I hadn't been so afraid of disappointing Clive, I might have taken the easy way out.

Somehow, Clive had never seen the similarities between me and the girls I taught. Because I'd been beautiful and eager to please. I'd been moldable into the kind of wife he wanted.

That had been the final nail in the coffin of our marriage. The realization that he had never seen me as a person at all. He had seen me as raw materials that he could sculpt into his idea of the perfect wife. The other half of the power couple he wanted to be.

But just now, when Max walked into this room and apologized to these girls, he'd had the opposite reaction. He had seen them. He had seen their intrinsic value.

Okay, I'm probably being overly dramatic. Imagining motivation and emotional depth that might not be there. After all, that is my fatal flaw.

Yet … And yet, Max is a completely different kind of man than Clive.

Not just on the surface either. Not just because Clive is handsome, charming, and has a closet full of tailored jackets. But because Max actually looks at people.

How could someone who appears to have so few social skills have done so much for my girls just now?

And why did I feel like he hadn't done it for them, but for me?

CHAPTER 16

MAX

I spend the next twenty minutes watching Holly interact with her students through the narrow window in the door.

Not because I'm a stalker, despite the accusations of Holly's student, Tria.

No, it's merely an issue of wanting something to occupy my time. I check my emails on my phone. While there are several I need to respond to, the only thing I hate more than answering emails is answering emails on that tiny keyboard. I even spend a full five minutes looking over the student work displayed on the walls outside the classrooms. It's not intellectually stimulating, so I end up watching Holly.

She is a completely different person here than she was in the lecture I watched at the university. There, she was in command of the room, a bundle of kinetic energy the students couldn't take their eyes off.

Here, the girls are the center of attention. They aren't in control—that's obvious in the way Holly steps in any time the conversation gets off track—but they are her focus.

Finally, at five forty-five on the dot, Holly ends the class.

She opens the door and indicates I can come back in. Like at her class on campus, a few of the students linger, asking her questions.

I can't help but watch her interactions. There's something about her that draws people in. It must be the way she focuses her attention on them. The way she listens. The way she actually seems to care. The soothing tone of voice she uses.

As each of the girls prepares to leave, Holly makes sure that they have a ride home and she hands them a brown paper sack with their name written on the front. There's no discussion or conversation about the bag. Each of the girls takes it, though several roll their eyes when they do.

When we're finally alone, I ask, "What was in the bags?"

Holly stills. There's something in her posture that makes me think she's about to tell me to mind my own business.

But then she slides her laptop into her bag and answers without looking at me.

"Two peanut butter and jelly sandwiches, an apple, and a Clif Bar."

"Why?"

"The first year I did this, one of the girls left her cell phone in the class. I had to follow her out to give it to her. I found her behind the school, digging through the cafeteria trash bin."

Holly zips her bag closed and then slings the strap over her shoulder. Finally, she meets my gaze. Her chin jutted out at a stubborn angle. Like she's ready to argue with me about it. Like she's daring me to push back.

"What was she looking for? Her retainer or something?"

I'd accidentally thrown away my retainer in middle school when I threw out my trash from lunch. My mom had been furious.

Holly's lips curve, but there's a bitterness to her smile. "The girls who take this class usually aren't from families who can afford braces."

She says it like I should have known that.

If there'd been clues about the girls' socioeconomic status, I'd missed them.

Before I can explain this, Holly says, "She was looking for food. She denied it, of course. But I knew she qualified for free lunch and breakfast. I realized those were the only two meals she ate a day."

"But she had a cell phone—"

Holly stalks toward the door. "That attitude is just—"

Then she cuts herself off and turns back to face me. She draws in a breath and then exhales like she's trying to calm herself down. Something I've never seen her do before.

I know I'm a pain in the ass to deal with. But this is the first time I've irritated her this much. My comment about the cell phone must have really pissed her off.

This wasn't the low-grade irritation most people felt when I annoy them.

This is a genuine roiling rage. The kind I feel when a grad student contaminates a sample.

"That attitude is not helpful," she hisses. "People are allowed to have phones. In the modern world, a cell phone is a basic necessity. Not a luxury."

"Sure, for an adult. For a parent, maybe, but—"

"My former student, Sarah, was an adult. She was eighteen. And she was a parent. She had a two-year-old daughter at home. Sarah qualified for free lunch, but her daughter didn't. So during the day, she ate whatever she couldn't bring home to her daughter, and anything else she stashed in her backpack to bring home to feed her kid. Fresh fruit, bread, rolls, anything she could keep. That meant on any given day, she lived on reconstituted dried eggs, pints of milk, and meat that she was afraid would go bad if she stored it in her backpack. Can you even imagine what it's like to live on such little food? Can you imagine what it's like knowing all you can give your kid is a roll or slice of bread?"

Holly turns back to the door and storms out, saying over her shoulder, "No. I don't imagine you can."

I race after her.

"My assumptions about her socioeconomic status—" I start to explain.

But Holly whirls back to face me just as she reaches the door out to the parking lot.

"Ever since then, every kid who's ever made it through one of my classes, gets a lunch when they leave. I don't care what they do with it. I don't care if they throw it away. We don't discuss it. Ever. That may be the only food they have to eat tonight. They may have to split it with their family of four. Or more. I don't know. I don't care. I don't ask questions. I just give them the food. Because they may need it or they may not. But I don't judge them. I don't *ever* judge them. And if you're going to, then this is over right now."

"I'm not, but—"

"There's no 'but' at the end of that sentence." Her hand cuts through the air like she's wielding a machete. "You don't get to judge."

"I was just explaining my position."

"This isn't your doctoral defense. I don't care about your position or your thought process. If you make a mistake, you apologize. And back there"—she gestures towards the building—"you made a mistake."

I open my mouth, imagining the logical and completely valid defense I could offer.

But if I'm honest, when have logical and valid defenses of my behavior ever helped?

Never. That's when.

So I nod and try again. "I'm sorry."

She looks at me through narrowed eyes, like she knows there's a defense hiding there behind the apology.

Then she walks away, heading for the car parked in the middle of the parking lot.

I follow, saying nothing, but a little in awe.

If you'd asked me a week ago, I couldn't have imagined her losing her temper like that.

I know what it's like to have that kind of rage. How hard it is to get it back under control, even when everything you're saying only makes things worse.

I follow her to a Toyota that's seen better years and wait while she puts her bag in the back seat. Then I say again, "I'm sorry."

"No, I'm—" She gives a little chuckle, that doesn't sound amused at all. "You know what? I'm not going to apologize for defending those girls."

"I wouldn't expect you to."

"But I did overreact. I just get so tired of the attitude in this country that people deserve whatever poverty they have. None of those girls chose to be born poor. And they're doing everything they can to change things, but they have so few opportunities. So few options. I do what I can, but I know it's not enough. Even if it's enough for one of them, it's not enough for all of them. Let alone enough for all of the girls in poverty."

I don't even know what to say. Because I have no idea what it's like to live in poverty. My childhood was comfortably middle class. My intellect has opened doors I didn't even know existed until years later.

Despite that, I know what it's like to feel trapped by circumstances. To feel like you have no options. No way out. I know the frustrations.

Suddenly, all I want to do is pull her into my arms and hug her.

I've never wanted to hug anyone in my life. Ever.

So I have no idea why that's the idea that comes to me.

Probably because that's what characters do on TV when they're trying to comfort someone. I don't know.

Right after my parents died, my aunt had tried hugging me. A lot.

She used to tell me people needed eight hugs a day to maintain their mental health. Tavey used to tell her that I wasn't most people, but that she needed extra hugs to make up for it. Because that was the kind of shit Tavey has always done. Automatically stepped into the space between me and the rest of the world.

I don't know if she does it to protect me or everyone else.

But Tavey would probably hug Holly now. Of course, Tavey isn't six-four. If I try to hug Holly, she'll probably pepper-spray me. If I don't crush her, that is.

Standing beside the open door to the car, Holly says, "I am sorry I overreacted. I don't normally get so . . . worked up." She straightens and looks up at me. "But very few people from the university know what I do here. And I don't think most people would understand. So if you could keep this between us, I would appreciate that."

"Of course."

Who would I tell anyway? Does she imagine I have friends at the university that I hang out with? That I might tell this story to someone else, and what? Criticize her for wanting to help people who would dare to own a cell phone and want to eat?

In retrospect, my comment about the cell phone was stupid. Because of course a young mother with a daughter at home would need a cell phone. Would need to be reachable.

I felt like a dumbass for not getting that sooner.

She glances at the cell phone in her hand. "Look, if you really need me to, I can try to get you a hair appointment tonight, but we might as well just wait until tomorrow."

"Okay," I say stupidly. Because I'm suddenly feeling very fucking stupid. And it's not something I'm used to.

But she must misunderstand my tone, because she tips her head to the side and says softly, "It probably won't be as bad as you think."

"What?"

"Shaving off your beard. It won't be that bad. I promise."

I don't tell her that just now I hadn't been thinking about the damn haircut that's been looming over me like a sword. That I hadn't even been thinking about my soil samples.

When I don't say anything, she just keeps looking at me, her gaze moving over the scarred side of my face, tracing the mangled tissue from its origin by my temple across my cheek to where it disappears into the growth of my beard.

Even in the relatively low light of the parking lot, I can't help but think she sees more of me than most people do.

"Can I ask you a question?" she asks.

I nod instead of pointing out she just had asked a question. I've learned from experience that those kinds of observations annoy people.

"When was the last time you looked at your face without your beard?"

It doesn't take a genius to see where she's going with this. "I know what my scar looks like."

"Are you sure?"

"Of course I'm sure. I've had this scar since I was twelve." I jerk my hand up to indicate my cheek. "I know what it looks like."

"That isn't what I asked." She does that head-tip thing again. "I didn't ask what it looks like. I asked when the last time you looked at it was."

I open my mouth but then snap it shut again. "I don't see what that has to do with anything."

"When I was in high school, I desperately wanted to be a cheerleader."

The abrupt change of topic surprises me into silence.

"I know." She laughs. "Shocking, right?"

"Actually," I say. "It's not particularly surprising given—"

"I was being sarcastic. Because yeah, I think on some level, all fourteen-year-old girls want to be cheerleaders. But that's not the point of the story. The point is, I was the smallest person on the team. Which meant I was supposed to be the top of the pyramid. But I was afraid of heights. Terrified, actually. To make matters worse, the first time we tried it, I got dropped. There was no lasting damage, but it hurt. A lot. I bruised my tailbone and it hurt to sit for weeks. Needless to say, I did not want to try again. But if I wanted to stay on the squad, I had to."

"I understand the analogy you're trying to make. You're going to say that you built this up in your mind to be something terrifying. But that when you actually did it, it was not as scary as you thought it would be."

"Actually, no." She lets out a rueful laugh. "The truth is I was a coward. I never tried again. The cheerleading coach booted me off the squad."

"That was extremely irresponsible of her. She should've been fired for that."

"That's not my point. My point is, I let my fear dictate my life. I gave up something I really wanted because I was afraid. I don't want you to do that. All my life, I've wondered if being at the top of the pyramid was really as scary as I thought it was."

She steps just a little closer and puts her hand on my arm. Even through the multiple layers of fabric, I feel the heat and the weight of her touch.

"Maybe you're right. Maybe the scars are just as bad as you remember. Maybe they're not. The point is you'll never know unless you shave. Be braver than I was."

Is that really what she thinks? That she's a coward? For not participating in some ridiculous high school ritual? It's absurd. Clearly she's very brave.

She's confronted me over and over again. She stole my fucking soil samples, which is just about the ballsiest thing I've ever heard of.

I want to tell her that, but instead I just say, "My memory is quite good."

"Oh, I have no doubt. You probably have an eidetic memory. Many brilliant people do."

"That's not what I meant. But when you spend years of your life looking in the mirror waiting for your beard to grow in enough to hide a scar, then you remember what the scar looks like."

"When was the last time you shaved your beard?"

"When I interviewed for this job."

My aunt had insisted. She and Tavey had helped me pick out a suit and took me to get my hair cut.

When Tavey and I went to live with our aunt and uncle after the accident, Aunt Jules had never quite known what to do with me, but she had tried. She had never stopped trying. Not when I blasted through high school and demanded that they let me go off to college at fifteen, even though she wanted me to stay close. And not when I skipped coming home for holidays for years, because life with her and Uncle Pete was just so different than life with my parents had been. I just never knew how to handle being around so much overt and obvious affection. But she'd always tried.

"So that was, what?" Holly asks now. "Five years ago? You know, scars fade over time."

"I appreciate what you are trying to do. However, the timing of this is not logical. Sometime in the next seven days, I need to send in a sample video for the fellowship. If I shave my beard now, the scar will be visible during that video."

"But if—"

"If you are correct, and my scar has magically healed in the past five years because I have been secretly wishing upon a star every night, then yes, I will be glad I shaved off my beard for the promo. However, if you are wrong, and the scar is still—" My tongue trips over the words. Because how can I describe the scar? Do I remember it? Yes. But how do I quantify it? I can't. So I choose the easiest way to describe it. "Unsightly, it may ruin my chances of getting the fellowship."

Her lips quirk. "First off, nice use of sarcasm. How about we compromise, then? You cut your hair, as we've already agreed. And then we trim the beard. I promise I won't go so close to the skin that the scar will show for filming."

Before I can agree or disagree, she does the unthinkable.

She reaches up and runs the tips of her fingers along the top of my beard. "We'll need to trim this up." Her fingers pause to trace the spot where the scar dips into my beard. "A little more of the scar will be visible here. That's unavoidable."

She is almost—not quite, but almost—cupping my cheek.

Inexplicably, I want to lean into her hand. To step closer until more of her is touching more of me.

Suddenly, her fingers freeze and her gaze darts to mine.

She drops her hand and takes a step back as she blurts, "And your neck."

"My neck?"

It's all I can do not to bring my hand to my cheek, to press the memory of her touch deeper into my skin.

"Yes. We'll need to shave your neck. I'll compromise on a neatly trimmed beard. But the neck scruff has to go."

She has no idea what she does to me.

How could she?

For her there's nothing even remotely sexual about this.

She has no idea that the feeling of her fingertips on my skin drives me wild.

A woman like Holly would never be attracted to me.

And it doesn't matter if I have a beard or not.

Maybe she's right; maybe the scars are less pronounced than I remember.

I've spent the better part of my life learning not to care about my physical appearance.

And the truth is, I suspect the scars wouldn't matter to Holly either. She's not that superficial.

She's vibrant and charming, caring and complex. She's loved and admired by everyone who knows her. I, on the other hand, am feared by nearly everyone.

No, Holly might not care about my physical scars at all. But I have plenty of other qualities, plenty of other defects in my personality, to drive her away.

Ultimately, there's no point in trying to hide the scars on my face, when there's nothing I can do about the flaws that actually scare people off.

"I'll text you the address of the barbershop," she tells me, opening the car door. Before she climbs in, she says, "It wouldn't kill you to text me back to let me know you've received it."

"Okay," I say again, feeling even more stupid. But then I step forward and ask, "What about my soil samples? Can I have them?"

She tips her head to the side as if considering the matter. "Of course. Tomorrow. After the beard is trimmed."

"Holly—"

She just laughs and shakes her head. "You heard me. I'm not falling for your sad, regretful biologist act. You'll get them back when you're less hairy."

Still smiling smugly, she shuts the car door.

That's when it hits me. She's enjoying this.

Not just that . . . but I'm enjoying this too.

And I don't know which is more shocking.

No one ever does that. No one ever jokes with me.

No one enjoys my company.

Maybe Tavey, I guess. But she's my sister. She has to put up with me.

All my life, my intelligence had set me apart from others.

It's not that I'm better than other people. Just . . . different. Meant for bigger things.

I don't mean to be a dick about it. It's just a fact of life. Some people go through the world just living their lives, caught up in the minutia of social media and TV and whatever the fuck normal people cared about.

My life was bigger than that. My job was bigger than that.

I was pulling back the curtain to reveal the inner workings of a universe humanity hadn't even known existed fifty years ago. That's what I was put on this earth to do: to improve the human race by uncovering knowledge through scientific discovery and hard work.

Yes, it set me apart from others. I'd always been okay with that. Because I knew it was important. Not just important, but the most important thing I could be doing with my time.

I had never doubted that. Ever.

Until now.

Until I saw what Holly did with her time.

CHAPTER 17

HOLLY

I text Max as soon as I get in the house.

Me: Pete's Flat Top Shop, 203 University Blvd. 7:00 p.m., Friday

Max: Holly?

Me: Yes.

Me: Who else would it be?

Max: You don't want to know.

Hmm.

Suddenly, I remember all the calls and texts he got that Saturday when I went to his house. I don't love the idea that he has so many women texting him that he can't keep us straight.

I set my phone down as I let the dogs out of their crates.

By the time I get back to my phone, there's another text from Max.

Max: I'll be there.

I type out a reply and hit send.

Then I slap my palm to my face. I scrub my hand down and stare at the phone in horror.

Me: It's a date

It's a date? Why did I type that? It's not a date.

I stomp into the living room and practically throw myself onto the sofa. What was wrong with me?

I don't want to go on a date with Max Ramsey.

A date with Max Ramsey would be a disaster.

Even if we weren't working together, a date would be a disaster.

Besides, I'd given up dating.

I mean, he probably didn't even read it that way.

I'm sure he didn't.

Why would he? "It's a date" was a common enough phrase.

Somehow, I push the train of thought out of my head long enough to grade some essays and rewatch an old favorite show on Netflix. The next morning, when I stumble out of bed, pull myself together, and head into work, I stop cold on my front porch.

There are three brown paper sacks sitting right in front of my door. Bags that were not there the night before when I arrived home.

I set my bag down and investigate.

The bags have the logo of the local grocery store printed on them. The first bag contains ten jars of peanut butter and ten jars of jelly. The second, several loaves of sliced bread. The third, six large boxes of Clif Bars.

I carry them to the kitchen, unload all three of the bags until the contents cover the surface of my kitchen table, then slowly sink to the kitchen chair as I take in the bounty.

This is the kindest thing anyone has ever done for me.

Max did this for me.

I can hardly reconcile it in my mind.

The gruff man who yells at me, bullies me, and has dismissed my work and my skill . . . he's the person who did this. He's also the man who apologized to a room of teenage girls. The one who shook their hands and treated them with kindness and respect. How is it possible that Max can be both those people?

The man who was supposed to have no social skills had seen what no one else saw. He realized how incredibly important my class is to me.

Yeah, I know the approximate value of each of these items. I've bought them enough to know. Financially, it's not an extravagant gift. Clif Bars are pricey, so it's more than dinner would be. But it's certainly less expensive than the unimaginative diamond tennis bracelets Clive bought me on Valentine's Day year after year.

But this . . . this is something else entirely.

This was thoughtful and kind. It was a revelation.

I absolutely do not know what to make of it. Because there is so much more to Max than I'd ever dreamed there was. And, no, I'm not just talking about his crazy muscles. There is so much more to his heart. Twenty-four hours ago, I never would have thought he was capable of this kind of sensitivity. But now . . .

Oh, God. Now, I want to date Max Ramsey.

CHAPTER 18

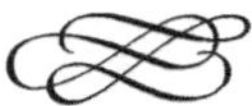

MAX

I put off talking to Tavey about the shaving situation as long as I can.

On one hand, I do not want to let anyone touch my beard. I'm comfortable with my beard. I haven't shaved regularly since I was a teen. I hated it then and I have no interest in adding an additional step into my morning routine now. Furthermore, I don't see how having a beard could possibly affect my chances of winning the McPherson Fellowship.

However, I am, admittedly, not an expert.

So as I walk from my lab to my car to head for the appointment with Holly, I call Tavey to get her opinion. Either she'll convince me shaving my beard is necessary or she'll arm me with additional arguments to present to Holly.

As soon as Tavey answers, I ask, "Do you know who Hagrid is?"

"From Harry Potter?" She pauses, and I hear the sound of fingers on a keyboard. Then the typing stops. "Wait. Do *you* know who Hagrid is?"

"He's the keeper of keys and grounds at Hogwarts."

There is an audible gasp of breath on the other end of the line. Then silence.

Then I hear a shuffling noise, before she says, "Wait a minute. Just one hot minute. You not only know who Hagrid is, but his actual title?"

"I do know how to use Google."

"Oh. For sure. Obviously, you know how to use Google. I'm just shocked that you bothered to use it for something that's not, uh, you know, about dirt."

"I google things that aren't dirt."

"Do you?"

"Yes."

I also google things about climate change, crop production, weather patterns, and deforestation.

I don't tell Tavey that, because I'm pretty sure she would argue that all of those topics are at least tangentially related to dirt and therefore don't count. She wouldn't be wrong.

"Your Google habits aside—which, by the way, you do know I could easily track, right?"

"Yes. I don't know why you would. But I know you can." I add under my breath, "And you tell me I need to get a hobby."

"Puh-lease. I have lots of hobbies. Meddling in your life is just one of them. Which brings me to my point. Your googling habits aside, why are you asking about Hagrid? Why do you even know who Hagrid is? Or Harry Potter, for that matter?"

"Someone recently told me I look like Hagrid. And I'm wondering—"

Before I can finish my question, Tavey cuts me off.

"Hmm . . . I wouldn't say Hagrid. I've always thought you were more of a grumpy, brooding Jason Momoa."

"Should I know who that is?"

"He's Aquaman."

"Who is that? Is he in charge of the lake?"

"The what?"

"The lake. With the giant squid."

"No, he's from the DC comic books. Wait a second. The giant squid? Like the lake and the giant squid at Hogwarts?"

"Yes. Isn't that what we're talking about?"

"No, I was . . ."

Tavey trails off. And I can practically hear her thinking. No one thinks louder than Tavey.

And it's never a good sign when she has to think longer about something than a few seconds.

"I'm almost to my car," I tell her. "I'll call you—"

"Holy shit," she mutters. "This is about that woman, isn't it?"

"What woman?" Though, obviously she means Holly.

"That woman who went to your house that Saturday. The one who is so into you."

"She's not—"

"And oh. My. God. You are into her."

"I'm—"

"Yes. You are. Not only are you upset that she said you look like Hagrid—"

"I'm not upset."

"You called me to get a second opinion about it. Do you know the last time you needed a second opinion about something? Or called me, for that matter?"

"I call you."

That's not true. I can't remember a specific time I've called her. Not in the past few years. But I don't need to call Tavey, because she calls me.

"It was five years ago when you were debating whether you should accept the job at Texas University or the one at DuPont. And before that, it was when you were trying to decide between universities for your graduate studies."

"That's ridiculous. I have called you more than twice in the past decade."

"No, you really haven't. You only call me when you have some massive, cataclysmic shift in your life. You didn't even call me to tell me about the McPherson Fellowship. And that was huge. But now, suddenly, you're calling me because some woman said you look like Hagrid? And not only did you run out and research who Hagrid is, you're reading the books."

"You can't possibly know that."

"Dude, give me a little credit. I'm looking at your Amazon purchase history right now."

My steps slow a little. "Tavey, you are kind of terrifying."

"Take that back. I am not kind of terrifying."

I can't tell from her tone if she objects to "terrifying" or "kind of." Through the phone, I hear her fingers flying over the keys.

"However," she says. "If I were limiting myself to characters within the Harry Potter universe, I would say you're more like a young Sirius Black."

"Who?"

"Don't worry. You're still in the second book, right? He doesn't show up until the next one."

How does she know not just which series I'm reading, but how far into the series I've read?

"I revise my earlier statement. You are more than kind of terrifying."

"Hey!" She almost sounds offended. "When my older brother falls in love for the first time, I'm allowed to meddle."

This time, my steps don't just slow. I stop dead in my tracks. Right in front of the doors to the building.

Students stream around me. Time seems to stop inside the bubble of my shock.

"What did you just say?"

"That I'm allowed to meddle?" she asks. Then the keyboard chatter on the other end of the line ceases. There's a pause and then an audible gasp. "Oh my God, you didn't know."

"I'm not . . ." I start the sentence, but it gets caught in my throat.

Because I'm not.

I am not in love with Holly.

The very idea is . . .

Yes. She's beautiful. And funny.

Yeah, I can admit that.

And smart. In her own way.

Do I admire certain qualities about her? Like the fact that she isn't intimidated by me and never backs down? Yes.

Did my chest feel tight and panicky when she texted me "It's a date"? Yes, it did. But then I realized, obviously, that the phrase "it's a date" is common parlance for "we have an appointment." And since an appointment with a work colleague has no romantic connotation at all, I was able to ignore that panic. Until now.

"You're wrong," I blurt out. "I'm not in love with her."

"Oh, Max."

The tone of her voice when she says it is soft and low. Almost a whisper.

That hits the hardest. Because there's regret there. And maybe a little bit of . . . I don't know what. Caution, maybe? Like she's afraid.

"Max, are you all right?"

Suddenly, I'm fighting the urge to bolt. To run to my car, get in, and just drive.

Which is stupid.

Because I don't run. Ever. My fucking hip doesn't allow me that kind of agility.

And I don't bolt. Ever. My fucking temperament doesn't allow me that kind of cowardice.

"Love isn't real," I blurt.

"Ouch," Tavey quips.

Her tone is light, but even I hear the sting in her voice.

Because she's my sister and obviously, I love her.

"You know what I mean," I grumble. "Romantic love is an illusion. A hormonal response brought about by the evolutionary drive to reproduce. The ability of a species to create lasting pair bonds is directly related to the fragility of that species' young. Therefore—"

"Okay, Professor Ramsey. I get it. You don't believe in romantic love as a philosophical concept. So what? You still have a physical body. You have all the hormones and biological reactions the rest of us have. So if you need me to put it in more scientific terms for you to accept it, I can. You feel the biological urge to create a pair bond with this woman."

"That's . . . I don't . . . You can't . . ." Once again, my heart is pounding and my thoughts can't keep up with my sputtering words.

Tavey laughs.

"You are speechless." She sounds fucking delighted. "The brilliant and enigmatic Dr. Ramsey is actually speechless."

"Shut up," I mutter.

"Do you know how long I've waited to win an argument with you?"

"Fuck off."

"My entire life. That's how long. My entire damn life. This is the curse of having a brilliant older brother who goes off to college when he's fifteen. You've been more knowledgeable and better educated than me since I was a single-celled organism. And I've found the one thing you don't know more about than I do—your own emotions."

"Seriously. Can you just fucking shut up?"

"Yes. I can." She gives a luxuriant, indulgent sigh. "Yes. I can shut the fuck up. I can enter a Buddhist monastery and take a vow of silence if you want. Because I won an argument with you. I never have to speak again."

"I didn't know you were this petty."

"My dear brother, this isn't me being petty. This is me being delighted. And not just because I won. But because I've waited my whole life for someone to work their way beneath your crusty exterior."

I have to endure several more minutes of gloating from Tavey before I finally get her off the phone.

My sister—the woman who has been tormenting me with practical jokes and pranks since she was five—has never been more annoying than she is right now.

I would like to think that this latest distraction is no worse than the time in college when she hacked my computer and translated every file into ancient Sumerian and wouldn't undo the damage until I agreed to come home for winter break.

No matter what I tell myself, I know in my gut this is much worse than that.

Do I think she's right?

No.

But I can't dismiss the possibility that she *could* be right.

Tavey is as smart as I am. Smarter, if I consider her aptitude for interpersonal interactions. Simply put, she gets people in a way I never have.

I can't dismiss the possibility that she gets *me* in a way I never have. She may, in fact, understand me better than I understand myself.

In any other matter, the idea might be puzzling, but hardly alarming.

But when it comes to Holly?

The idea that I might be forming an emotional attachment to Holly is unacceptable.

CHAPTER 19

HOLLY

Because I know how anxious Max is about this, I bargain with my friend Carl, who owns the barbershop near campus, to let me cut Max's hair myself. Even though I'd cut hair professionally in college for four years, I haven't cut anyone's hair in nearly a decade. Which is the only logical reason for me to be nervous about cutting Max's hair.

Yes, I suppose a professional with more recent experience might do a better job. But I'm less worried about giving Max the perfect haircut and more worried about him not showing up at all. Or panicking halfway through the shave and having Max end up looking like a rush hazing gone wrong.

I arrive at the shop early enough to chat some with Carl. Even though I've known him for years, I have no idea why he owns a barbershop named Pete's. I've never asked. The university tends to go a little crazy with their traditions. I've always just assumed it has something to do with that.

Pete's caters to a very masculine clientele, so Carl doesn't cut my hair. However, I know him because I send a lot of business his way as part of my how-to-prepare-for-job-interviews workshops I give at the university. I figured he owes me a favor. He must have agreed, because he didn't even blink when I asked if I could use his shop after hours on a Friday.

Carl and I chat as he shows me around. I've been there before and I know my way around a barbershop, but I still appreciate his help. Plus, he's leaving his baby in my hands.

When Max shows up, stomping in with his cane, dripping rain all over the floor, Carl gives me a skeptical look. "You sure about this?" he asks under his breath.

"Yep!" I lie.

Because no, I'm not sure. And the sight of Max standing in the door to the shop doesn't calm my nerves or dismiss my reservations. It's raining tonight and he's wearing his duster again. He seems to take up even more physical space than normal and I tell myself that it has nothing to do with how much emotional space he's been taking up in my head.

Despite that, I'm sure this is the right course of action. The right course for Max, that is. And I'm not a wimp. I'm not a scaredy-cat. I don't let anyone intimidate me.

Besides, after all the manipulation it took to get him here, I'm not letting him go.

That is, I'm not letting him *leave*.

The shop.

Without a haircut.

Yeah, that's what I mean.

Max stomps the rest of the way into the shop, looking around critically. "Where are all the other people? Isn't this a business?"

Carl looks at Max and then back to me. "If you're sure . . ."

He lets the question dangle there in the air.

"I am."

With any luck, the smile I give Carl is more reassuring than it feels.

"Okay, then." He slaps the keys to the shop into my open palm. "We open at nine tomorrow, so make sure I get these back before then."

He walks around Max to the front door to the shop and turns the bolt. On his way back past Max, he gives him a look that seems to say, "Don't forget I know what you look like and that you were the last person to see her alive."

As he walks past me, he gives my shoulder a squeeze. "Good luck with that one."

A moment later, Max is still glaring after him when the back door to the shop closes behind Carl.

"Where the hell is he going?" Max asks.

"Home for the night. The shop closes at six thirty on Fridays."

"Then who the hell is going to cut my hair?" He looks around the shop like he's expecting someone to pop up from behind one of the sinks.

I cross over to him and start to guide him toward the sinks in the back before I answer. "I am."

"You?" He jerks his arm away from my touch and stops to glare at me. "You can't cut hair."

Naturally he's going to argue with me about this. Why did I ever imagine he wouldn't?

"I can, in fact, cut hair."

He gives me a suspicious look. "To cut hair in the state of Texas, you have to have an active cosmetology license issued by the Texas Department of Licensing and Regulation. Do you have a—"

"Let me stop you right there. No, I don't have a Class A Barber Certificate issued by the Texas whatever board." He narrows his gaze and opens his mouth, but I cut him off. "However, I did have a license in Georgia. It's expired, of course. And they don't transfer from state to state. So yes, technically, I'm not legally allowed to cut your hair." Then I tip my head and consider. "Or maybe I'm just not allowed to charge you." I shrug. "The point is, I was licensed in Georgia. I worked in a barbershop for four years in college."

"Of course you did." Somehow this seems to annoy him.

Of course it annoys him. Everything about me annoys him.

I blow out a breath, trying to remember all of the reasons I was not going to let him egg me on tonight.

It doesn't work.

I think I need a new mantra, because dealing with Max has just about worn my old one out.

I prop my hands on my hip and face him fully. I'm in my Chucks, because only a fool cuts hair in heels. I was a fool in college and it earned me great tips. I'm not a fool now.

"Look, I thought you would be nervous. Given how protective you are of all that mess"—I gesture to the beard—"you might be more comfortable getting your hair cut and your beard trimmed by someone you know. In an empty barbershop. But if you're going to be a—" I have to bite back the word I want to use and remind myself of all of my momma's idioms about nasty language. I blow out another breath. "If you're going to be a jerk face about it, then—"

"A jerk face?" he asks.

Ugh. This man.

He is seriously testing the strength of my calming mantra.

"Yes. A jerk face. As in a man who is such a jerk, he doesn't need to say a word, because it's all right there on his face. Does that definition work for you or do I need to get creative?"

"That works," he says.

And I swear to God I see his lips twitch. As if I amuse him.

I better not amuse him. Because I am ready to peel his skin off with a filleting knife as it is. If I get any more worked up, I'll be in the back making a shiv out of a safety razor and hair pick comb before the night is over.

"My point is, I went out of my way to make this experience as comfortable for you as possible. But if you're going to be a jerk face about it—" I pause briefly, but he doesn't so much as blink at my use of the phrase "jerk face," so I continue. "Then we can leave right now. I can make you an appointment with Carl tomorrow morning and you can come in here to get your beard trimmed in front of a dozen other barbers and customers. What's it going to be? Do you want to do this now or with an audience?"

"Now," he says with a scowl.

The jerk face doesn't even have the good grace to look cowed.

"Good." I point to the hair-washing station in the back. "Now get in that chair."

He glares at me for a minute before stomping off toward the chair. And then glares at it for a moment before sitting down. Still in his duster and his suit jacket.

I sigh. Sometimes it feels like he's never been out of the lab. Like, ever.

Once again reaching for calm—but this time finding it—I say, "You need to take off your coat. And your jacket."

"Oh." He says it like it genuinely didn't occur to him.

This man is ninety percent arrogant jerk and ten percent newborn fawn.

He stands up and shrugs out of his wet duster. I take it from him. It's still dripping, so I walk into the back to hang it up in the work area where it can drip on the linoleum instead of the wood floors. When I turn back, I see Max has also shucked his jacket and draped it over the back of a nearby chair.

And he's unbuttoning his shirt.

My steps slow. Then stop.

He's looking down, so he doesn't see my mouth drop open as he shrugs out of his oxford shirt. He's wearing a white T-shirt on under his oxford.

I never, not in a million years, would have thought wearing a white shirt under a dress shirt would be inherently sexy. It shouldn't be.

It's oddly formal. It calls up images of old-world elegance and cuff links.

But it's also just . . . hot.

Because while all of Max's other clothes are ill-fitting—including the pants he's still wearing—the crisp white undershirt is snug. It highlights every one of those perfect muscles I've been trying not to think about since I saw them at his house that day.

Every. Single. One.

From his stupidly broad shoulders to that narrow waist.

I'm still staring—who am I kidding? I'm still drooling—when he looks up from carefully draping his shirt over this jacket.

I must look like a pervy cartoon with bugging eyes and a long, dangling tongue, because he clears his throat and says awkwardly, "I don't like having hair caught in my collar."

I nod mutely.

"So I took off my shirt."

I nod again. Still dumbstruck.

But surely I'll be able to speak again sometime in the next couple hours.

"I hope that's okay."

I clear my throat.

Because the whole struck-dumb-by-his-muscles thing is starting to get ridiculous.

"Yes." I swallow. "Absolutely. Whatever you need."

God, I hope that didn't sound like a proposition.

I clear my throat again and quickly add, "To feel comfortable. You should do whatever you need to feel comfortable. That's the point, right? You should be comfortable and I should be . . ."

Silent.

I should be silent.

Because, oh my God. Dumbstruck was so much better than this rambling mess.

"Firmer is better," he blurts.

"Excuse me?"

He blushes and presses his lips together, before saying, "When you're washing my hair. Or touching me. A firmer touch is better than a light one."

I nod, the pieces falling into place. I had read that people with sensory issues and people on the spectrum sometimes find light touches over-stimulating.

"Thank you for telling me." I want to say more. Something that will get him to open up to me. But is that really a good idea? Do I really need more ideas about how Max likes to be touched?

Um . . . that is a big, fat no. No, I do not. Because I'm only touching him to cut his hair and trim his beard. I do not need to be getting ideas beyond that.

I snap my mouth closed and just point to the chair.

Thankfully he seems to get my meaning and walks over to sit down. I turn the water on, letting it warm up in my hand. When it's about the right temperature, I pull down a towel and drop it around his shoulders. I do the same with the cape.

As I'm snapping the cape at the back, my fingers brushing the nape of his neck, I realize what a profoundly stupid idea this whole thing was.

Will he be more comfortable?

Yes. Maybe.

Will I make a damn fool of myself drooling over Max?

Yes. Definitely.

I drop the chair back and cup my hand at the back of his head until it rests on the dip in the sink. His eyes are closed, and his thick wavy hair spills back into the sink.

If I had to guess, it's been at least a year since he had it cut.

It's long and shaggy. There's nothing about it that is elegant or refined, but as I run my fingers through it trying to gauge its texture, it feels surprisingly soft. I try to do what he asked and keep the pressure of my fingers firm.

"Let me know if this is too hot," I say as I dampen his hair.

"It's hot," he says. His voice even lower and more growly than normal. But then his eyes snap open. "But not too hot. The temperature is fine."

He blurts the words. Like he knew just what I was thinking.

Because, yeah, washing his hair is hot.

Definitely too hot for me.

I turn off the spray and slide the nozzle back into its slot.

"Do you have a scent you prefer?"

"I like lemon," he says sharply.

Okay. That's an odd choice for a man. But I consider the shampoo choices.

"I don't see anything citrusy." I twist a few of the bottles. "There's a bergamot."

"Oh. For shampoo," he says, sounding almost disappointed. "Anything. You pick."

I don't ask what he thought I was talking about, but pick something woodsy. So I'm basically doubling down on his natural yumminess.

Again, probably it's not my best idea. But I'm about five hundred miles south of good ideas by now.

As I squirt the shampoo into my hand, he gives me the side eye. "You're just going to wash my hair?"

"Yes. You've had your hair cut before, right?"

I get the stink eye again.

It's probably a good thing the guy is such a jerk sometimes. Right now, it's the only thing keeping me from climbing into his lap and licking his neck.

I lather the shampoo between my hands. "Okay, here's the deal. I am not just going to wash your hair."

"You're not?" he asks suspiciously before I can continue. He moves like he's going to sit up and bolt.

"No." I use a non-soapy elbow to push him back down. "Think of this as a relaxing scalp massage."

"I don't think I'm going to like that." He tries to sit up again.

I elbow him back down. "You will. Trust me." More side-eyeing. "Seriously, Max. You have to give this a shot. I'm good at this, too. Besides, this is an important part."

"How?"

"How is it important?"

"Yes. How? Don't some people do dry cuts?"

"Yes. Some do. But this part is actually important for you. Because as I massage, I want you to relax and talk about your work."

"Huh?"

I have to elbow him back down, but I finally get my fingers into his hair. And, just as I start to work the shampoo in, running my nails over his scalp, I finally feel him start to relax.

"Better," I murmur. "Now, start talking."

"About what?"

"About dirt. Or soil. Or whatever it is you study."

He opens one eye to glare at me.

"If I'm going to help you write a lecture for the audition," I tell him, "I need to understand what you're studying. More importantly, I need to understand why you love it."

It takes several more minutes of coaxing, but eventually he starts talking. I massage, letting my fingers work on the tension in his scalp and neck, letting the slippery strands of hair slide through my fingers. I rinse. I massage some more. I condition and rinse again.

And he talks some more.

He talks about how soil isn't dirt. How it's a complex web of organisms that work together and depend on one another and how modern farming methods have messed it up. How he's working with researchers and farmers all over the world to inoculate over-farmed, "dead" dirt and transform it into living, thriving soil.

I finish washing, move him to another chair, and start cutting. Aside from the occasional suspicious look, he just keeps talking. I'm pretty sure he doesn't believe I'm smart enough to follow his research. Clearly he's forgotten that I was married to his boss for six years. I ask questions. I make sure they're good ones. And eventually he seems to buy that I might be smart enough to follow along.

By the time I get out the clipper to trim up his neck and beard, he seems to have almost forgotten why we're here. I turn him away from the mirror and tip the chair back so he can't watch, but he doesn't even notice.

I'm starting to see why the McPherson committee short-listed him in the first place. Once I get past his blustering, his work is fascinating. Moreover, his enthusiasm for it is catching. I start to see just how important it could be, how it could change the way people grow food and how it could affect humanity's relationship with the planet.

I get lost in the work and in his words. Cutting Max's hair is both second nature and completely different.

Sure, in college, I always flirted with the customers. Nothing too overt. Just enough to keep them coming back and tipping well.

But it was always just a job. I never felt aware when I was cutting someone's hair. Aware of how close you have to stand. How much you have to touch them.

When I lean back Max's chair and start to trim the beard and shave his neck, everything feels much more intimate.

His words slow. My heart rate speeds up.

I am painfully aware of the heat of his skin under my fingers, the pulse in his throat.

As I slide the blade of the razor down his neck, he stops talking entirely, but I can still feel his breath against my skin. I follow the razor with a clean warm towel, wiping away the last of the shaving cream. Then I move on to his cheeks. I leave most of the beard intact as promised, but clean up the stragglers on his cheeks, shaving his right cheekbone smooth. And then I move on to the left side, where his scar is.

Despite my promises that it won't be as bad as he remembers, I'm nervous. And the more skin I reveal, the tighter the knot gets in my belly. I'm terrified I might nick his skin. Shaving around scar tissue is different that shaving normal skin. God knows I had enough trouble getting him in the chair at all; I certainly don't want to cut him.

But more than that, now that all of my concentration isn't focused on trying to cut his hair and understand his research, now that this transformation is nearly complete, I'm getting a better picture of what Max really looks like.

His unruly curls are shorter and back off his face, which somehow makes his eyes look even brighter. More blue than gray. I can finally see his lips, which are ridiculously full. Max has been hiding the mouth of a sensualist beneath all that hair. As for the scar? Yes, the scar slashes down his left cheek, thinner at his temple, nearly a half inch wide where it enters his beard.

I run my finger along the length of the scar, down to where it meets his beard, where it doesn't quite disappear. Now that his beard is trimmed, the scar leaves a visible gap. It makes him look . . . roguish. Dangerous.

He reaches his hand up and wraps my fingers in his hand, stopping my progress down his cheek.

My gaze meets his and I can hardly breathe past the intensity of the questions in his gaze.

"How bad is it? Is it horrible?"

I swallow and shake my head, unable to put my thoughts into words:

"Oh, God." He groans. "It's as bad as I thought, isn't it?"

I blink rapidly and pull my gaze from his jaw to meet his eyes. "It's worse." I let out a nervous laugh. "Much worse. You're handsome."

CHAPTER 20

MAX

I scramble to my feet awkwardly, too aware of Holly's gaze following my movements, cursing my damn leg, because the muscles spasm slightly when I put weight on it after sitting for so long.

"Don't lie to me."

I bark the words at her. I don't mean to. But the pain spiking down my leg pisses me off. Even worse than the pain, I hate it when people lie to me to spare my feelings. Like I'm some kind of child who can't take the truth.

I hate even more that Holly is lying to me. Because I'd thought better of her. Because I'd thought I could trust her. Because the thought of her coddling me like a child is repulsive.

I'm not a toddler.

I'm a man. Who just spent the past two hours being caressed by the most beautiful woman he's ever met.

And, yeah, I know she wasn't caressing me. I know she was just cutting my hair. Just shaving my neck. But my body didn't seem to know that. My cock sure as hell didn't.

Thank God she asked about my research, because the only thing that kept me from getting a raging hard-on was my attempts to condense years of research into a single conversation.

It's the only thing allowing me to stand upright.

All this together—the pain, the hard-on, her total lack of awareness of me as a man, and the fact that she feels like she has to lie to me—the combination tips my mood from irritation into anger.

"Don't ever fucking lie to me," I say again. "I'm not a child. I don't need to be coddled. I—"

"I'm not lying." She shakes her head, giving another one of those hysterical-sounding laughs. "And you would see that if you would stop yelling long enough to look at yourself."

"I—" I cut myself short.

Because I haven't looked in the mirror yet. I went straight from looking at the ceiling to focusing on her. Partly because she is always the thing I want to look at in any room. But also out of habit.

In a room with mirrors, I usually look anywhere else.

I barely have to move to face a mirror. The man I see there is me, and somehow not at all what I expect.

My hair is short on the sides, but longer on top. The wavy mess I never know what to do with is somehow tamed and sculpted. With the scruff on my neck gone and the beard trimmed nearly out of existence, I look . . . handsome isn't the word I would have picked. It's too foreign a concept. But I don't look frightening, either.

Beside me, Holly gives another laugh and this time she sounds amused instead of nervous. "Well, maybe scowl less."

"I don't scowl." I turn away from the image of us standing side by side, because there's something about it that unsettles me. She's still tiny to my tall, but we look less ill-suited than we do in my mind.

"You're scowling now."

"I am not. This is just what I look like."

"You are without a doubt the most argumentative man in the universe. No, not the most argumentative man. Person."

"I am not."

"Yes, you are. If I said the sky was blue, you would say—"

"The sky isn't blue," I say automatically. "It only appears blue because the density of Earth's atmosphere happens to scatter more of the blue light."

She raises her eyebrows but says nothing for a moment. Then notches them higher as if that makes her point.

"I—" I start to argue that I'm being precise rather than argumentative, but her phone rings.

It's not a normal ringtone, but it's clearly one she recognizes, because her eyes widen and she actually jumps when she hears it.

She lunges for the phone with a clumsiness that's not at all like her.

"Hello?" There's a pause while the person on the end greets her. And then, "Hang on a second. Let me go out to my car."

She's already moving as she says this, grabbing her bag and umbrella and digging out keys. She pats her pockets absently, looking like someone who's forgotten something important but is too distracted to care.

"Holly?"

Her gaze darts to mine.

"Oh, right." She gives her head a shake. It's apparent I was the something she'd forgotten. "I have to take this. Can you . . ."

She looks around the shop as if surprised to find herself there.

"Is everything okay?"

"I . . . yes. I think." She gives me a tremulous smile. "Yeah. I think so."

"Do you need me to lock up? So you can go?"

"Yes! Thank you!" She pulls out the keys Carl left with her and presses them into my hands. She practically runs for the door. And then hurries back. "You need to turn off the electricity. And there are two locks on the back door. A deadbolt and—"

"I think I can figure it out."

The smile she gives me is luminous and damn near stops my heart.

"Thank you!"

Just like that, she's gone. And I'm alone in the shop, staring at the door she just left through.

What the hell just happened?

Who had called her this late on a Friday and why?

I've never seen Holly looking flustered. But she was definitely flustered.

Why does that bother me?

Is Tavey right? Do I care about Holly?

I don't know what to think about that.

When she first floated the idea, I'd dismissed it. But what if she's right?

I push the question aside, and start to clean up. I'm not sure what cleaning procedures Carl usually performs, but sweeping up the hair off the floor seems like a good start. As I sweep, I force myself to look in the mirror. To catalogue the changes.

I don't usually look at myself. Not ever, if I can help it. Not since I was a teenager, when I spent months—years, maybe—staring at the scar on my cheek. Hating the scar on my cheek. The visible, undeniable proof that my life would never be the same. That I'd lost my parents, my home, and my body as it had once been.

The scar, much like the pain in my leg, was with me always. It had faded over the years. Somedays I barely noticed it, but it was always there in the background. A relentless reminder that the only two people who might have loved me were gone. That I had lived and they hadn't. That I had no one. That *my sister* had no one. That we were alone in the world.

We weren't of course, not really. Aunt Jules and Uncle Pete had taken us in. Without children of their own, they had showered us with attention. Tavey—younger, cuter, and eager to please—had welcomed their attention and affection.

I had not.

I know from experience that it's not only my physical scars that make me . . . unlovable, for the lack of a better word. I know I'm difficult. Arrogant. Rude. And—what was the term Holly used? A jerk face?

Yes. I am all of those things.

I will continue to be all of those things regardless of the length of my hair. I'm smart enough to know that. Is Holly?

CHAPTER 21

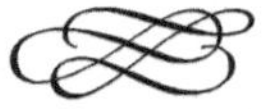

MAX

When I leave the barbershop, I have every intention of heading home.

However, I had taken my time cleaning up and closing the barbershop, erring on the side of doing more than is necessary, rather than less. Over an hour has passed since Holly left the shop. I still don't know if she was upset or excited when she left. If the news she got was good or bad. It's only reasonable to go check on her.

Besides, I still have the keys to the shop, which she had told Carl she would return to him. Furthermore, she still has my soil samples.

So, really, going to her house instead of going home is only logical. I try not to be disconcerted by the fact that I easily come up with so many reasons to visit her.

Though I've never been to her house, I'd gotten her address from Clarissa the other day when I sent her the grocery order, so finding her house is easy enough. Her neighborhood doesn't have enough streetlights. Tomorrow, I'll ask Tavey to look up the crime statistics for Holly's neighborhood.

I park on the street and walk past Holly's Toyota in the driveway to reach the door to her ranch house. My knock is followed by a cacophony of barking, the clatter of nails on a floor, and . . . is that the screech of a bird?

She opens the door after my third knock and I'm greeted with her standing there looking disheveled. She's changed out of her earlier skirt and blouse into yoga pants and a T-shirt for a local animal rescue group. Her eyes are red-rimmed and she's got a wineglass dangling from one hand. Her sexy-as-fuck lips part, then she frowns.

She looks . . . sad.

"What do you want?" Then she sniffs and steps out of the way allowing me entrance into her home. "I'm sorry, that wasn't kind."

"Why are you sad?" I ask and my voice comes out angry and harsh. I'm not angry with her, but with whatever has made her cry. Sounds filter through from the back of her house. "Is someone else here?"

"What? No, that's just my dogs. I crated them before answering the door."

I step fully inside and close the door behind me.

She walks further into the living room and takes a drink from her glass, looking vaguely surprised to find it nearly empty. She sighs. "Look, I know I still need to get your soil samples back to you, but I just can't tonight. I just—"

Her voice breaks and she raises her hand to rub at her forehead.

The sight of Holly like this . . . Holly, who is normally a ball of cheerful energy, a force of nature . . .

The sight of her like this damn near rips a hole in my chest.

Because she shouldn't ever look like this.

Defeated. Exhausted. Worn.

I'm used to life kicking me in the teeth. Fuck it. I probably deserve all of it and more.

And, yeah, I know no one makes it to adulthood without being kicked around by life at least at little. She's already been divorced. And if all the gossip I try not to listen to is right, it's because her dick of a husband cheated on her. So, yeah, I know her life hasn't been perfect.

But it should be. Because if anyone deserves a perfect life, it's Holly, who does so many things for so many people.

I hate—I fucking hate—that she's crying. And even worse, I hate that I have no idea what to do to make her stop.

So I do the only thing I can think of. Something that feels totally unnatural and completely right all at the same time. I cross over to her and gently take the wineglass from her hand and set it on a nearby console table. Then I open my arms and pull her towards me.

Her body jerks a little. "What are you doing?"

"You're sad, so I was going to give you a hug. Or is that not appropriate given the nature of our relationship?"

She folds her lips together. "You're adorable. And under the circumstances, it's appropriate." She leans into me.

I fold her into my body and I'm instantly surrounded by the crisp, lemony scent that's been driving me crazy since the first moment I met her. Her petite form is so much smaller than mine, but it feels incredibly perfect pressed against me. I can place my cheek on the top of her head and her brown locks are soft against my skin.

The feel of her in my arms and her scent in my nose all hit me in the gut so hard I almost can't breathe. There's the hot rush of desire, of need, but there's also a burst of panic. Because she is clearly in emotional pain.

Which makes this exactly the kind of situation I will undoubtedly fuck up.

I'm the kind of guy who can't send a damn thank-you email to a business colleague without somehow insulting the person. A sobbing woman that I care about—if Tavey is to be believed—is so far out of my skill set I might as well be trying to cross a high wire stretched between two skyscrapers. Or two continents, for that matter.

I have got to get the heck out of here before I say whatever the hell it is that I'll inevitably say that will make this worse for her.

"Is there someone I can call to come be with you?" I clear my throat. "Maybe that English lit friend of yours? The one who told me you had classes in Bryan on Thursday nights."

"Liz is out of town." She sighs. "And, no, there's no one else I want to see right now."

Somehow she sounds even more sad.

Which just about guts me.

Her arms are around my waist and one of her hands is rubbing small circles against my back. It instantly reminds me of when I was a boy and my mother would gather me on her lap and hold me tight. When you have sensory issues like I do, sometimes you need that tight hold to feel safe. I didn't know until this exact moment that I missed it. That I still want to be held. That I still need to be held.

I walk us backwards until my back hits the wall. I slide down, until I'm sitting with my back to the wall and then I pull her down on my lap. She fits perfectly with her head tucked under my chin, her cheek pressed to my chest. It's now my turn to rub the circles on her back.

"What happened?" I ask.

"I got disappointing news."

"About?"

"Does it matter?" she asks.

"Apparently it does."

She tilts her face to look up at me. She shakes her head and gives me an eye roll despite her sorrow. "God, you are such a jerk sometimes."

But she doesn't sound mad as she says it. Maybe amused. Or maybe that's grief and I'm confusing the two.

"Why?"

"Why are you a jerk? Or why am I noticing it now?"

"The former."

With a sigh, she tucks her head back under my chin with her cheek once again against my chest. Her free hand is still rubbing gentle circles, though her hand has shifted from my back to my obliques. "You're a jerk because only you could be sarcastic and kind in the same moment."

"I wasn't being sarcastic. Your news is obviously important to you. Therefore, it matters."

I instantly want to tell her that everything in her life matters to me. That she matters to me, but that doesn't make sense.

I'm just here to return Carl's keys and get my soil samples.

Despite that, I have zero interest in asking for my soil samples.

Since she seems to be floundering, I prompt, "Sometimes it helps to talk about things."

"Does it help you?" she quips.

I frown. "No. But it's been documented that for women, having a supportive social network slows the degradation of their telomeres, so—"

"Max," she says my name on a breath and my heart tightens.

"Holly."

Then she tucks her head and exhales, the warm breath caresses the newly exposed skin of my neck. My dick takes instant notice of the current situation.

Fuck.

Like she needs me getting turned on right now.

Jesus. And she thought I was an asshole for being sarcastic.

I shift her slightly.

"Talk," I say.

She sighs again. She's silent for so long, I think she's going to ignore me. The only reason I know she's still awake is her fingers are still doing their mind-blowing magic on my abs.

When she does finally start talking, her voice is soft, her words slow. Her tone . . .

I don't know how to describe it other than small.

It's almost like what she's saying is so important to her, so delicate, she's tucked it away into a tiny package.

"I want to be a mother. More importantly, I want to adopt from the foster care system. I've been through the training, had my home study and had everything approved and now I'm just waiting for kids. My case worker had submitted me for this amazing sibling group and things were looking good." There's another pause. Another deeper sigh. "But then their case worker found a married couple who is interested and they're getting the kids."

"I don't understand. You were in line first?"

She releases a humorless chuckle. "It doesn't really work like that. Married couples always trump a single mom. A loving, two-parent home is the preference for any child."

"Even a child who is stuck in a system moving from one stranger's house to the next?"

"Sometimes even then."

"That is asinine."

"Well, I can't do anything about the way the system works. Now I just have to wait for some other kids and hope I get approved for them."

"Unless another married couple shows up?"

"Yeah, unless that."

"So you need a husband."

"I tried that once. It didn't work."

"I'll marry you. Then you can get whichever kids you want." I don't even know what I'm saying. The words just come out of my mouth.

Because, fuck it, this is Holly.

Right now, in this moment, I would do anything for her. Anything to make her not sad.

She looks up at me then and her entire face is full of wonder and disbelief. Like when a child sees the moon for the first time. I'm just about to ask her what she's thinking when she cups my face and kisses me.

I still for a moment because I'm not sure if this is a mistake. If she's going to pull back from me with apologies or if it's meant as a sweet thank-you. But then her tongue slides across my bottom lip and it is all the invitation I need. I growl into her mouth as I slant mine and devour her. The way I've been wanting to. The way I've been fantasizing about every time I fist my cock in the shower.

She shifts herself on my lap, straddling me, her yoga pants bringing her hot core right against the ridge of my now full-blown erection. She arches and her breasts press against my chest.

Our kiss is wild, all tongues and teeth and lips. Like she's been wanting me the way I've been wanting her. Which doesn't make any sense. But until she pushes me away, I'm going to kiss her.

I grip her hip with my left hand while I slide my right hand up her torso until my fingers rest right beneath the rise of her breast. My hands are so big, it will take barely any movement for me to scrape a finger across her nipple. So I do. Because if she wants me to stop, she'll tell me. Holly isn't a shy woman.

When my thumb brushes against that tight little bud, she tilts her hips and rubs herself against my cock. Holy fuck that feels good. I growl again. She breaks the kiss and I think this is when she's going to shove me away and balk at touching me. Instead she surprises the shit out of me when she grabs the hem of her T-shirt and rips it over her head. She's braless, which I wasn't prepared for, and now I'm staring at the most perfect pair of breasts I've ever seen. Rounded in just the right way with small, pert nipples. Rosy pink nipples that beg for my mouth. I lean in and flick my tongue against one, while my thumb scrapes against the other.

She arches into my mouth. "Yes," she hisses.

I suckle her hard, nearly pulling her entire breast into my mouth, and she rubs her pussy against my erection again.

Vaguely I feel her fingers at the buttons on my shirt, tugging my undershirt from the waistband of my pants, and then her hands are pressed to my bare chest. They map every line and muscle as I continue to lave her perfect tits.

Then her fingers are at my belt and my eyes fly open. I search her face, but she's looking downward at what she's doing.

It takes everything in me to say her name. It doesn't seem to faze her, so I grip her wrists until she looks at me.

She seems to know what I'm asking because she leans in and kisses me. "I want you to fuck me, Max."

I close my eyes and exhale slowly. God, that word on her lips. I haven't ever heard her cuss. To hear her do it now somehow makes her request even hotter.

Her lips kiss from my jaw to my ear, where she sucks on the lobe.

"Fuck me, Max," she whispers. Her crafty hand has unfastened my belt and pants and she's reaching into the front of my boxers and wrapping her fingers around my hard length before I can even process fully what's happening.

Abruptly she stands and shimmies out of her yoga pants and panties. Plain white cotton, I note as she kicks both behind her. Her pussy is practically eye level and so pink and beautiful that I want to lick every inch of it. I lean forward and she stops me with a hand to my head.

"Later. Right now I just want you inside me."

Fuck, we're really doing this. I shift upwards to pull down my jeans and boxers to free my cock. It slaps against my stomach and Holly's eyes are like a goddamn laser beam on it. She licks her lips and a drop of precum beads at the tip.

She crawls back onto my lap and I realize something. "Holly, I don't have any condoms. I don't . . ." I don't carry them because, well, hell, it's not like this has ever happened to me before. But I can't say that out loud.

"It's okay. I'm on the pill. And I'm clean." She searches my face. "Are you?"

It takes a second for her question to break through the sex fog clouding my mind. She wants to know if I'm clean? As in clean of STDs? I haven't been with a woman in nearly a decade.

I just nod. "I am." I almost say more, that I've only ever been with one woman. That I always wore a condom with her and have been tested since then. But before I can say any of that, she slides her pussy against my cock and I'm pretty sure I black out for a minute. It's wet and warm and I want inside. Now.

As if reading my mind, she notches herself on me, then slowly sinks down. We moan in unison as she takes my entire length. She's perfection. Like she was made specifically for my body.

"Oh God, you feel good," she moans. Then she begins to ride me. I grip her hips and just watch her as she chases her pleasure, using my body to do it.

An overwhelming feeling of pride shoots through me. I'm honored that she'd want to use me for this. Which is damned nonsense. This is why I don't sleep with people. Stupid damn hormones make your brain mushy.

Those perfect tits of hers are bouncing right in my face, so I lean forward and capture one, sucking the tight nub. I slide my tongue across it as I suck. Holly continues to ride my dick and grind herself against me. Her movements are getting jerky and her moans louder.

"Oh, oh, I'm gonna come," she says. "Max . . ." She moans as her body shudders over me.

I wait for her to finish riding out her pleasure before I shift our position. I lay her against the floor and brace myself above her. I pull almost completely out before plunging back in. Her eyes widen.

"Do that again," she says.

So I do. Again and again. She's so tight and so wet and she's squeezing my dick and I just want to come, but I want her to come again first. So I mentally go through the periodic table. In alphabetical order.

By the time I hit gallium, she's coming again with such force that I come with her. The climax starts at my spine and then explodes outward, ricocheting through my entire body so much so that I'm pretty sure I go blind for a nanosecond.

I have enough presence of mind to not collapse on top of her. Instead I fall next to her and wait for the shit storm of awkward to hit. Until then I'm going to bask in the most incredible sex of my life.

CHAPTER 22

HOLLY

In the fantasy, romance-novel version of my life, after we had sex, Max would have gently swept me into his arms, bride-style, and carried me off to my bedroom. Possibly to ravish me several more times. Because holy shit, that was amazing sex.

However, I do not live a fantasy, romance-novel-style life.

Instead, I obviously live in a horror novel.

I am still recovering from the most mind-blowing, knee-weakening sex of my life, when several things happen in quick succession.

First, I feel Max's body go rigid. He scrambles off of me. "What the hell is that?"

His obvious alarm sends a jolt of panic through me and I scramble to my feet as well. I look around, searching for whatever has Max reaching for his pants, like he may have to flee the house or fight off an invader.

Automatically, I grab my own clothes, pull my panties back on and then my T-shirt. "What is it?"

He points toward the door that leads to the bedrooms. "What the hell is that?"

"Oh." I breathe out, relieved. "That's Tinky. My rabbit."

Max stills, his jeans on, but still unzipped. His shirt is clutched in his fist. "That thing is not a rabbit."

Before I can tell him that Tinky is, in fact, a Flemish giant rabbit, Iago—who's been asleep—wakes up. He bleats a nervous, "Fuck off," and then starts plucking out his feathers. His words wake Skip and Lou. They start barking excitedly.

And then, the coup de grâce. The doorbell rings.

I look from Max to Tinky to Iago and finally to the door.

I know who it is.

Only Clive gets the animals this worked up. He's like a foul wind blowing in before a storm.

"Oh, for the love of Fudgsicles," I mutter, reaching for my yoga pants.

"Who—" Max starts to ask.

But I shush him, adding in a keep-your-mouth-shut glare for good measure. Aloud, I say, "Give me a minute."

Of course Clive is already ringing the doorbell again. Which sets off a whole 'nother round of cacophony.

"Just a minute," I call again, more loudly this time in case Clive wasn't able to hear me over the barking. I smooth down my shirt, push my hair out of my face, and glance around the room, taking in the epic disaster my life has become.

Iago stress plucking. Tinky hopping slowly towards Max—because Tinky is overweight and does everything slowly. Max tugging on his clothes as he backs away from Tinky, looking for all the world like he expects Tinky to transform into one of those bloodthirsty rabbits from Monty Python and the Holy Grail.

I hurry to the door, which isn't even locked, and send up a silent prayer of thanks that Clive didn't let himself in. I open the door and slip out, hopefully before Clive can see the chaos on the other side.

I close the door behind me, keeping my hand on the knob. Praying I look calmer than I feel, I smile up at Clive. "Hey, what's up?"

He's been pacing, because he's at the far end of my porch. He takes a step toward me, like he expects me to let him in.

He stops when I don't, giving me a concerned look. "Holly, what's going on?"

I feel his gaze moving over me. Not in a good way, but in a way that makes me very, very aware of how disheveled I must look. I am braless. I probably have beard rash on my neck and cheeks. My panties are wet. And I am entirely too aware that I just had two earth-shattering climaxes in record time.

I know I'm fooling no one when I blurt, "Nothing. Why?"

"Can I come in?"

"That's not a good idea."

His eyes move from me to the door behind me, and then dart to the window beside the door, where—damn it!—the play of shadows make it obvious there's someone there.

"You have someone here," he says, looking stung. He takes in my appearance again, clearly putting two and two together and coming up with coitus interruptus.

My instinct is to deny it. Or tell him to mind his own business. Because we've been divorced for years. I could have the entire cast of Meet the Press in there for an orgy and it wouldn't be his business.

Not that I—or probably anyone—wants to have an orgy with the entire cast of Meet the Press.

Before I can say anything, Max opens the door behind me.

I still have my hand on the doorknob. I tighten my grip, trying to keep the door closed, but Max doesn't take the hint and just gives it a firm tug. The door flies open. Off-balance, I stumble back a step, landing squarely against Max's chest. His arm goes around my waist, clamping me to him.

Clive narrows his gaze into a razor-sharp glare that he aims at Max. Giving a stiff nod, he says, "Ramsey."

Max mimics Clive, keeping his nod just as stiff and his tone—if possible—even colder. "Thorndyke."

I lean slightly forward, hoping Max will pick up on the sign I want him to release me. He doesn't.

Since Clive's head looks like it's about to explode, I don't push it.

"Is there something I can do for you, Clive?" I ask, my tone sounding stupidly formal given the circumstances.

He doesn't even look at me, but continues to glare at Max. If the tension in Max's arm is any indication, he is glaring back.

Basically, we're one whistling theme song and a tumbleweed away from a show-down at high noon.

Or low midnight or whatever.

"Clive?" I ask again. "Do you need something?"

Finally, he looks at me. He gives me a cold smile. "I came by to check on Lou."

Ouch. It's a low blow, hitting me in my dog soft spot. The jerk.

"Lou?" Max asks.

I say, "My dog," at the same time Clive says, "Our dog."

Clive recovers and continues before I point out that while we did settle on joint custody of Skip and Lou, Clive hasn't ever had them to his house. I even have to hire a pet sitter when I go out of town. As far as I'm concerned, our "joint custody" agreement became moot years ago.

"I thought I might take Lou out for a walk," Clive says.

"It's after eleven," Max says.

"I was going to come back to pick her up in the morning."

"So you came here in person late at night to tell Holly you wanted to take her dog for a walk tomorrow? That seems like a lot of work."

"I wanted to plan ahead."

"But you didn't text first?"

"I never do."

"Oh look!" I jump in before the testosterone overload starts taking out the electric grid. "There goes a tumbleweed!"

Both men frown and then look in the direction I'm pointing.

While they're momentarily distracted, I pry Max's arm from around my waist and grab his hand, pulling him back into the house.

"Okay, sounds good. We'll see you tomorrow, Clive." I wave my free hand in a gesture that's a little too Mickey Mouse Club enthusiastic. "Thanks for stopping by. Lou will be excited. See you then. Bye now!"

I practically have to drag Max over the threshold before slamming the door on Clive. Who, for a second there, I thought might try to follow us in.

As soon as the door is shut, I drop Max's hand and throw the deadbolt. A full minute passes before I hear Clive moving on the porch. In that time, I imagine him glaring at the closed door trying to Jedi mind-trick his way inside.

"Fuck off," Iago says miserably as he plucks out another feather.

When I hear Clive's footsteps head across the porch and down the steps, I whirl around to face Max.

"What was that?"

"What was what?"

"That." I jab a finger in the direction of the porch. "That weirdness that happened out there. What were you doing?"

Max's expression hardens. "I wasn't doing anything. What about Clive? What was he doing? Why was he here?"

"I have no idea."

"Does he usually come over late on a Friday night?"

"No. Not that it's any of your business."

Pained surprise flickers across Max's face. "Why wouldn't it be my business?"

Something about his expression makes a knot of panic unfurl inside my chest. This has all happened so quickly. One domino tumbling into the next so fast I haven't had a chance to even breathe since I got the call from the social worker.

I've spent the past two hours trying to get in front of the dominos, to stop the cascade, but now that I'm in front of it, I see my mistake. The dominos have too much momentum. I didn't get in front of it soon enough to stop them falling. I got in front of them just in time for them to land on top of me and squash me flat.

I sink to the sofa and scrub my hands down my face trying to buy myself a few seconds to think.

When that doesn't help, I hop up and move. I nearly trip over Tinky, so I scoop up nearly twenty-five pounds of giant rabbit into my arms, stroking his dense fur like he's my lovey.

"Why wouldn't it be my business?" Max repeats. When I turn to look at him, he recoils back a step. "And what the hell is that thing?"

"He's not a thing. He's a Flemish giant."

"I think you meant 'fucking giant.'"

I let out a bark of laughter—hysterical, of course, and befitting my mood. Sitting back down, I cradle Tinky in my arms. I'm tempted to bury my face in his fur, but somehow I think a mouth full of bunny fur is not the solution.

"Tinky is a rescued Flemish giant rabbit."

Ignoring my words, Max asks a third time, "Why wouldn't it be my business?"

"Why would it be?"

"Because you're my fiancée."

My hands clench, and I inadvertently squeeze Tinky, who jumps down in protest. Which is for the best, since I also leap to my feet. "I'm your what?"

"My fiancée."

"Your what?" I repeat. "We're not . . . We just . . . Why would … Why would you think that?"

Max's normal frown has deepened into a scowl. "I offered to marry you. Then you kissed me. And then we had sex."

I can't look at Max. Not because he looks mad—I mean, he almost always looks somewhere on the spectrum from grumpy to furious—but because he doesn't look mad. He looks genuinely confused. And maybe even a little hurt.

And—okay, if I'm honest, he still looks so damn handsome it makes my heart feel too big for my chest. And, if I'm really honest, because when I look at him, I can't help but remember the expression on his face when I took off my shirt. He looked at me like I was a goddess. And when I think about that, I remember what he felt like inside me. Huge and hot and perfect in every way.

The combination—all of that together is just all too much to process. So I don't look at him. I pace because every cell in my body is screaming at me to move. If I can't run for the hills, the least I can do is pace in circles.

But because Max is Max, he doesn't take the hint that I need time to think and to process and to just be, so my circle pacing dead-ends when he steps in front of me.

I look up to see his brow furrowed in confusion. "You kissed me," he says again.

"I did."

"I asked you to marry me. And then you kissed me. How was that not a yes?"

How can I explain it? How can I defend my actions?

"It just wasn't, okay?" I throw out my hands in a how-do-you-not-get-this gesture. "Sometimes a kiss is just a kiss."

Which is clearly the wrong thing to say, because he points out the obvious.

"That wasn't just a kiss. That was a kiss that led to you taking your shirt off, sticking your hand down my pants and begging me to fuck you."

Right. Good point.

My clit pulses, as if to remind me that we could totally do that all over again.

Which, for obvious reasons, would make everything so much worse.

No, not worse. But so much more complicated.

"I know!" Just looking at him makes my heart feel tight, so I whirl around and start pacing again. "I screwed this up. I get that. I don't know what you want me to say to make this better. I should have set better boundaries. I knew this thing between us could be a problem, but I thought I could handle it. I thought I was in control. And if I hadn't just lost those kids, if you hadn't come over, and if you hadn't been so damn nice when I least expected it, I would have had it under control. But all of that did happen. And it was just the perfect storm."

I stop again, forcing myself to look at Max. Because I owe him that much.

His expression is unreadable and for the life of me, I can't tell if my rant made any sense to him at all. If I made things better or worse.

Finally, he asks, "What did you mean when you said, 'this thing between us'?"

"This." I gesture from me to him and then back again. "This chemistry. This tension. This thing that I think we've both felt from the first day. At least, I know I have."

I force myself to meet his gaze, wanting—no, not wanting, *needing* confirmation that he's felt it, too.

Because, he is absolutely right. I threw myself at him. I stuck my hand down his pants and begged. He wouldn't be the first guy in the history of the world to sleep with a woman he didn't really want just because she begged him.

It doesn't help that Max can be so hard to read.

"Am I wrong?" I ask, hating how small my voice sounds.

Thank God when he meets my gaze, I see naked hunger in his eyes.

Still, the question he asks takes me by surprise.

"Was the sex insufficiently satisfying?"

"What?" I gape.

"Did you climax? Because I thought you did. But if you didn't, we can try again. As I understand it, it takes time to learn an individual woman's body and erogenous zones."

"No!" I cut him off, because the last thing I need is to imagine the kind of attention a man like Max could apply to this situation. Especially when he's looking at me like that. "That's not the problem. Trust me."

"Because I can learn—"

"The sex was great. Fantastic. It was …" It was perfect. Hot and sweet and—for the love of Gobstoppers, I came twice. Which I've never done with a man before. I have no idea what I'm supposed to say in this situation, but I know if I admit that, there's no way he'll walk away. So instead I use his word. "It was definitely satisfying."

"Then what's the problem?"

"The problem is us, Max. We don't fit."

His jaw tightens and I see that familiar glint of determination in his eyes. Only this time, it doesn't irritate me. It turns me on, because it's layered with heat and desire. And the last time I saw that glint in his eyes, he wasn't arguing with me, he was rubbing my clit, and all that determination was focused on making me come again.

And when he speaks, his voice is low and growly and deliciously familiar. "I thought we fit together perfectly."

"Yeah. But that was just sex."

As soon as I say those words, I know I've said the wrong thing.

Or the right thing.

He flinches, like I've slapped him. And then he turns and walks away. He walks out of my house. Maybe out of my life.

Which is exactly what I want.

I think.

I'm right. I know I'm right. I know that Max and I don't fit. Not in any of the ways that really matter. I also know that a relationship based on sex alone won't be enough for a man like Max. A man with two PhDs who was short-listed for the McPherson Genius Award needs the mental stimulation that he can't get from someone like me.

Moreover, I need more than just sex, too. I need someone who can love me.

I don't need functional companionship. I need love. Big, deep, and all-encompassing.

I don't know if I'll ever have that, but I know I can't settle for anything less.

Despite all of that, being around Max makes me stupid and reckless. It makes me want things I shouldn't want and do things I definitely shouldn't do. The condom-less sex, for example. If a girl in one of my classes admitted to doing that—to merely asking a guy if he was clean and then taking his word for it—I'd roast her alive. Because you can't just take chances like that with your life and your health.

Do I believe Max was being honest with me and he's clean? Yes, absolutely. Because this is the man who scrubs his hands for three minutes before handling dirt. So, yeah. I think he's disease-free. And I've been on the pill since I lost the baby. Because having one ectopic pregnancy increases your risk of having a second and I can't ever do that again. I won't survive the pain of having my fallopian tube burst, of nearly dying from blood loss, of waking up in the hospital to learn I'd lost the child I desperately wanted. I am vigilant about birth control pills because I can't ever do any of that again.

The fact that I forgot all that, even for a few minutes, only proves how stupid Max makes me. Obviously, if I was irrational enough to have condom-less sex, then my feelings for Max have gotten way out of control. Wanting him makes me reckless and desperate.

Reckless and desperate Holly makes very bad decisions. I.e., if Max asks me to marry him again, I might just be desperate and reckless enough to say yes.

CHAPTER 23

MAX

I go to the lab first thing on Saturday morning. Thank God I don't see anyone on my way across campus.

The last thing I need is someone stopping me to make small talk. No one else is in the lab either. Again, thank God, because Gwen, Jaxon, and Priya often come in on the weekends to finish up work.

However, that's where my luck runs out.

Not that I believe in luck. But if I did, this is definitely where mine fucking ends.

I make it all the way into the clean room before I remember that all my sample bags are full of fucking Miracle Grow.

I'm this close to texting the dumbass grad students to ask why none of them threw out the Miracle Grow, but I know the answer. They don't do anything with any of my samples unless I specifically tell them to. It's taken me two years to train them on the protocols for how I want my lab run. So, no, I don't get to yell at them when they follow my directions.

Besides, I know it's not them I'm mad at. It's me.

Because I'm the one who went over to Holly's expressly to get the soil samples. I'm the one who fucked her. And then fucked everything up. And then left without even getting the samples.

Though, even I can't imagine how that conversation would have gone down.

Hey, I know you're pissed that I revealed our relationship to my boss and your ex-husband, and you just said you didn't want to marry me or have sex again, but do you mind telling me where my soil samples are?

This is my curse in life. I'm a genius when it comes to unraveling the connections between microbes, but a dumbass when it comes to reading people. But even I'm smart enough to know better than to ask Holly for the samples now.

Which leaves me here. At the lab. On a Saturday. With the entire damn weekend stretching ahead of me. And nothing to do.

I never have nothing to do. I can always find work. There are simulations to run. Samples to analyze. Work to review. Papers to write.

But today, for the life of me, I can't focus enough to settle on anything.

I don't want to go home. Last night, I stayed up until three finishing the puzzle Tavey sent me and I've already done my workout today.

Which is why I'm still at the lab, staring at my open computer, when fucking Clive Thorndyke shows up just after lunch.

I've been sitting at the computer for over an hour, stewing on the events of the previous night so long the monitor had gone black. I see his reflection on the screen when he enters the room.

I push back my chair and stand, hating the way my hip spasms even more than it normally does.

On the bright side, it is the only thing keeping me from crossing the lab and decking the fucker.

Clive isn't exactly my favorite person.

Sure, his early research was intriguing, but he moved into administration early in his career. To me, it's a sign he was never passionate about his work. Besides, he's too slick and too polished for me to take him seriously as a scientist.

Until yesterday, those all seemed like valid reasons for me to dislike the guy. But none of those explain the pure rage that fills me when I see him today.

I've been doing Tae Kwon Do since I was thirteen and my physical therapist recommended it to strengthen my leg muscles and provide additional support for my hip.

I've been sparring for exercise almost as long. I'd like to think I could handle myself in a fight. But I have never wanted to actually punch someone until now.

Now? Now, I want to beat Clive to a fucking pulp.

Because I can't help but think that if he hadn't shown up last night, things might have gone very differently. For the past sixteen hours, I've been playing out what-if simulations in my mind.

Why had he shown up on her doorstep after eleven on a Friday night?

Was that normal?

Why hadn't Holly wanted him to know we'd slept together?

Was it just because he was my boss?

Or was it because they used to be married?

And—this one was the kicker—if he had shown up before I had, would she have slept with him instead?

Last night she'd implied there was something between us. Was there? She had all but said that she'd wanted me even before I conveniently showed up at her house when she happened to need a release. That she had felt an attraction to me from the moment we met.

Could that possibly be true?

Or was that just something she'd told me to make me feel better about what had happened?

Was I just a convenient placeholder for who she really wanted?

Was she still in love with Clive?

Was that why she was upset that he'd seen us together?

And if she was, why did that idea bother me so much?

Jesus. Was Tavey right?

Do I have feelings for Holly?

Was that why I'd offered to marry her?

Is that why I want to punch Clive?

He doesn't say anything. I don't either. We just stand there, glaring at each other.

Finally, he says in that polished voice of his, "You're lucky I don't condone violence, because I am sorely tempted to punch you."

I let out a bark of laughter. "You are welcome to fucking try."

No, I'm not enough of a dumbass to punch my boss.

Plus, the guy is easily ten years older than me. And I'm in better shape, despite my hip. I don't ever punch down.

So I'm glad he doesn't give me the temptation by taking the first swing. Decking Clive would feel good, but it's sure as hell not going to get Holly back in my bed.

Still, there's a moment when he just studies me, like he's trying to decide if he can take me.

I don't have to study him to know he can't.

He must see that in my glare, because after a minute, he shoves his clenched fists in his pockets and paces the length of the lab between the door and the clean room.

When he turns back in my direction, he says, "If I had known you were going to seduce her, I would never have introduced her to you."

There's so much ignorance in that statement, I don't even know where to start. I ignore it entirely and tell him, "You don't get to have an opinion on her love life. You're not her husband anymore."

"I still care about her."

"Your emotions are irrelevant."

Clive takes a step closer to me and I can tell from the way his arm muscles are moving that he is clenching his hands inside his pockets.

"I don't want to see her hurt. She deserves better."

"Again, you don't get to have an opinion. You had your shot. You had *her*. And you were too much of a dumbass to keep her."

"You don't know what you're talking about," he says.

"If you didn't want her to get hurt, you probably shouldn't have slept with someone else."

He rocks back on his heels. "I didn't pin you for the type to listen to gossip."

"It's not gossip," I tell him. "It's common knowledge."

"Okay, well, here's what you don't know. My affair isn't what ended our marriage. She had an ectopic pregnancy. She lost the baby. It nearly destroyed her. It did destroy us. Our marriage was over long before I ever slept with anyone else."

Jesus. No wonder she was so desperate to foster kids. And so heartbroken last night when she got the news about the sibling pair.

But one bit of information bubbles up through my surprise. "Did you really just admit to having an affair while she was grieving the loss of your child?"

To my surprise, Clive laughs. It's the bitter, hard laugh of a man with regrets. "Well, you weren't wrong when you called me a dumbass. You're right. I had my shot and I blew it, big-time. I'm not here picking a fight with you because I want her back. I know that's not ever going to happen. But she deserves better than a guy like you."

I know he's right. Because of course she deserves better than me. Does he think I don't know that?

But I'm sure as hell not going to give him the satisfaction of agreeing with him.

So instead, I say, "She's a grown woman and she's smart enough to make her own choices. She deserves to be with whomever she chooses."

"Yeah. I know that." Clive scoffs. "I'm just not sure she does. Have you seen her dogs? That stupid parrot of hers that can't stop plucking out its own feathers? She collects misfits. She prides herself on being able to love the unlovable. And sure, if she wants to surround herself with a whole ark of rescue animals, I'm not going to argue about it. But she deserves better than a misfit boyfriend."

"Is that supposed to hurt me? You think I don't know I'm a misfit?"

Clive just shakes his head. "This isn't about you. This is about Holly. I wasn't the man she needed me to be. What makes you think you can be? You really want to be the guy she's fucking out of pity?"

And all of a sudden I want to punch Clive all over again. Because I'm not smart about people. Not at all.

But I'm not too stupid to know he's right.

CHAPTER 24

HOLLY

It is a truth universally acknowledged that if you linger outside an open door listening to two people talk about you, you will probably hear things you don't want to hear.

I know this. I know better.

But when I approach Max's lab and hear him talking, I still listen.

When I realize the two people in the room are Clive and Max, I know I should interrupt. Obviously. No good has ever come from listening to an ex and a current paramour discuss you.

So why don't I knock loudly and enter immediately?

I have no answer for that.

Maybe it's that my brain is still sluggish from my epically sleepless night. Maybe I'm too stunned by the idea that Clive still cares enough to even bother warning Max off. Maybe I just can't resist the temptation of hearing what Max really thinks about me.

Yeah. It's probably that.

After all, resisting temptation has never been my strong suit, and this weekend, my willpower seems to be at an all-time low.

What did I expect to hear?

Some passionate declaration of love?

No. Not really. Not from Max.

But I guess I was hoping for something a little more emotional than, "She's smart enough to make her own decisions."

Maybe if I stand in the hall outside Max's office, I'll get it. But I don't think so.

And I'm sure as hell not going to stand there while Clive calls Max a misfit and implies I slept with him out of pity.

So that's the moment I knock on the doorframe and saunter through the open door.

Both men whirl around to look at me. Their expressions move through an almost identical cycles of surprise, confusion, and then embarrassment.

I try to memorize the moment. Someday in the future I might feel like laughing again, and when I do, this moment will probably be humorous. Maybe. In the very distant future.

Until that day, I'm just thankful I know enough beauty tips that my eyes don't look like I was crying all night.

Since both men are still staring at me in horrified silence, I merely nod at Max and then turn to my ex. "Clive, can I talk to you in the hall for a minute?"

Max looks like he wants to argue. So does Clive, for that matter.

After another old-Western-showdown moment passes between them before Clive nods and heads for the door. Before he can take my elbow and steer me out, I cross to Max, pulling an insulated lunch bag out of the tote over my shoulder. "You might want to get these back in the fridge."

He frowns at the bag. "My samples?"

"Yep. They were kept at the correct temperature the entire time. Clarissa gave me very specific instructions as well as a few vivid threats of how she would eviscerate me if I killed your precious microbes."

I press the bag into his hands and follow Clive out into the hall. I make sure to shut the door to the lab. Maybe if one of these geniuses had thought to do that, I wouldn't be struggling to keep my temper.

Out in the hall, I walk all the way down to the elevators, because I want to make sure that Max doesn't hear this.

Clive follows. When I reach the bank of elevators—which is far enough away from any of the rooms anyone might be working in on a Saturday—I turn to face Clive. He's got his hands tucked into his pants pockets and his head ducked.

Before I can say anything, he speaks. "Look, I know you're mad."

I tip my head to the side and quirk an eyebrow. "Do you?"

"Yes." He gestures in the general direction of my face. "You get really still when you're mad."

"How observant of you."

"And you smile too much."

"I appreciate the feedback."

"And—"

"Do you want some kind of sticker as a reward for knowing me so well, or are you going to apologize for acting like a colossal jack apple by meddling in something that isn't any of your business?"

His hand slips back into his pocket and his head bobs down, giving every appearance of being suitably cowed. I don't buy it.

"I get it," I tell him, my tone sharpening. "You think you know what's best for me. You think you're so smart that you know—"

His head snaps up. "That's not it. Not at all."

"Then what is it?"

"It's just . . ." He shakes his head.

"It's okay. If you use small enough words, I'm sure I'll understand."

"Stop it."

"Stop what?"

"Stop acting like that. Like I think you're not smart enough."

"Why? Isn't that what's going on here? You think I'm not smart enough to make decisions about my own life? That I'm still that ignorant girl from Georgia that you plucked out of obscurity? That you think you still need to help me along? To guide me? To sculpt me into the best version of myself?"

"No."

"Then what is it?"

"Holly, I—" He meets my gaze, and for once the arrogance he wears like a shield is completely absent. "I know I was a shitty husband. I know you put up with crap from me that you shouldn't have had to put up with. And I know how hard you tried to make it work. Do you really think I want to watch you go through that again? That I want to stand by and watch while one more arrogant asshole makes you miserable? Because if you thought I was hard to live with, I promise you that he will be much worse."

Yeah. That hurts.

I try not to show it though. Instead I just shake my head. "Fine. That's your opinion. And it still doesn't matter. Because you're not my husband. You're not even my boss. You don't get any say in what I do with my life." To drive my point home, I punch the call button on the elevator. When the door slides open, I gesture him inside. "And don't ever show up at my house unannounced again. It upsets the dogs."

I don't wait for him to answer. I don't even wait to see if he gets on the elevator and leaves. Because I am so over him right now.

Instead I march back into Max's lab.

When the door opens, Max looks up, clearly surprised. "How—"

I waggle my faculty key card. "I had maintenance grant me access to your lab. It's how I stole the samples to begin with."

Max scowls, clearly annoyed.

I try not to find it sexy. It's hard.

It's even harder not to enjoy that I bested him. And that I surprised him.

Frankly, it's kind of a miracle that I have the energy for either of those things after the twenty-four hours I've had. And probably a sign of just how dangerous Max is.

Because he should not be as distracting as he is.

Determined to stay focused, I rattle off the explanation before he can ask. "I knew eventually I would need to return the soil samples and figured it would be easier if I could get in whenever I needed to. Besides, I didn't know you'd be here today. I thought I could just slip in and leave them for you." He's still glaring at my key card, so I add, "Don't worry, I'll have access to your lab removed from my card on Monday."

"I'm not worried about that."

"Since you are here—" I reach into my bag and pull out the other thing I have for him and place it on the counter. "I might as well give you this."

He picks up the file folder and flips through it.

I don't wait for him to ask about it. "It's a speech I wrote for you."

"This is about my research."

"It wouldn't be a very good speech if it wasn't." He continues to flip through the pages, pausing to read every so often. "I've been working on the speech with Gwen and Priya. I asked one of my students who studies graphic design to do the slides."

He holds up a page and points to a paragraph in the middle. "This bit right here. Those are my words. My exact words."

I nod. "Yes. Yesterday evening while I was cutting your hair, I recorded our conversation. I didn't tell you I was doing it because I thought it would make you nervous. I needed to hear you talk about your work while you were distracted. I had already written the bulk of the speech with help from Gwen and Priya based on some of your published papers. But I needed to hear you talk to get the cadence right."

He's still frowning. "I don't understand."

"Look, you need to submit a taped speech to the committee. I wrote it for you. Abby did the slides. A former student from the media department is going to film it and do the editing. I have a couple dozen student volunteers who will sit in the audience. All you have to do is memorize the speech and show up on Monday night wearing the suit Rodrigo will deliver to your house on Monday morning. You'll be able to submit it to the committee by the end of the week."

"You recorded our conversation?" he asks.

"Yes."

"And didn't mention it? Is that legal?"

"Since I'm not planning on submitting it to a court of law, I don't think it matters."

"This was a lot of work," he says.

I just shrug. His field of research is dense and complicated, but Gwen and Priya broke down anything I didn't easily grasp. "I've emailed you a digital copy of both of those, in case you need to tweak things. You should read it over and make sure we got all the details right."

He flips back to the first page and starts to read.

I stand there for just a moment watching him, my heart pounding faster than it should. Then I turn and leave.

I make it almost out the door when he says, "I don't understand."

I turn back, ready to explain again, but the folder is closed now and he's not looking at the speech anymore.

"About what?"

"How much did you hear of my conversation with Clive?"

His question surprises me and I have no idea how to answer it. How to admit that I stood there listening to them talk about me, hoping . . . Hoping what? That he would say something that might help me understand what happened last night?

Because I have no idea what to say, I just shrug. "Some."

"He told me you'd had an ectopic pregnancy."

I nod, again, unsure what to say.

Max is a smart guy, but a lot of people don't understand exactly what an ectopic pregnancy is or the kind of damage it can do to your body. And even those who do don't understand the damage it can do to your heart. To your marriage.

To want a child so badly, and then through sheer bad luck and quirk of nature not only lose that baby, but possibly the ability to ever carry a pregnancy to term, is devastating.

Logically, I know it wasn't my fault. There was nothing I did or didn't do that affected where that fertilized egg implanted. It was a fluke.

Just one of those things that sometimes happens.

Max studies me, somehow understanding that the topic is off-limits. Though he does say, "And that's why you want to adopt."

Again, I just nod.

"That's what I don't get." He rounds the counter, never taking his eyes off me. "You want to adopt. You were devastated yesterday when you found out that you weren't going to get those kids. That's how badly you want to be a mom."

His words seem harshly critical, even for someone as blunt as Max.

"You don't get it? Fine. Not everyone wants to be a parent, but—"

"No, I get that. What I don't get is why you would turn me down. If you marry me, you can have everything you want. You want to foster kids? We can do that. We can adopt. We could do both. You want more dogs and parrots and weird rabbits? You can have them."

I laugh at the image.

"Listen to yourself, Max. You don't want kids. Or dogs. Or rabbits."

He juts out his jaw, looking like a stubborn child. "You don't know that."

"Okay, so do you want kids?"

He frowns. Not his normal, adorable grumpy scowl, but a thoughtful frown that gives me the impression he's thinking it through. After a moment, he nods. "Yes. Yes, I do."

His tone is so serious, I almost laugh, despite the circumstances. "Okay, next question. Have you ever thought about whether or not you want kids before this moment?"

"Does that matter?"

Does it matter that this man—this smart, sexy, amazing man—clearly decided just now that he wants kids solely because I said I wanted them? I don't even know what to think about that, about how tempting it makes him.

"I don't know. But I do know this—my life is messy. Really messy. I'm a flibbertigibbet."

"No, you're not."

"Do you even know what a flibbertigibbet is?"

"No." He looks offended, like he should know and he's disappointed in himself for not knowing. "But you said it like it was a bad thing."

I resist the urge to rub my hands down my face. I hate having to explain this. I hate how vulnerable and needy it makes me feel. Like I'm making excuses for myself, when that's not what I'm doing.

But Max deserves an explanation. I owe him that much.

"When I say I'm a flibbertigibbet, what I mean is I have ADHD."

He frowns when I use the term, and I can practically see him mentally pulling up what he knows about ADHD and comparing those characteristics to my behaviors.

I cut him off at the pass. "I wasn't diagnosed until high school, because ADHD in girls looks different than it does in boys, and most teachers don't know the symptoms well enough to suggest testing. For me, it shows up in a lack of impulse control, disorganization, and horrible time management. I've learned to cope. I don't expect special treatment. But it makes everything just a little bit harder."

He's still frowning, but this time it's his intense-thought frown. His puzzling-things-out frown.

So I keep talking. "All my life—from childhood straight through my marriage—I've felt like a disappointment. Like an irritation everyone else had to learn to live with. I'm the grit in the bottom of their shoe they can't shake out. I could say my marriage to Clive ended because of the ectopic pregnancy or because he cheated, but neither of those is the whole picture. The truth is, I annoyed him. The person I really am—the flibbertigibbet with ADHD—irritated him. I spent a lot of time trying to be the person he wanted me to be instead of the person I really am. It was exhausting. I won't ever do that to myself again."

And I won't do it to you.

I don't say that part out loud, because if I do, he'll just argue with me about it.

When I asked Clive for a divorce, he gave it to me, not just because he felt guilty for cheating on me, but also because he was relieved. He was as tired of all my annoying traits as I was of trying to hide them. I think we both wanted the excuse to end things.

"I've seen your life. I've seen your house." I gesture to the clean room on the other side of the lab. "I've seen your clean room. I don't have any place in this. And I can't imagine why you would think I do."

For a moment, I think he might argue with me about that. Just the smallest instant when I think he might tell me what I want to hear. That I could fit in his life. That maybe we could make it work.

But instead, he says, "You should get to have kids if you want them."

"Yeah. I agree. And maybe someday a judge will too."

"But if we got married—" he starts to protest again.

"Can I ask you a question?"

He blinks as if surprised I would dare interrupt him, because, after all, he is still Dr. Maximillian Ramsey, rising star of soil restoration research. He's not used to being interrupted.

I don't wait for him to answer, but instead cross to the spot by his computer where his cane rests against the desk—a good twenty feet away from where he is now.

I pick up the cane, looking pointedly at it and then at the distance to where he sits.

"Why do you have a cane?"

"Because I was in a car accident when I was twelve. It's how I got this damn scar." He jerks his hand up to his check. "My hip was shattered and—"

"Yes, and now you walk with a limp and a cane." I nod. "But you don't actually use it that often. You don't seem to need the cane. Oh, you stomp around with it when you're upset. You wave it around at me when I've irritated you, but how often do you *need* it?"

His frown turns into an outright scowl, but I'm not sure if it's my line of questioning that's annoyed him or the fact that I reminded him how irritating he finds me.

"I need it if I've been on my feet all day. If I overexert myself."

"So not that often."

"No. Not often. Exercise helps." His scowl deepens. "Are you implying I don't really need my cane?"

"Are *you* implying you don't really need it?"

"Even if I don't need it that often, I'd rather have it with me and not need it than go through the fucking embarrassment of not having it when my leg spasms."

"That's fair."

"But you think I don't need it," he accuses, sounding like a petulant boy.

"I didn't say that." I set the cane back down where I found it. "I don't know what your muscles or joints are feeling. I can't tell you whether or not you're in pain. Only you know that. I'm just observing that I haven't seen you actually use your cane. I think your cane is a crutch."

"Of course my cane is a crutch," he snaps. "That's the very definition of a cane."

"Okay, then, I think your physical crutch is an emotional crutch as well." I have to fight back a smile as I say it, but oh, God, it's a bittersweet smile. Because I am going to miss how cute he is when he's being obtuse. "I think you carry it because it brings you comfort, knowing that it's nearby if you need it."

"Do you have a point?" he practically growls.

"When we first met, you were terrified of giving these speeches."

"You make me sound like I was being irrational."

"I agree. Your fear was irrational. But you don't seem nearly as afraid anymore. Why aren't you?"

"Are you making fun of me?" he blurts.

"Not at all. You don't seem worried about giving the speeches for the McPherson committee. Why?"

He pushes himself off the stool and stalks over to stand in front of me. He looms over me, as huge and overbearing as always. When we first met, I constantly wanted to push back against his strength. Now, I want to lean into it. I want to soak it in and hold it close.

I can't let myself do that, so instead I push. "Why aren't you worried?"

He reaches out a hand, using a single finger to brush my hair off my cheek. "I trust you. If you say I can do it, then I can do it."

It's the answer I knew he'd give, but it's not the one I wanted.

I step back from him to pick up the cane again. This time I push it into his hands. "You already have one crutch. You don't need another."

He's still frowning at the cane in his hand when I turn to leave. Even accounting for the fact that people with Asperger's don't easily understand metaphors, I know he'll figure it out. He's a smart man.

I almost make it out the door when he asks, "Is the idea of being with me really so bad? You don't want to try, even if it means you get everything you want?"

The way he says it—like the problem is with him—nearly breaks my heart.

"You forget I've done this whole marriage thing before. I know how this story ends for me. I may not have two PhDs, but even I'm smart enough not to make the same mistake twice."

I turn and leave before he can say anything else, because if he keeps offering, I might not be able to resist.

CHAPTER 25

MAX

I stare at the bag of soil samples long after Holly leaves.

Eventually, I get up and transfer them from the insulated lunch bag to the refrigerator. I follow the same protocols I normally would, logging them into the computer, tagging them with RFID chips to make it easier to track them. Normally, the routine would be comforting. Familiar.

Not today.

Today, nothing is familiar.

The bulk of the weekend stretches ahead of me, vast and empty.

I pull out the file folder Holly handed me earlier and start to read the speech she wrote.

For the first time, the thought of actually giving a speech, in front of a crowd, in front of a camera, doesn't fill me with dread.

I still seriously doubt anything I say on camera is going to sway the committee in my favor. I'm simply not that guy. I will never be that guy.

My work is dense and esoteric. I have trouble making my students understand it.

And, sure, I get that Neil deGrasse Tyson—the example Holly always uses—explains dense and esoteric topics to the public all the time.

But he is charismatic and well-spoken. He's charming. Everyone loves him.

I am none of those things, and the only person in the world who loves me is my sister.

Dangling a five-million-dollar carrot in front of me isn't going to change any of that.

But fuck it.

If trying to be that guy will prove to Holly that I might be worthy of her, then I will try. Despite her insistence that she's undereducated compared to her colleagues, she's clearly brilliant. If she believes I can do it, then I can. And I don't think my faith in her faith in me is a sign I see her as a crutch.

I think about the things she said. That she thinks I somehow can't handle her. That somehow the problem is with her, not me. Which is the stupidest fucking thing I've ever heard.

I'm still in the lab, hours later, when the door opens and Gwen walks in.

She's got her phone in her hands scrolling through something. She hangs her bag on the hook by the door distractedly. She doesn't look up from her phone until she turns back around and is halfway across the room.

When she does look up, she jerks to a stop, lets out a yelp, and drops her phone.

"Damn it! What the—?" She just stares at me for a second like she doesn't even recognize me.

It takes me a second to realize that she doesn't. I'd been so lost in thought I'd actually forgotten about the haircut.

Gwen's gaze moves over my face as she says, "Whoa . . . Max?" Then she pulls the glasses off her head and slides them on to her nose. Somehow she misses getting the arm over her ear and she leaves them perched cockeyed and precariously on her nose. She shakes her head and then quickly corrects herself. "I mean, Dr. Ramsey?"

She takes a step forward. Momentum plus gravity work against her and her glasses tumble to the ground.

"Shit!" She bends to pick them up.

I just wait. Gwen has worked for me for over a year now. I'm familiar with her Rube Goldberg-esque reactions.

After several moments and enough curse words to shock even me, her glasses are back on and she's sitting on the stool opposite mine.

"I don't . . . how did . . . I just . . ."

"It's just a haircut."

"I know, but . . ."

I know I'm going to have to wait her out. I return to making notes in the margin of the speech.

I don't look up again until I hear the *click* of her cell phone. "Did you just take my picture?"

She blinks, wide-eyed. "No."

I keep staring.

"Okay, yes. I took your picture. Holly put me in charge of your social media."

I don't say anything. Basically, because the mention of Holly's name sends a bolt of something through my stomach. Maybe excitement. Maybe anguish. It's too soon to tell.

But Gwen apparently thinks I'm trying to stare her into a confession, because she jabs a finger in my direction defensively. "I need pictures for your Instagram. And she told me to get them, and I quote, 'Even if Professor McGrowly doesn't like it.' She said I shouldn't let you bully me."

"I didn't growl."

"You always growl." She blinks and then says slowly, "Did you not know that?"

I do know that, but I don't like being called on it. So instead of answering the question I ask one. "What are you doing with the picture?"

"I'm posting it to Instagram." She clicks away on her phone, eyeing me warily like she thinks I might snatch her phone away from her. "Let me just . . ." She trails off as she keeps typing. "And I changed your profile pic on Insta and Twitter."

"Why?"

"Um, because . . . social media." She waggles her phone like I'm supposed to piece together meaning out of that. "Did you read the document Holly sent over outlining the steps you're supposed to be taking to increase your social media presence?"

I have a vague memory of getting emails from Holly with attachments. Lots of them.

I glance over at Gwen to see her cowering a bit.

"What?" I bark.

"Um, you're growling again?"

"Shut up." But I try to soften it with a smile.

Her eyes go wide and she looks back down at her phone. "Well, Priya read them all and then forwarded them to Jaxon and me. And—"

"What?"

"Um . . ." She looks quickly up and then back down again. "I just . . . Are you smiling at me?"

Fuck. Why is this shit so hard?

"I am trying to seem less like a 'misanthropic dick who gets off on being mean.'" I use the phrase one of my former grad students yelled at me when he quit. I don't know why I keep thinking about that or why knowing Holly has made me start questioning everything.

"Oh." Still looking at her phone, Gwen nods. But after a moment she looks up, frowning. "Topher shouldn't have said that to you. That was mean of him. I don't think you're misanthropic. Or a dick."

"Good," I blurt. I don't try to smile again, since that seemed to freak her out. Instead, I add, "I don't want you to be afraid of me."

"I'm not," she says quickly. And then adds tentatively, "But you do growl a lot." Then she goes back to her phone, says, "Thank God you have us. According to the documents Holly sent, your official account needs one to three tweets a day. Insta needs two stories a week and one post."

"That's the stupidest—"

"Don't worry. We're taking care of it." She turns the phone around to face me, as if I care or even know what she's showing me. "And, can I just say how impressed I am by how fast your following is growing. It is off the charts."

I try to return my attention to the notes in front of me, but she clicks some more and then slides the phone across the counter so I can't avoid looking at it.

It takes me several moments—far too long—to realize what I'm looking at.

"This is me," I say, picking up her phone.

"Yeah." There's an implied *"well, duh"* in her voice.

Which I resent.

I'm not a stupid man. And it's not like I haven't looked at myself in the mirror since Friday night. I have.

But it's different seeing a picture of myself. Imagining the picture seen through the eyes of a stranger. It's both me and not me.

The tag on the photo reads, "I don't just study dirt. I study the connection between every living creature on this planet. We can't heal our world until we understand that connection."

I look from the phone back to Gwen, and cock my eyebrow, more than a little annoyed.

"What the fuck is this?"

"That's a quote."

"That's not a quote."

"Yes. It's a quote." She gives me another "duh" look and points to the papers in front of me. "Didn't Holly tell you I helped with the speech? I listened to the audio clips from Friday night. That's a direct quote. That's how you described research to Holly. I think there's even a transcript at the back."

I flip through the pages to the end and, sure enough, there's a section titled "Transcript."

"When exactly did you and Holly do this?"

"She DMed me last night. We met up this morning at the pancake house."

Great. That is just fucking great.

She DMed Gwen last night? Was that before or after she begged me to fuck her and then practically kicked me out after her ex showed up?

I don't ask Gwen for details on the timing there, because frankly I don't want to know.

It doesn't do my ego any favors. Any way I look at it, I asked Holly to marry me and then she spent the next twelve hours hustling to write this speech for me and getting Priya and Gwen to take over my social media. Basically, she finished all the work she has to do with me so that her obligation to spend time with me is over.

So, in other words, it wasn't just, "No, I don't want to marry you," it was, "Hell, no, I won't marry you. And I don't really ever want to see you again."

"You're growling again," Gwen says.

"If I'm growling, it's because you and Holly managed to twist my words."

"Again, it's a direct quote. We didn't twist anything."

"At best, this is a heavily romanticized description of my research." I scoff. "'The connection between every living creature,' my ass."

"Personally, I think it's a fabulous description for your research. It is exactly what you study. How every organism on this planet is connected and bound to some other living creature. How we can't survive without one another." Gwen gives a small smile. "But maybe Holly just brings out your hidden sentimentality."

"I don't have hidden sentimentality."

Gwen opens her mouth again.

Before she can say anything, I jab a finger in her direction. "And if you tell me I'm growling again, you're fired."

She snaps her mouth closed. If I didn't know better, I'd say she was laughing at me.

I'm about to tell her she's fired anyway when a text comes in on my phone.

I give her one last (mostly) silent glare before standing and walking a few feet away to unlock my phone and read the text that came through. It's one of several, actually.

But not from Holly, damn it.

Tavey: OMG

Tavey: Super-hot picture of you on insta

Tavey: love it

Tavey: BTW

Tavey: you're welcome

Okay, not only is it not Holly, but now I'm sickened by the idea that my sister thinks a picture of me is hot.

Me: What is wrong with you?

Tavey: Besides an incurable case of the awesomes? Nothing.

Tavey: What is wrong with you?

Tavey: Also, you're welcome.

I hold my phone farther away and glare at it.

Me: What is wrong with you for telling me I look hot? You're my sister and that's unacceptable.

Me: Also, why are you using punctuation? You never punctuate your texts. Is this code that you've been kidnapped? If so, in the future, can we discuss and agree on these things ahead of time?

Tavey: Eeewww

Tavey: Calm down, perv

Tavey: I said the picture was hot

Tavey: don't make it weird

Tavey: Also, I do too use punctuation. I am a well-educated woman, with a full command of the English language and its many idiomatic forms, who sometimes chooses not to use punctuation so as to conform to the popular parlance of this informal format.

Tavey: So there

Tavey: Also, I tweaked the algorithms on your insta and twitter

Tavey: And now you have over 200k followers

Tavey: That's why you should thank me

God, Tavey is a pain my ass.

Still, I type out a thank-you, only slightly worried that she may demand some sort of blood sacrifice at a later date. Frankly, my sister is terrifying, because who the hell can just casually "tweak the algorithms" on Instagram and Twitter? Surely that can't be legal.

I'm sliding my phone back in my pocket when Gwen says, "Oh my God."

"What?"

Gwen's phone dings in her hands. "Oh my God."

"What is it?"

She hops off the stool and hurries around the counter, once again thrusting her phone at me.

"It's your Instagram."

"What about it?"

"Well, Lily McPherson herself just liked your post."

"You mean your post."

Gwen is shaking her head, but I can't tell if she's disagreeing with me or if she's in shock. Based on how wide-eyed she looks, either is a possibility.

"No. Your post. It's your account, right? The point is, she liked the picture of you. And then DMed you."

"So?"

"So?" Gwen's eyes go even wider. "So? This is Lily McPherson we're talking about. She has a million followers. And she's the head of the selection committee and"—Gwen looks down at the phone and then back up at me—"she wants to meet with you."

"Well, I'm sure she's meeting all of the candidates. It's probably part of the selection process."

Gwen's mouth opens and closes mutely several times. Then through clenched teeth, she says, "Are you being willfully ignorant?"

"What do you mean?"

"It's not part of the process." She jabs at me with the phone, like she's trying to fence with me. "Didn't you even read the materials from the McPherson Foundation?"

"No," I answer honestly. "I gave them to you to read."

"Well, I did read them. And Holly read them. And I guarantee that personal visits from billionaire socialite Lily McPherson are *not* part of the selection process. Especially not when the invitation is DMed to you over Instagram ten minutes after your account posts a picture of you looking like this!"

Gwen once again thrusts the phone at me.

I look down, once again taking in the picture. It's not that different from how I normally look. Is it?

"You seem . . . perturbed by this," I say eventually. And slowly. Because everything I've said to Gwen today seems to set her off.

Which, frankly, seems to be on par for my track record with women today.

Gwen narrows her gaze. "You are a moron."

"I'm aware of that fact." I sigh. "Can you just tell me what to do?"

"No."

"Please?"

"Maybe."

Gwen's expression softens infinitesimally. She sets her phone on the counter and starts pacing, massaging her temples like that will somehow help.

After several laps, she gives me a shrewd look. "Just how bad did you mess things up with Holly?"

"Why do you assume I messed things up?"

She gives me another one of those *"well, duh"* looks that I'm really starting to hate.

I honestly don't know what the right thing to say here is. So I settle on, "Holly is a work colleague. And I'm not comfortable discussing our relationship."

"Oh my God!" Gwen says. Again. For what must be the twentieth time today. Except this time she follows it with, "You're in love with her."

"Why do people keep saying that?"

"Oh my God! Who? Who else has said that? How many people have you talked about Holly with? Does she know you're in love with her?" Gwen's voice rises with every sentence until she finally ends in a final, "Oh my God!"

Then she drops back onto the stool and buries her head in her hands.

I don't do well with hysterical women.

To be honest, I never deal with hysterical women at all. I've pretty much organized my life to avoid it. Them. Whatever.

So the fact that this is the second hysterical—or even emotional—woman I've had to deal with in the past twenty-four hours is more than a little disconcerting.

And while my instincts told me exactly what to do with Holly, Gwen is something else entirely. She's normally so level-headed. Clumsiness aside.

When she doesn't say anything for several heartbeats, I say, "My sister."

Gwen raises her head and blinks up at me. Obviously, she's forgotten the first of her many questions.

"My sister, Tavey. She's the other person who said I'm in love with Holly."

Gwen nods. "Okay, that makes sense."

Even though she sounds a lot calmer, I ask, "Are you okay?"

She frowns, but then shrugs and give a head bob. "Yeah. I guess. I know this isn't about me, but I just . . ."

She gives another shrug. And then sighs.

"Oh my God." Fuck. Apparently that's contagious. "You're not in love with Holly too, are you?"

Gwen blinks in obvious surprise. And then laughs. "No. Not even a little. I mean, she's awesome. But it's just . . . well, when your reclusive, misanthropic genius boss finds love before you do, it really throws into sharp relief how pathetic your love life is."

"Oh."

Once again, I don't know what to say. Because I've never considered the love lives of any of my colleagues.

After a moment, Gwen stands and picks up her phone from where it's been sitting on the counter between us.

"So what are you going to do?" she asks.

"About what?"

"About Holly. And Lily McPherson."

"I have no idea," I admit.

"That's what I was afraid of." Gwen nods. "Okay, so we just need to figure out how to get you this meeting with Lily McPherson and get you the grant. And we have to do it without you sleeping with Lily McPherson so that you can also woo Holly."

"Why would I sleep with Lily McPherson?"

"It's cute that you didn't get that's why she's DMing you."

CHAPTER 26

HOLLY

I have legit never been more miserable getting praise than I am at this moment.

"You've achieved the impossible," Dean Rogers says heartily.

He accompanies his praise with a congenial slap to the shoulder, in some kind of good-ol'-boy ritual. I guess I should just be thankful that he doesn't pour a bucket of Gatorade over my head.

Once again, I wished I'd been able to talk Liz into tagging along as my plus-one, but when I'd invited her, she'd laughed heartily before saying, "An evening with bloated windbags? No way. Not even for you."

"Thank you." I barely keep my voice from lilting up at the end and making that a question.

The dean raises his glass in salute and then tosses back the remainder of his drink.

I mimic his actions but sip rather than gulp my wine.

I learned a long time ago that the key to surviving any kind of faculty mixer is to pace your drinking.

I may not have the innate intelligence to hold my own in this crowd, but I can definitely hold my liquor. So I do.

It's been eight days since I trimmed Max's hair. Eight days since he asked me to marry him. And then we slept together . . .

No. We didn't sleep together.

We had sex.

So, eight days since we had sex and I told him I wasn't going to marry him.

Eight days. It feels like an eternity. But only to me.

Apparently.

Max and I haven't spoken—not alone, at least—since Saturday morning. Since I outlined all the reasons why we were a horrible match.

Some part of me had expected him to protest, because that's what we do. I say something. He argues.

It's our thing.

But he hadn't argued. He hadn't put up a fight.

Which was good, right? I don't know how long I could resist him if he did put up a fight, even though I know I'm right.

Which doesn't make being here at this event meant to honor Max any easier at all.

It's not like I have a choice though. As soon as Lily McPherson reached out to Max saying she wanted to visit him personally, the wheels of the university had kicked into high gear.

Gwen had immediately contacted me. Unfortunately, she'd included Clive in the same text. Just over a week later, and everyone with a shred of power and influence in a hundred-mile radius had descended on this cocktail party to praise Max and kiss Lily McPherson's ass.

I almost felt sorry for them both.

Max because he was clearly uncomfortable with all the attention. Lily for other reasons entirely.

I mean, I saw the picture Gwen posted of Max on Instagram that morning.

I'd been in the room with him mere hours before the photo was taken. Frankly, it was a miracle my panties hadn't burst into flames the second I saw him.

He'd looked even hotter in the picture. Collar unbuttoned, sleeves rolled up, his freshly trimmed beard looking scruffy, hair even more tousled than normal . . . and glasses. Where had those come from? He'd had his notes in front of him, his pencil in one hand, the arm of his glasses just grazing his lower lip. And then he'd looked up just as she'd snapped the photo.

The whole thing was very sexy-professor-with-extra-broody-sprinkled-on-top.

And Lily McPherson had DMed him from her personal account—not the foundation's account—less than twenty minutes after that picture went up? Well, it doesn't take a genius to figure out what she actually meant when she said she wanted to meet Max in person.

Except it took someone who wasn't a genius to figure it out.

Because here I am, surrounded by geniuses, and it has occurred to none of them that Lily might be more interested in Max's full bottom lip than she is in his full research proposal.

Maybe I was projecting.

Or maybe everyone here—except Lily McPherson and me—is so focused on the pursuit of intellectual greatness that they can't imagine a young, rich, beautiful heiress hopping in her private jet and flying to Texas for a hookup.

But me?

I can imagine it all too well.

It's what I would do if I was Lily.

I turn my most congenial smile on Dean Rogers. "You do know that this doesn't guarantee he's going to get the fellowship?"

Alarm flickers over the dean's face.

Clive, who hasn't left my side all evening, gives my elbow a squeeze. "What Holly means is that we can't announce anything yet. Of course. But surely it's just a formality at this point."

I'm tempted to yank my elbow from his grasp. Clive hasn't stuck this close to me since the early days of our marriage when he was always afraid I might say the wrong thing in public.

I didn't like it then, but I tolerated it because I'd assumed he knew better than I did about a lot of things.

Now though? In this moment? When I'm ninety-nine percent sure Lily's motives are more carnal than philanthropic? And I'm the only person in the room who seems to have noticed?

Now, I don't yank my arm away, but I shift my foot just enough to press the heel of my pump onto his loafer as I say, "Let's not forget that Ms. McPherson is just one person on the committee. And this is her first year. Her personal opinion might not hold much weight when it comes to the final decision."

I dig my heel in a little harder on the word "personal."

Clive grunts, jerking his gaze to mine.

I smile sweetly while looking pointedly at the other end of the room where Lily clutches an empty tumbler in one hand and strokes Max's bicep with the other. He doesn't have his cane with him. Even though I'm the one who pointed out how rarely he uses it, I don't know how I feel about that.

I swear to God, I can see Lily squeezing his muscle from across the room. The woman is that obvious. Like he's an avocado she's thinking of buying.

Max is looking down at her with a frown.

From here, I can't tell if it's a frown of horror or mere confusion. Or—oh, God. My stomach clenches—if he's interested.

Frick, frick, fricketty, frick-frick.

Do I even want to see what happens next? Can I look away?

Before I can flee (or not), Clive excuses us from the conversation with the dean and drags me away. His tone has the forced joviality of a cut-rate Santa—a sure sign he's trying not to freak out.

As soon as we're out of the dean's hearing range, he hisses at me, "What are you saying? You think Lily is here for personal reasons? Not as a member of the selection committee?"

"I don't know," I answer honestly. "Maybe."

"Why didn't you say something before now?"

Clive's face is starting to flush.

"I did. Literally every time we spoke this past week, I told you that we should take this slowly and not make a big deal out of it." I gesture to the room at large, to the gathered university dignitaries, and the waiters with canapés. "And somehow this still happened."

"I thought you were exaggerating."

"Why would I do that?"

"Because you wanted an excuse to keep working with Ramsey, obviously." He gives me a bug-eyed look and then adds, "Because of the personal nature of . . . whatever is happening between you and Max."

There's a pettiness in Clive's gaze, as well as a flash of jealousy that I might not have recognized if I didn't know him as well as I do.

It makes me a little sad—and a lot relieved—because his pettiness isn't my problem anymore.

Which is probably a good thing, since I clearly have enough pettiness and jealousy of my own to deal with right now.

"I wasn't exaggerating. My concerns about Lily McPherson have nothing to do with the personal nature of whatever is between me and Max." Clive's gaze narrows and I hastily add, "I mean, if there was something between me and Max. Which there isn't. So it's a non-issue."

"Are you sure about that?"

Clive looks from me to where Max is standing on the other side of the room. Where he's been standing ever since he arrived.

He's barely glanced in my direction.

"Yes, I'm sure about that," I snap. "Do you think I don't know how ill-matched Max and I are? That I don't know we would never work together?"

"Do you know that?"

Oh, sure, on Saturday, when I overheard him talking to Max about it, he made it seem like Max is the problem. Like Max is some kind of misfit. But I know Clive. That was just him hitting below the belt. Saying what he thought would hurt Max the most.

"Look," I tell him now. "We both know I can't keep up with Max intellectually. I know I'll bore him or irritate him or whatever. I get that. I know that when he asked me to marry him, he was just being nice, but—"

"Back up," Clive cuts me off. "He asked you to marry him?"

"Yes. Friday. Right before—" I stop myself mid-sentence and autocorrect. "Right before you showed up."

"To *marry* him?"

Clive's incredulity says it all.

"Yes. As unbelievable as it is that someone would want to marry me, with my misfit pets and my application for Hoarders not even accepted yet, he did ask."

"That's not what I meant," Clive protests.

I roll my eyes, because I know that's exactly what Clive meant. Max and I are mismatched. I don't need Clive to explain it to me.

"What did you tell him?" Clive asks.

"What do you think I said? I'm here talking to you while he's over there chatting up Lily McPherson, so obviously I said no."

Clive brings his tumbler to his mouth and drains the Scotch in a single gulp.

"Still," Clive murmurs, shaking his head. "He asked you to marry him."

"Yes," I repeat.

Because, oh, God. Let's please talk about this some more. Because this isn't awkward and horrible at all.

Clive waves down a waiter and orders another drink, snagging a full wineglass from the tray and pressing it into my hand before waving the guy off.

"And you think . . ." Clive shakes his head, looking like he can't believe what he's about to say. "You think Max asked you to marry him because he was being nice?"

"Yes."

"Nice?"

"Yes."

"You think Max was trying to be nice?"

"Stop saying nice like that. Max is nice. He is a nice person."

"No. He's not a nice person. He's an asshole. *Everyone* thinks he's an asshole."

"Well, everyone is wrong, okay? Just because he isn't polished and doesn't say the right thing every time he opens his mouth does not mean he's not a good person."

"I—"

"He found out I wasn't going to get kids, okay? That's the only reason he asked me to marry him. There was a sibling pair I thought I might get to foster-adopt, and some judge gave them to a couple instead. And Max felt sorry for me. That's it. That's the only reason he would want to marry someone like me. Out of pity. And I know that. Is that what you wanted to hear?"

"Jesus. No, of course I don't want to hear that. Why would you think that?"

I just shake my head. "I don't know, Clive. I don't know anything anymore."

The waiter comes back with Clive's drink. He downs it in one gulp.

From across the room, he watches Max and Lily interacting. He looks as miserable as I feel.

"Holly, I'm sorry. I'm sorry I got you mixed up in this at all."

He gives me puppy-dog eyes full of pity and regret.

What the hell am I supposed to say to that?

Am I supposed to lie to make him feel better? Tell him that it's okay? That no harm was done? That I don't feel like my heart is breaking?

I say nothing, and after a few minutes, he says, "Do you really think Lily McPherson came all the way down here just to meet Max because of some picture she saw in his Instagram feed?"

"I think she's the heiress to a multibillion-dollar fortune with a private jet at her disposal. And she's here. So maybe."

"What do you think he's going to do?"

"About what?"

"About Lily McPherson."

Calling on depths of restraint I never imagined I had, I don't hit Clive upside the head as I ask, "Are you asking me if I think Max will sleep with her? Honestly?"

Clive steps closer and mutters, "I thought you said there was nothing going on between the two of you. That he asked you to marry him out of pity."

"I was being discreet. Besides, if you believed me when I said there was nothing going on between us, why did you go to his office on Saturday and act like a total jack apple?"

Clive runs a hand through his hair. "I don't know. I panicked. And now I'm even more panicked. If she propositions him and he turns her down, it could hurt his chances of getting the fellowship."

Again, I fight the urge to do bodily harm.

Because all of my sound logic and reasonable reasons aside, if she propositions him and he doesn't turn her down, it will be worse than bad. At least for me.

I hand Clive my glass. "If you're so worried about it, maybe you should go offer to sleep with her."

And with that, I leave. Because there's only so much indignation a woman can take in one night.

CHAPTER 27

MAX

The only thing worse than being in a group in public, is being in a group in public at a party.

And the only thing worse than that is a party in my honor.

How the hell did this happen to me?

Of course, I know the answer to that.

The woman beside me is to blame.

Lily. Fucking. McPherson.

If she hadn't decided to join the selection committee and "update" the requirements, then I wouldn't be here. More to the point, if she hadn't reached out to me via Instagram, this party would not be happening. And she would not be standing at my side, her hand on my arm. Her annoying laughter ringing in my ears. And worse . . .

And this is the absolute worst part . . .

Her damn floral perfume clogging up my nose.

She smells like a fucking garden.

Specifically, she smells like my grandmother's garden.

And she does not smell like lemon pancakes.

Which is completely beside the point.

I don't want her to smell like lemons. It's just that if I have to have some damn woman flipping her hair in my face all the time, the least she could do is smell like something that doesn't make me feel awkward and uncomfortable.

Not that I have any expectation of *not* feeling awkward and uncomfortable around Lily McPherson. For starters, this is a party. With what has to be damn near a hundred people. Most of whom I don't know and probably don't have anything in common with. I see Dave over by the bar. Maybe I should go talk to him. Ask him if he's read Harry Potter yet.

But first I would have to ditch Lily McPherson, who—so far—is more tenacious than a parasitic invasive species. Something with fangs.

Though, based on the way she's digging her fingers into my arm, perhaps claws would be more appropriate.

She gives my arm another squeeze, drawing my attention from the room at large back to her. She seems to be waiting for me to speak.

But I can't remember the last thing she said. Or the last thing I said, for that matter.

Jesus.

Why the hell is this so hard?

Her hand slips up my arm to my bicep.

"Did you—" I start to say.

"You must—" she says at the same time.

We both break off, but she's the only one who laughs.

It grates on my already-frayed nerves. Two people talking at the same time is not funny.

"Please," I say. "Continue."

"You must work out."

"Exercise is important for both cardiovascular health and mobility. So, yes. I do."

"Of course you do," she says with a smile that can't possibly be real.

Her smile is disproportionally wide, therefore it can't be genuine. It is also dispropor-tionally white, given that most people have some discoloration in their teeth by the time they reach their mid-twenties.

Instead of pointing out either of those facts, I blurt, "Did you know that many amateur gardeners consider caterpillars to be parasites?"

She blinks, looking a little surprised. "I didn't."

"However, they're able to complete their life cycle beyond their host plant. So they're not true parasites, like fleas or ticks, which depend on a host species for all stages of their life cycle."

For a second she just stares at me, her mouth falling slightly open. Then, slowly, her lips curve into a smile, except this time, it looks like a real smile. Not that fake shit she was throwing my way before.

Her hand falls away from my bicep. "Am I the butterfly or the tick in that analogy?"

"I—"

Well, fuck.

I am colossally bad at reading people.

And even by my standards, this is an epic fuckup.

"I'm sorry," I blurt. "I didn't mean . . ."

She laughs. Not the loud artificial laugh from earlier, but a soft chuckle.

"No. Don't." She looks around the room, before taking my elbow and nudging us both toward the double doors that lead out onto the patio.

I let her guide me, which is surprising in and of itself. Ten minutes ago, I wouldn't have gone anywhere alone with this woman.

It's not that she's not beautiful. She is undeniably gorgeous, with sleek dark hair and the kind of cheekbones and lips you'd usually see on a sixties pinup. It's the preda-tory undercurrent of everything she's done since the moment we met that I have a problem with.

But all of a sudden she seems less predatory insect and more . . . human.

So I follow her out onto the patio. Even though it's after eight, the temperature is still in the nineties. The staff set up fans and a mister, which makes it almost bearable to be outside. Almost. It means we're the only people on the patio, despite the stunning view of campus the sixth-floor balcony allows.

As soon as we're alone, she drops her hand from my arm and walks over to the railing to look out at the view.

I follow more slowly, more cautiously, because I don't know what the hell is going on, but clearly I've already fucked things up.

At some point, she glances over her shoulder at me, gives me a shrewd look and then sighs. "This isn't going to happen, is it?"

"What?"

She makes a huffing sound. "Yeah. If you have to ask, then it really isn't." She turns to fully face me, leaning back against the railing, her long legs stretched out in front of her. "What a shame. You are so pretty. And smart, too. Fucking you would piss off so many people."

I nearly blow out a sigh of relief. Because as shitty as I am at reading situations, I was starting to wonder if I'd misunderstood. My gut said she was coming on to me. But what the hell do I know?

A week ago, I'd thought Holly was agreeing to marry me, so clearly I'm a fucking idiot.

It feels like Lily's waiting for me to say something, so I say, "I'm sorry."

She gives a sigh that sounds purposefully dramatic, and then rolls her eyes. "I'll live." Then she pushes away from the railing and seems to perk up. "If you don't want to fuck me, maybe we could just pretend. Spend a few days together, make everyone think we'd slept together. I can definitely make it worth your time."

"Are you suggesting that if I either sleep with you or pretend to sleep with you, you'll make sure I get the fellowship?"

She tips her head to the side and then laughs again. "Oh, yeah. I guess that is what that sounded like, isn't it? And that would look really bad for you, huh? I can see why you wouldn't want to do that." Suddenly, she grips my arm. "I don't suppose you'd want to marry me instead?"

I take a startled step back. "I'm sorry. I didn't mean—"

She waves a hand dismissively. "Yeah, I didn't think so."

"Why would you . . . why would you ask that?"

Jesus, is this what Holly had felt like when I asked her?

She shrugs. "I'm impulsive. It's kind of my thing. Which you might have guessed, given I'm here. I mean, come on, what kind of person sees a guy on Instagram and flies halfway across the country to meet him on a whim? Am I right?"

"I don't know how to answer that," I say honestly. Though I am seriously beginning to question a lot of things about Lily McPherson. Rich? Yes. Objectively, inarguably beautiful? Yes. Emotionally stable? That one is a big question mark for me. Which is not a great sign since she controls a billion-dollar empire. "Why *did* you do that?"

Instead of answering my question, she turns back to look out over the campus again. Then she pushes her hair off her forehead and says, "It is miserably hot out here. How do you people live in this weather?"

"Air-conditioning. Though Texas does have more deaths per capita from heatstroke than any other state."

"What?"

If the look of horror on Lily's face is any indication, my conversational skills have just hit a real low.

"Would you like to go back inside?" I ask.

"No. I'm not any better at handling the fawning crowds than I suspect you are. I'll take the heat." She braces her hands on the railing, and then pulls her hands away. The stone is undoubtedly hot. "You know the worst part of being rich?"

Several possibilities come to mind, but given my track record so far tonight, I keep them to myself and just shake my head.

"It's the other rich people." She leans toward me and whispers, like she's sharing a secret. "A lot of billionaires are such assholes."

"That makes sense. The latest research in neuroscience indicates power kills off the empathy portion of the brain."

Her eyes go wide and she grins. "Exactly!"

"It's undoubtedly an evolutionary response—"

"Yeah, yeah. I'm sure there are reasons." She circles her hand in a *speed-it-up* gesture. "My point is, everyone I come in contact with is either a rich dickhead or a social-climbing, pandering sycophant. It's exhausting."

Was she . . . was she asking for advice about how to make friends? Because I am not equipped for that.

Thank God she doesn't pause long enough for me to feel like I'm supposed to answer her.

"I thought things would change when I joined the committee. Like, maybe I would meet new people. There is one assistant professor from MIT, Dr. Tia Wang, who is pretty amazing, but most of them are so damn old. And they all think I'm a dilettante. I suppose I am, but some of them are outright mean about it. I swear one of those women is actually Delores Umbridge."

"I know who that is!" I blurt.

Lily grins again. "Then I read your work and found it fascinating. So when I saw your post—"

"You've read my work?"

"Obviously," she scoffs. "You didn't think I came all the way down here just based on the photo, did you? I mean, you're hot, but there are hot guys in New York. Quite a few actually."

Am I supposed to say something about her calling me hot? I don't know.

"Sorry, my work isn't widely read," I say. Or understood, for that matter.

She lifts and lowers a shoulder before giving her hair a toss. "Everyone looks at me and sees my mother. Very few people consider that I got her looks and my father's brain."

"Sorry," I say again. Because I had assumed that as well.

"Don't be. Though, for the record, my mother was no dummy. But my point is I don't fit in anywhere. Or with anyone. I'm a socialite who hates rich people. And a genius trapped in the body of a game show hostess." She pauses like I'm supposed to know what she means by that.

I don't. Instead, feeling like I finally have something useful to contribute to the conversation, I say, "Do you know why I study soil?"

"Okay, weird segue. But I assume it's because it's an emerging field of research with wide-reaching implications for food security and for the health of our planet."

I nod, but add, "Beyond that."

"Beyond the ability to feed our growing population in an environmentally friendly way? What is there beyond that?"

"All of that is the result of my research, but it's not what brought me to it. I started studying soil because of how it all fits together. Fifty years ago, a hundred years ago, everyone thought bacteria were the bad guys. These microscopic monsters that destroyed everything. The more we studied, the more we realized it's not that simple. The bacteria, the protozoa, the fungi . . . it all works together. Everything has a place and everything has a job. And it's all unique to a specific location. The species in Arizona are different from the species in Texas which are different from—"

"The species in the Amazon. Which is why you can't just buy a bag of Miracle Grow with a chemical fertilizer included at Home Depot and expect it to actually help improve the soil in your yard because it doesn't have the microbial diversity your yard needs."

"Yes! Exactly!" Now it's my turn to laugh. "You really are familiar with my work."

"Duh."

"Then you know everything in this world has a place. Every creature belongs somewhere. But the fungus that thrives in the desert might not survive in Central Park."

I half expect that I'll need to explain the analogy, but I don't.

Instead, she laughs. "So I'm not a butterfly or a tick. I'm a fungus."

"You're an integral part of the ecosystem. You're just not in the right ecosystem."

She gives me a thoughtful look. "Are you sure you don't want to get married?"

"Oh, I do want to get married." My gaze drifts through the glass doors to seek out Holly. The last time I saw her, she was talking to Clive, but now I can't find either of them in the crowd. "I'm just not sure how to convince her of that."

Lily whips around and follows my gaze. "Ooooh . . . is she in there?"

"She was earlier."

"Then why were you hanging out with me at all? You should have been with her."

"Because when I asked her to marry me, she said no. Pretty emphatically."

She gives me a shrewd look. "Okay, break it down for me. Tell me exactly what happened."

"Why?"

"Well, so I can help, obviously. I mean, clearly me being here has made things worse, so I'm obligated to help fix things. Besides, if you're not going to sleep with me or marry me, then the least you can do is befriend me. And friends help their friends. Unless you're just a creepy stalker. In which case I don't want to help. Are you a creepy stalker?"

"I don't think I am."

"Then like I said, you're going to have to tell me everything that happened."

"I don't see how this is going to help."

"Well, is she your fungus or not?" She rolls her eyes. "And by fungus, I mean your soulmate."

When she phrases it like that, it's a punch in the gut.

Is Holly my soulmate? I don't know.

I'd never considered whether or not soulmates were real. Or that if they were, I might have one.

But is she the one person who makes me feel complete? Who makes me feel like my ecosystem can run smoothly forever, just so long as she's nearby?

"Yes," I say, my voice sounding unexpectedly gruff. I clear my throat and say again, "Yes, she is."

"Okay, then, you just need to figure out how to woo her."

For the first time in days, the pressure in my chest lessens. Maybe, just maybe, I could make this work.

And now it's my turn to give Lily McPherson a shrewd look. "You know for a dilettante socialite, you have a strong understanding of biology."

She grins. "I do, don't I?"

"You should consider graduate school. I have a hell of a time finding competent students."

CHAPTER 28

HOLLY

For the first time in my many years at the university, I cancel my office hours on Monday afternoon. For the past thirty-six hours—basically ever since I watched Lily McPherson fawn all over Max—I've been fighting an epic and unexplained panic attack. I make it through class, but only because in class, it's socially acceptable for me to pace in circles and talk too loud. But I know myself well enough to know I don't have the patience to sit in my office and listen to students with anything approaching the compassion and attention I normally give them.

So I slap a note on my office door and head home, where, hopefully, I can calm the heck down by doing . . . I don't know what. Taking the dogs for a walk? Spending a few hours grooming Lou? Carding her excess fur and spinning it into yarn to knit a sweater?

All I know is that I can't sit still. I picture Max leading Lily McPherson out on the balcony at that stupid frickin' party. And then not coming back inside for over an hour.

I know it was over an hour, because I left at the hour mark and they were still out there alone. Talking.

Who does that?

Okay, sure.

Lots of people talk for over an hour alone. But I checked the weather app on my phone. It was ninety-three degrees out.

No one—no one!—stands around in ninety-three-degree heat talking for that long unless the person you're talking to is the most interesting, fascinating person you've ever met. I wouldn't talk to Lenny Kravitz in ninety-three-degree heat for that long. And I'm pretty certain he wouldn't talk to me that long either.

What were they talking about?

Is Lily McPherson that fascinating?

If it was Clive or Dean Rogers or anyone of a dozen other people, I would say, "Well, it's Lily McPherson. She's powerful and rich. And, at this very moment, she holds his future in her impeccably manicured hands. Anyone with any sense at all is going to stay out there as long as she wants to talk."

But Max? He doesn't have any sense. He has logic and brains to spare. But it wouldn't occur to him to stay out there talking to her in that heat out of polite deference to her power. The only reason he would talk to anyone that long, no matter the weather, is if he found that person fascinating. If he thought he really needed to hear what they had to say.

That is the realization that sends me home sick.

Yep, that's the word I use when I put up the sign. Because I actually feel sick to my stomach at the thought of Max wanting to talk to another woman.

If I'm going to feel sick and panicky, I want to do it at home, surrounded by people I love. And by "people," I mean animals.

Animals I love.

Because right now I am too grumpy and miserable to force my company on another human.

I know something's wrong the second I open the door to my house.

It's quiet. Totally and completely silent.

My house is never quiet.

Usually the dogs start barking the second they hear the key in the lock. And that's on days I come home earlier than normal and they're not already circling their kennels in anticipation. And as soon as the dogs bark, Iago starts in on his pathetic stress plucking. Poor guy is still hoping his previous owner will come home. Maybe someday I'll be able to afford parrot therapy.

A silent house is not a good thing. I drop my purse and computer bag by the door and all but run for the kitchen, where the dogs are usually crated. I hit the light switch on the way in and then skid to a halt at the sight before me.

The crates where my dogs usually spend their days are gone. The dogs too, for that matter.

Someone stole my dogs.

What the hell?

I run back to the living room to dig my phone out of my purse. Clive's phone is already ringing as I turn and stare at Iago's cage.

Or rather, the spot where Iago's cage normally sits in the corner of the living room.

The cage is big. Like, coffin big, because African grays need a lot of space. I don't know how I missed this on my first dash through the living room, but the cage is gone.

In its place is a fancy brass perch, with a bird swing hanging from an arched pole. On the swing sits a stuffed parrot.

Not a dead stuffed parrot—thank God—but a brightly colored stuffed animal.

My steps slow as I cross to the plushie.

"Holly?" I hear Clive's voice as if from afar.

I'd lowered my hand as I walked toward the perch, and now I bring the phone back to my ear.

"Sorry, Clive," I tell him. "I can't talk right now."

"You called me," he says, sounding a little annoyed.

"Yeah. Sorry about that. It was a mistake."

My first thought when the dogs were missing was that Clive had them. After all, according to the divorce settlement, he had the right to take them for the weekend twice a month. He never did, but that seemed like the only logical explanation.

But he hates Iago. And Iago cusses nonstop when Clive is around, because Iago is magically capable of reading my mind and giving voice to my thoughts. There's no way he'd take my bird.

I hang up on Clive and reach for the stuffed animal. There's an oversize pet tag on the collar around the bird's neck. Iago's name is etched on a tag in big letters. In smaller letters under that are two words, "so I."

I stare at the words for a long moment, then tuck the stuffed parrot under my arm and go look for the other animals. I find one stuffed dog under the kitchen table. He's a normal-sized stuffed animal, but one of his legs has been removed and the spot clumsily sewed closed. His tag reads "Skip" followed by the words "You took."

In the bathroom I find a stuffed bunny, with a tag that reads, "Whatever the fuck this is," above the words, "took yours."

On my bed is the biggest stuffed dog I've ever seen. That tag reads "Lou" and "my pets."

I line them up on the bed—small dog, big dog, parrot, and rabbit—so that the tags read, "You took my pets, so I took yours."

What the hell . . .

I took his soil samples. Not his pets.

But still, who else could this be?

I have played pranks on no one else. I haven't taken anything from anyone, unless I count that one time I accidentally took the ceramic mug from my favorite coffee shop last year when I was distracted and forgot I hadn't asked for a to-go cup. And I returned the mug the next day.

This has to be Max.

But . . .

Then I remember his speech. The whole point of his research. Soil is a living organism. A complex ecosystem full of thousands of tiny life forms. But pets?

Surely that's a stretch.

Baffled and confused, I grab my purse and head for . . .

Where?

His house? His pristine, monochromatic McMansion? I can barely imagine the stuffed versions of my pets there, let alone the living, breathing, shedding, pooping versions.

But where else could he have brought them? Not his lab. That's for sure.

Maybe his office?

I head for campus, but call Clarissa on the drive.

"Hey," I say when she answers. "Do you know if Dr. Ramsey is in his office today?"

"Not that I know of."

Which isn't exactly a firm answer. "Is there anything . . . odd going on in the building today?"

Like, maybe a compulsive jerk filling his office up with my pets in some crazy act of . . . What?

What was he doing?

Was this revenge?

No, I don't believe that. Because Max isn't cruel.

"No," Clarissa says slowly. "Wait a second. I think I got an email from him this morning."

I am not fit to be operating a motor vehicle right now, so I pull off the road into the parking lot of a Sonic while I wait for Clarissa to find the email.

"Yep. Here it is. He's taking a week of personal leave."

What the . . .?

A week of personal leave?

In the middle of the semester?

Who does that?

Worse still, it was a week of personal leave, in the middle of the semester, thirty-six hours after meeting a beautiful heiress who'd been hanging all over him.

A knot starts to form in my stomach.

Because, for the love of pumpkin-spiced lattes, if I had spent all this time and effort just so Max could get laid by a socialite, I would legit lose my mind.

"Okay, thanks, Clarissa."

"Oh, wait. There's another note here. It says if anyone asks, he'll be at his house all week."

"Oh."

Does that mean he's not in Tahiti with Lily Frickin' McPherson?

Or does that mean he's at home in bed with Lily Frickin' McPherson?

And if he is at home in bed with her, what did he do with my animals?

"Thanks, Clarissa." I hang up.

I just sit there and stare at the Sonic menu.

Maybe a cherry limeade will help.

Right. If it was half vodka.

But how does he not get it? The pranks I played on him were fun and they were . . .

Okay. They were flirty.

When I pranked Max, I was flirting with him.

Shit.

Why hadn't I seen that before now?

Duh. Because I've been in deep denial about how I feel about him.

Oh, frick-sicle.

I'm in love with Max.

Yep. A cherry limeade was definitely not going to help.

I order one anyway.

When it arrives, I just sit there in my car, drinking my cherry limeade and staring at the menu out the window.

Okay. So, I'm in love with Max.

What does that mean? Exactly?

Well, for starters, it probably explains my compulsion to make a Lily McPherson voodoo doll and then feed it to my blender. And then bury the pieces in my pets' waste.

So, yeah, I've been a teeny bit jealous of the attention Max was paying her. And it also explains my panic attack and nausea today.

But what do I do with this knowledge?

Sure, life-altering personal revelations are great. Go, me.

But—the intrinsic gratification of self-knowledge aside—this gets me nothing.

Because Max obviously doesn't feel the same way. He doesn't love me.

Yes, he asked me to marry him, but like I told Clive, he was just trying to be helpful.

Despite what Clive obviously thinks, Max is a good person. He's a problem solver. I have a problem, he had an easy solution.

It wasn't emotional. Not for him, anyway.

The only thing I do know is that he has my pets at his house. And unless I'm going to gas up my car and disappear Thelma and Louise–style (minus the dramatic death), I need to get my animals.

Which means I need to go to his place no matter what, because even if I was going to leave town Thelma and Louise–style, I would definite bring my pets with me.

I do the only thing I can do. I throw out the cherry limeade—which didn't sit well with my anxiety anyway—and head over to Max's house.

I know he has my animals as soon as I pull up in front of his house because parked in front of his house in place of his sensible sedan sits a rental truck, the kind you can rent by the hour from the hardware store. Even more tellingly, Lou's crate is still in the back.

Did he honestly drive from my house to his with my dogs in the back of his truck in their crates? Surely even he wouldn't be that dumb.

And while I'm not one hundred percent sure it would be dangerous for them, I am one thousand percent sure they would hate it.

By the time I'm out of my car and up the walkway to his house, I am mentally halfway into an epic lecture about animal safety. I don't just ring his doorbell, I poke it so many times and so hard I'm pretty sure I break the damn thing.

The resulting cacophony assures me my animals are here, but does little to soothe my anger and indignation.

When he opens the door, I launch straight into my rant. "I don't know if you thought this was going to be funny or what, but this was very irresponsible. And—"

I break off as I take in the scene before me.

Yes, Max is there, looking decidedly more disheveled than he usually does. And that is saying something. He's barefoot and wearing jeans and a teal T-shirt that makes his eyes look almost aqua. The T-shirt is tucked in, but only on one side. The untucked side appears to have—

"Did someone take a bite out of your shirt?"

Before he can answer, two things happen at once.

Somewhere in the house, a voice says, "Baaaaaaa," and, with the usual clatter of dog nails, Skip and Lou come running for me. And the open door behind me.

"The dogs!" I yelp, because if they make it to the freedom of an unfamiliar street, they will bolt.

Max seems to understand this, because he grabs my arm, jerks me into the house and slams the door shut behind me.

He doesn't just pull me into the house.

He pulls me into his arms.

My hands automatically go his chest. His hands land on my butt and he lifts me off my feet as the dogs skitter to a halt, prancing around us in excited joy.

Despite myself—despite my anger and anxiety—my heart starts pounding in a decidedly non-angry, non-anxious way.

I suck in a breath full of Max-scented yumminess and meet his gaze.

A second passes. Then several more. He doesn't put me down, but just holds me against him, every delicious bit of his body pressed to mine. My legs dangle uselessly as I just stare into his eyes.

I swallow. "Are you going to put me down?"

"No."

"Oh."

Who am I to argue with that logic?

It's not like I want him to put me down.

"But isn't this hard on your hip?"

"You hardly weigh anything." He shakes his head, his gaze never leaving mine. "Besides, someone told me recently that my cane was a crutch."

A minute ago, I was ready to roast him over a pit, but now all I can do is breathe and try to resist the urge to wrap my legs around his hips and kiss him.

Like he can read my mind, he turns, still holding me in his arms, and takes two steps until my back is pressed against the wall and kisses me.

Everything inside of me melts the second his lips touch mine. One hand snakes up to bury itself in his hair. My other goes to his neck, anchoring his mouth on mine. My legs give in to the impulse to wrap around his hips. The second they do, he adjusts his hold on me, cupping my ass more fully in his huge hands and seating me fully against his dick, which is rock-hard.

I groan, rubbing myself against his dick.

Okay, as much as I don't want to be the girl who looks a gift horse in the mouth . . . or in this case the girl who questions a hard cock . . . I pull away from the kiss to look at him. "Does this . . ." I rock my hips on the word "this." "Mean you didn't sleep with Lily McPherson?"

"Why the fuck would I have slept with her?"

I don't answer but pull his mouth back to mine, because it feels so good to be held against him. It feels so right. And it's what I need after the past thirty-six hours of not knowing what was going on between him and Lily. After the past eight days of not being with him.

His lips must be sprinkled with magic dust, because they make me forget all the reasons why this is a bad idea. Right now, in this moment, I don't need more. I don't need him to love me. I don't even need him to fuck me. All I need is for him to keep kissing me like it's more important to him than breathing.

He does just that.

He keeps kissing me like it's the only thing he wants to do. Like it's the only thing he's ever wanted to do.

He steps away from the wall and, for a second, I'm afraid that he's going to set me down, but he doesn't. Instead, his mouth still on mine, his hands still cupping my ass, keeping me firmly pressed to that amazing cock of his, he carries me out of the living room.

I barely notice the walk down the hall, through a doorway I assume leads to his bedroom.

He pauses just inside the door, lifting his mouth from mine, searching my face. "Is this okay?"

I nod. "Yes."

"This is what you want?"

"Yes."

He takes a step backwards, nudging the door closed with his back.

And then he's kissing me again, his mouth moving over mine in a cascade of delicate kisses as he carries me to the bed.

He lays me down in the center of the bed, his hips between my open legs, rocking against my core, sending pulses of pleasure through my whole body.

He braces his forearms on either side of my head and raises up to look at me again.

"Because I don't want this to be like last time," he says, his voice low and growly as he buries his face against my neck. The scruff of his beard sends a flurry of tingles along my nerve endings. "I don't want this to be just once. I don't want to be quick. I need more."

I nod desperately before realizing he can't see me nod when he's kissing my neck. So I say aloud, "Yes. All of that. Yes."

And just in case he needs more encouragement, I reach down and tug his shirt out of the waistband of his jeans. I press my hands to his waist, reveling in the feel of the taut muscles that clench in response to my touch.

And then, he lifts his head, again. "Holly—"

I nearly scream in frustration. "Yes, I want you. I want this. I want you to fuck me. And I am definitely going to want you to keep fucking me for a very long time." I rock my hips up, grinding myself against him. "But mostly I want you to start now, because you are killing me."

His lips—those gorgeous full lips of his—curve into a smile. "Holly, I was just going to ask if the dogs are okay out there on their own or if I should crate them."

"Oh."

Oh God. This guy.

This guy is going to kill me.

Because no other man would worry about my dogs at a time like this and it's the sweetest, sexiest thing in the universe that he does.

"They can wait." I wrap my legs around his waist again and pull him back to me. "I can't."

I reach for his jeans, unbutton them and slide my hand down inside, cupping his cock in my hand. And he is so hard and huge and, oh my God, I cannot wait to feel him inside of me again.

Except . . .

This time I pull back. "Unless you're worried they might destroy your house."

He kisses his way down my neck, tugging at the front of my dress until the buttons pop open. "They can tear the fucking house down for all I care."

His fingers work quickly through the last few buttons of my dress and then he peels it off of me before flicking open my bra. He sucks one nipple into his mouth as he rolls off of me, baring my now nearly naked body. He skims his hand down over my abdomen, under the edge of my panties. It's like he knows exactly how to touch me. Exactly what I need.

His thumb finds my clit, rubs gentle circles across it that make my whole body tremble.

And he's the one who groans, like it's his body that feels like it's about to fly apart.

"God," he murmurs. "You're so hot. You're so wet." He lifts his head.

My eyes flutter open to see him gazing at me, wonder and heat and need in his eyes.

His thumb keeps up that steady pressure on my clit. His finger pushes deeper inside of me, pressing my G-spot, hitting it just right.

He holds me tightly as tremors wrack my body. Wreck my soul.

Then, while I'm still shaking, he quickly shucks off the rest of his clothes and moves above me, rubbing his thick cock over my entrance, wetting himself with my juices, before sliding deep inside of me.

"How the fuck are you this wet for me?" he whispers.

"Because it's you," I gasp, shattering again as he drives into me, bringing me to the brink of pleasure so intense the entire universe seems to implode.

CHAPTER 29

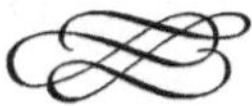

HOLLY

I'm still a quivering, incoherent bundle of nerves when Max rolls off of me and returns a few minutes later with a wet washcloth. His jeans are back on, but his chest is still bare. He lies down beside me, cleaning me off. His hands and gaze skim my body like it's worthy of worship.

I know it's not, but, dear God, the way he looks at me is addictive. Intoxicating.

He tosses the washcloth aside and pulls me against him. He's propped up on one elbow, gazing down at me as he brushes a lock of hair off my forehead.

He presses a single, soft kiss on my forehead, then pulls back and says, "There was rabbit shit on the floor."

My fingers slip from his hair. "Oooookay?"

"That's why I picked you up."

"Huh?"

"I didn't want you to step in the rabbit shit."

"Oh."

So, he picked me up because he didn't want me to step in rabbit shit. Not because he felt like he couldn't live without kissing me.

Bummer.

"I think I'm confused," I admit.

He's saying this all like this is a perfectly normal topic to discuss after he's just made me come, not once, but twice. After he's damn near fucked my brains out. While he's still running his hand over my body like it's his new favorite toy and gazing at me like he can't decide which part he wants to lick next.

He leans down to lave my nipple and then suck it into his mouth. Releasing my breast, he says, "I just wanted you to know that I didn't plan on fucking you. I picked you up because I didn't want you to step in rabbit shit and then the fucking-you part just sort of happened."

"Oooookay," I say again.

I push my palms against his shoulders until he leans away, his expression surprised.

I roll away from him, scrambling off the bed, snagging my dress as I go. I stand on the other side of the bed, yanking my dress on, fumbling with buttons, as he props himself on his elbows, just watching me, his massive bulk spread out on the bed. All those glorious, stupid muscles of his practically begging me to touch them.

But what the actual hell?

And because he's still staring at me and I don't know what to do or say and my fingers are barely working and I can only get about half of the buttons done, I say it out loud, too.

"What the actual hell, Max?"

For a second he just stares blankly at me. Like he one hundred percent does not understand why I'm upset.

"Ten minutes ago you were like, 'I don't want this to be like last time,' and, 'Oh, baby, baby, I need you more than once.'"

He's shaking his head. "I never said, 'Oh, baby, baby.'"

"Yeah, well, I thought it was implied. But apparently not, because, apparently, you fucked me by accident."

Shit.

Fuck.

God damn it.

This guy has me twisted into so many damn knots I can't even talk anymore.

Me!

I can't talk.

Which is a fucking embarrassment.

I stomp over to the bedroom door, ready to flee.

Max scrambles out of bed after me.

He slams his hand on the door just as I go to open it.

"I think I said that wrong," he says, planting his other hand on the other side of my head.

He's got me caged in his arms. I turn around, pressing myself to the wall because those extra millimeters help me resist the temptation to plaster my body against his bare chest.

Again.

We all know how *that* would turn out.

"No shit, genius," I snap. Then turn back to the door and tug on the knob.

He steps back, letting me open the door.

The second I step into the hall, Skip and Lou come barreling toward me.

I squat to give belly rubs and pets, saying, "Did this horrible man pet-nap you? Did he? Did you try to fight him off?"

"I didn't—"

Without his amnesia-inducing lips on mine, my irritation is back. I stand, cutting him off. "Forget it. It was an accident. A mistake, whatever. But this—" I circle my hand around to indicate the abduction of my pets. "This was irresponsible and unforgivable. Taking Skip and Lou is one thing. But Tinky gets car sick."

He shoves a hand through his hair, looking baffled and confused. "Yeah, I noticed when he puked all over my car."

I head down the hall to the living room, determined to get out of here, but catch a glimpse of Iago's cage—which is now in the corner of Max's living room. I don't even want to imagine how it got there, because it's huge and heavy. So I just gesture toward it. "And Iago doesn't like change."

At the sound of his name, Iago gives a squawk and plucks out a feather, muttering, "Hell in a handbasket."

"And—"

Before I can even come up with anything to say after the "and" there's another "Baaaaa" from the other room, followed by the click-clack of hooves on tile flooring.

A tiny goat trots out from the kitchen, a piece of teal fabric dangling from its mouth. The goat stops a few feet from us, and gives its head a shake. "Baaaa."

The fabric—which this goat clearly ripped from Max's shirt at some point before I arrived—must be stuck between its teeth or something, because every time it opens its mouth to baaa and shake its head, the fabric just hangs there.

Skip trots over to the goat and starts nipping at the goat's heels to herd it back into the kitchen. The goat—clearly having none of this nonsense—hops up onto the coffee table. The red puzzle Max was working on the last time I was here is now complete. At least until the goat lands on it. And starts eating some of the pieces. Just then, Tinky hops out from behind the sofa like he's coming to greet me, but he gets distracted by a tasty-looking lamp cord and pauses to gnaw on it.

Finally, even I can't take the chaos. "What the hell is happening? Why is there a goat here? I don't have a goat. And you don't have a goat. So whose goat is that? And why did you kidnap my pets when there was a goat here?"

"This is Bubble. Short for Beelzebub. She's a miniature silky goat."

Skip, clearly frustrated that Bubble is beyond herding range, barks at the goat.

Bubble jumps, her legs going stiff as she topples over.

"She's a little dramatic," Max says.

A moment later, she stumbles to her feet and takes a defiant bite of puzzle.

From his corner, Iago mutters, "Hell in a handbasket."

"I don't think I thought this through." Max shoves his hand through his hair again, and then grunts as Lou leans into his leg.

"I don't understand what's happening."

It's the only thing I can say. Because—seriously!—what the hell is going on?

Max, taking a big step to avoid the rabbit poop, crosses to the table and scoops the goat in his arms, as he gestures to the sofa. "Maybe you should sit."

I follow him to the sofa. What else can I do? I can't just take my animals and leave. I have no idea how to get them home. When I agreed to foster Iago, it took three college students to move his cage into my living room. Even if I could get Tinky and the dogs to the car, I'd have to leave Iago here. And I'm not doing that.

Besides, I still have no idea why Max took my pets. And then kissed me. And then fucked me, apparently by mistake? And now he has a pet demon goat.

"What is going on?" I ask.

"You said you couldn't marry me."

"Right."

"Because your life is messy."

"Right."

And at the time, I'd meant it. At the time, I'd genuinely thought that was why I shouldn't—or couldn't—marry him. Now, I'm not so sure.

Was that really it? Or was I just protecting my heart, because he asked me out of pity? Because I'm afraid he can't ever love me?

And I'm terrified of getting hurt again. Because this shit that's happening right now? Where he made love to me like I was the most precious thing in the world and then said it was an accident? I can't take much more of this.

"That's why I have a goat." He gives a firm nod. Like that explanation should be enough.

"Because I said I wouldn't marry you?" I ask.

As if Skip senses my discomfort, he makes a jumping move, so I scoop him up into my lap. I reach out a hand, expecting Lou to come bump it with her hand, but instead, she walks over to Max and puts her head on his knee.

Without seeming to notice he's doing it, Max strokes his hand over her head.

"You wouldn't marry me because you think I can't handle how messy your life is. But now my life is just as messy. And when I said I didn't mean to fuck you, what I actually meant was that I meant to explain all of that first. Because when I said I needed you more than once, I meant it."

Almost absentmindedly, he reaches over and wiggles the bit of cloth until it pulls free from Bubble's mouth. She makes a bleating noise and then settles beside him, tucking her legs under her body and chewing contentedly on red puzzle pieces. There's a piece stuck to her lips, and when she blows out in a huff, it flies free and lands on his knee.

He stares at the puzzle piece for a second, but when he reaches for it, Lou bumps her head against his palm again and he goes back to petting her. He doesn't even stop to flick the puzzle piece off his leg.

Instead, he just looks at me and says, "So if my life is as messy as yours, then you have no reason not to marry me. And then our lives can be messy together."

My heart swells, because this guy . . . oh, man, this guy just won me over. Forever. And he better be serious. He better love me. Or just be willing to fake it for the rest of my life. Because this moment right here, when he let himself be bullied by my dog, is the moment I become a goner forever.

"Let me see if I've got this right. You bought a goat to prove to me that you can handle messiness?"

"Rescued," he corrects. "I rescued a goat. Because apparently her previous owner didn't know that miniature silky fainting goats actually faint."

"Why a goat?"

He shrugs. "They didn't have any Flemish giant rabbits. And I didn't think a dog would cut it. They had an iguana." His gaze meets mine. "Do I need to go back and get him too?"

I shake my head. "No." I lean forward, bracing my elbows on my knees. And as much as I want to just jump in with both feet, I can't. Because I need to know— really know—that he knows what he's getting into. And I need to be honest—with myself and with him—about what I need. "But I have to be honest here. I think I was wrong when I said I couldn't marry you because my life is messy. The real reason I said no is because I can't be in another marriage with a man who wants a smart, professional wife but gets a hot mess. I need to be with someone who loves me. Who loves me for me. Who loves the me who's a good speaker and can help you pick out a suit, but also the me who rescues animals and volunteers on the other side of town. With Clive I always felt like I was hiding who I really was. I can't do that again. If you don't think that someday you'll be able to love me like that, then this isn't going to work."

Max stares at me for a long minute and then shakes his head. "I don't think I'll be able to love you like that someday."

I stand, clutching Skip to my chest so tightly he yelps and struggles to get free.

"Wait," Max says, standing too.

Before I can bolt for the door, he's right in front of me again, "What I meant was—"

He cuts himself off and stares at me for a long second. Then he pulls me to him, one hand on my jaw, the other on the back of my head, and he kisses me.

This kiss isn't sweet or reverent. Even though he can't pull me flush against him because Skip is still in my arms, it's deep and long and fierce. Like he's trying to pour words into me through the kiss. Then, abruptly, it's over. He drops his hands back to his side and steps away.

"Fuck," he curses. "I'm no good at this. What I meant was that I don't think I'll eventually love you someday, because I love you now. I know you think you annoy people. Like grit in the bottom of someone's shoe. I know what that feels like."

Hearing his words, I feel like I can't breathe. My heart is racing and maybe I'm having a heart attack, because he loves me? But also … "You think I'm as irritating as grit in your shoe?"

"No. I know what it feels like to be grit in people's shoes. If anyone knows what it's like to irritate people, it's me. I annoy everyone. If you're grit, then I'm bigger grit. If you're willing to put up with all my annoying quirks, I can definitely put up with yours. All my life, I've been waiting for someone who made me believe that I fit with them. It's like, if you have a single protozoan in a soil sample in a petri dish and you keep it cold enough, it'll hibernate and survive, but it can't live like that. That lone protozoan can't survive on its own. Not forever. It needs other protozoan and fungi and bacteria and microbes. It needs a whole ecosystem. Otherwise it's starving to death. I've been that lone protozoan. I wasn't living. Before you, I was just hibernating. But you're my fungus."

My breath catches. Because I think I know what he means. But I don't say anything, because I need to hear him say it.

"You are the other part of the ecosystem that I need to survive," he says. "You and your pets. And my pet. And whatever kids we can have, whenever we can have them.

All of us together will be our own ecosystem. If you aren't ready, I can wait for someday. I waited my whole life for you. I didn't do all of this, I didn't steal your pets, and get a goat, and step in rabbit shit without being sure I wanted you. I can wait if you need more time, but I want you *now*."

I drop Skip and launch myself at him. Because if he stepped in rabbit shit and still wants me, then it must be love.

EPILOGUE

MAX

I get home later than I meant to. I don't like working late, especially now, but Priya is defending her dissertation next week and needed help.

The house is nearly silent when I let myself in. Iago is snoring softly in his cage in the corner of the living room. The rustling coming from the kitchen means Holly has already crated the dogs for the night. I leave my shoes and briefcase by the front door and head down the hall to the bedroom.

I try to be quiet in case Holly already has the younger two asleep, but who am I kidding? I don't do anything quietly.

I pause at Eli's door and stick my head in. He's got headphones on and the Switch console in his hands. He looks up when the door opens. I look pointedly at the stack of textbooks beside his bed.

"I'm done," he mouths, then taps his fist to his chest like he's making a promise. His attention is back on his game before the door even shuts.

I will come back and check on that homework later, just to be sure. When he first came to us three years ago, his definition of "done" differed greatly from mine, but we're working on it.

Somehow, weirdly, miraculously, I have more patience with him and his slippery standards of success than Holly does.

That is something I never imagined. That I would be the patient one.

I knock on Rosa's door and wait for her quiet "come in" before entering. She's the one we never have to worry about when it comes to homework. She gets her shit done with a ferocity that impresses even me. So I'm not surprised when she's still at her desk pecking away at her keyboard.

The smile she gives me is friendly, but not relaxed. I stay by the door, because she's still not completely comfortable here and the therapist we've been working with says she needs to know we respect her space.

Maybe she'll never be completely comfortable with me. I can live with that. I wasn't completely comfortable with me for a long time.

I had no idea when Holly said just over three years ago there was a sibling pair she wanted to adopt, that Rosa—the girl I'd met in Holly's class—was part of that sibling pair.

I hadn't known there were specific kids she wanted. That she wanted to create a forever home for Rosa before the girl aged out of the system. I don't know that it would have mattered. Because at that point, I was already all in with Holly.

She could have told me she wanted to adopt an interdimensional demon and I would have found a way to make it happen. As it turned out, the other couple the judge wanted to give Rosa and Eli to changed their minds. Rosa and Eli ended up with us after all. First at Holly's house, while I went through the training and certification to become a foster parent.

Now, Rosa gestures to her laptop. "I'm just finishing up this paper for my poli-sci class."

"Okay," I say. It's not that late and I trust her to go to bed at a reasonable time.

I nod and am about to leave when she says, "When I'm done, do you think . . ." She trails off when I look back at her, then after a minute she blurts, "Do you think you could look at my Calculus homework in the morning? I'm not sure I got it all."

"Of course," I say, suppressing a smile. Because, holy shit. This is the first time she's asked me for anything.

She's at the university now. She could live on campus, but she chose to continue living at the house. She says it's because she wants to be there for Eli, but Holly has a different theory. She thinks Rosa was without a real home for so long she's still a little afraid it will all disappear.

I know how she feels. Sometimes this new life of mine feels bigger than I deserve. Tenure. The McPherson Fellowship. My research team. Yeah, those are all things I wanted. But the other stuff? Holly? The kids? This life we've built? It's all more than I could have ever imagined. Bigger than anything I had ever wanted or imagined for myself.

So, yeah, I can't blame Rosa for wanting to stay at home a little longer.

When Rosa doesn't say anything else, I shut the door and head to the next room, imagining the victory dance Holly will do when I tell her that Rosa asked me for help on her homework.

I don't knock on the door to the twins' room because I can hear Holly's voice, so I know they're still awake.

I open the door, slip inside and just stand there, looking at my wife.

She's cross-legged on the floor between the two beds with an open book on her lap, but she's not reading from it. Instead, she's running her fingernails down Bella's back, while Luna, who is lying next to Bella in the same bed, rocks a stuffed parrot in her arms.

The two girls are the glue that holds this crazy family together. They're the reason this crazy family exists at all. Because they are the reason the other couple decided not to take Rosa and Eli.

The week Rosa and Eli were supposed to go to that other couple, their birth mom showed up at CPS pregnant with the twins. The mom, who had signed over parental rights to Eli and Rosa, was wise enough and loving enough to realize that she couldn't do right by the twins either. That other family wanted two kids, not four. And weren't ready for infants, let alone twins.

Now, Luna kicks her legs out—a sure sign she's exhausted—but says, "Tell us again about the night we were born."

Holly sighs. "It's late, baby. You need your sleep."

The room is dark and somehow the girls haven't noticed me standing in the doorway yet.

"I wanna hear it, too, Momma," Bella says. "Tell us the story about how Daddy was dying and you saved him."

Holly chuckles. "Well, he wasn't dying, but he was very, very lonely."

"Like a zoan in a dish all by himself," Luna says, clearly proud of her command of language.

"And you were his fungus," Bella adds.

Holly reaches over to run her hand over Bella's mass of dark curls.

She looks up at me, her smile hitting me so hard I almost can't breathe. "Yep. He's my protozoan and I am his fungus. And together we're all one tiny ecosystem. Perfect and complete."

Bella rolls over, snuggling up against her sister, but frowning a little. "What if the other momma has more babies?"

"Well," Holly answers, running a soothing hand down Bella's shoulder. "We might have to get a bigger petri dish."

Holly looks up at me again, as if to see if I agree.

This isn't something we've ever discussed.

Still, I nod. Because there will always be room for more. More kids or more animals. More of everything. As long as we are together.

ABOUT THE AUTHOR

I write the kinds of books I want to read. Fast-paced books with lots of world-building, snarky heroines, and swoony heroes. I love story, pop culture, gossip, and baked goods. I'm a modern-day hippy and certified LEGO nerd.

I live in the Austin, Texas hill country, with my geeky husband and two extremely geeky kids. We have dogs, chickens, cats, and more LEGOs than should be allowed by law. Oh, and I stress bake. So if my characters talk about food a lot, that's why.

Emma Lee Jayne also writes as Rita award winning author Emily McKay.

Find Emma Lee Jayne online:
Facebook: http://bit.ly/3aYlucC
Instagram: https://bit.ly/3523Y3x
Goodreads: http://bit.ly/3aWXAhO
Pinterest: http://bit.ly/3866I1W
Website: http://emmaleejayne.com/

Find Smartypants Romance online:
Website: www.smartypantsromance.com
Facebook: www.facebook.com/smartypantsromance/
Goodreads: www.goodreads.com/smartypantsromance
Twitter: @smartypantsrom
Instagram: @smartypantsromance
Newsletter: https://smartypantsromance.com/newsletter/

ALSO BY SMARTYPANTS ROMANCE

<u>Green Valley Chronicles</u>

<u>The Love at First Sight Series</u>

Baking Me Crazy by Karla Sorensen (#1)

Batter of Wits by Karla Sorensen (#2)

Steal My Magnolia by Karla Sorensen(#3)

<u>Fighting For Love Series</u>

Stud Muffin by Jiffy Kate (#1)

Beef Cake by Jiffy Kate (#2)

Eye Candy by Jiffy Kate (#3)

<u>The Donner Bakery Series</u>

No Whisk, No Reward by Ellie Kay (#1)

<u>The Green Valley Library Series</u>

Love in Due Time by L.B. Dunbar (#1)

Crime and Periodicals by Nora Everly (#2)

Prose Before Bros by Cathy Yardley (#3)

Shelf Awareness by Katie Ashley (#4)

Carpentry and Cocktails by Nora Everly (#5)

Love in Deed by L.B. Dunbar (#6)

<u>Scorned Women's Society Series</u>

My Bare Lady by Piper Sheldon (#1)

The Treble with Men by Piper Sheldon (#2)

The One That I Want by Piper Sheldon (#3)

<u>Park Ranger Series</u>

Happy Trail by Daisy Prescott (#1)

Stranger Ranger by Daisy Prescott (#2)

The Leffersbee Series

Been There Done That by Hope Ellis (#1)

The Higher Learning Series

Upsy Daisy by Chelsie Edwards (#1)

Seduction in the City

Cipher Security Series

Code of Conduct by April White (#1)

Code of Honor by April White (#2)

Cipher Office Series

Weight Expectations by M.E. Carter (#1)

Sticking to the Script by Stella Weaver (#2)

Cutie and the Beast by M.E. Carter (#3)

Weights of Wrath by M.E. Carter (#4)

Common Threads Series

Mad About Ewe by Susannah Nix (#1)

Give Love a Chai by Nanxi Wen (#2)

Educated Romance

Work For It Series

Street Smart by Aly Stiles (#1)

Heart Smart by Emma Lee Jayne (#2)

Lessons Learned Series

Under Pressure by Allie Winters (#1)

www.ingramcontent.com/pod-product-compliance
Lightning Source LLC
Chambersburg PA
CBHW021122190726

48288CB00008B/2454